HOT

little

HANDS

HOT
little
HANDS
fiction

ABIGAIL ULMAN

Spiegel & Grau *New York*

Copyright © 2015 by Abigail Ulman

Published in the United States by Spiegel & Grau, an imprint of Random House, a division of Penguin Random House LLC, New York.

SPIEGEL & GRAU and Design is a registered trademark of Penguin Random House LLC.

Originally published in Australia by Hamish Hamilton, an imprint of Penguin Random House Australia, in 2015.

Library of Congress Cataloging-in-Publication Data

Ulman, Abigail.
[Short stories. Selections]
Hot little hands: fiction/Abigail Ulman.
pages; cm
ISBN 978-0-8129-8917-5
ebook ISBN 978-0-8129-8919-9
I. Title.
PR9619.3.U53A6 2016
823'.914—dc23
2015028878

Printed in the United States of America on acid-free paper

randomhousebooks.com
spiegelandgrau.com

2 4 6 8 9 7 5 3 1

First U.S. Edition

Book design by Liz Cosgrove

For my mum,
with love and thanks.

CONTENTS

HOT

little

HANDS

Jewish History

All the Jappy girls are on a new diet. It's called the Is-raeli Army Diet. I hear a couple of them talking about it at their lockers.

"It's two days apples, two days cheese, then two days chicken," Rachel Hoch says.

"And nothing else?" asks Maya Levine.

"Exactly. So the trick of the diet is—" Rachel looks over her shoulder to see if anyone's listening. She sees me there and turns back. "The trick is that you get so sick of each food, you stop eating it by the end of the first day."

"So what do you eat?"

"Nothing, that's the point. That's how you lose all the weight."

"Wow."

The bell rings and I close my locker. The two girls stay where they are, and I go to Jewish History.

. . .

Yulia has saved me a seat in the corner. I spot her as soon as I come in. As I make my way over, I glance around the room, looking for Bradley Ruben. He's talking to Josh Mellinger and laughing and, just as I'm about to turn away, he looks over, taking in—with one up-and-down swoop of his eyes—my synthetic-leather shoes, the secondhand sweater with the holes in the sleeves, my reddening face. Before I have time to smile or say something, he goes back to his conversation. Inside my school dress, I break into a summer sweat. When I get to my seat, Yulia can tell something's going on.

"Are you okay?" she asks me in Russian.

Irina turns around to look at me. "Yeah, your face looks funny."

"Okay everyone, quiet," Mrs. Kansky calls out. Her skin is heavily powdered as usual, and today her eyebrows are drawn on with what looks like lead pencil. The long sleeves of her blouse hide the line of numbers on her arm that we all saw once, when she lifted her hand to write on the board and the cuff slipped down. "Daniel," she says, though in her accent it is *Dani-ell,* "enough with the Game Boy. Good, thank you. Now let's begin. Who's brought in their testimonials?"

Last lesson we were doing the Spanish Inquisition, but Thursday is Yom HaShoah so this week we're doing the Holocaust. Over the weekend, we were supposed to interview any survivors in our family, or find out what happened to them if they're dead now, and today we're supposed to tell the story to the class.

"Who wants to go first?" asks Mrs. Kansky. No one volunteers, so she chooses Josh Mellinger. He goes to the front of the room and she makes him put on his kippah. Then she tells him to tuck in his shirt. While he's pushing the shirt under his belt, the top button pops off his pants, falls onto her desk, rolls to the edge and off onto the floor. He tries to stop it with his foot but it continues its arc until it disappears under the desk. Everyone laughs.

"My grandfather Isaac was nine years old the day he arrived at Auschwitz. He was separated from his family immediately—his two brothers, his mother, and his father—and he never ever saw them again. He didn't get to say goodbye."

Next up is Natalie Greenblatt. "The kapo liked my grandmother," she says, her fingers twisting the dial on her TAG watch as she talks. "I don't know why. But she always used to try and give her some extra food if there was any."

"He found out later that his mother was gassed two days before liberation, and half a kilometer away from where he'd been."

"She was sick for years after the war, and to this day her stomach is too weak to digest orange juice or the peel of an apple."

One by one, the students who have stories get up to tell them, and the mood in the room changes. Everyone is dead silent, listening. The noise of kids outside shouting to one another on the quadrangle just creates a sense of hushed community inside our classroom. Even the blackboard dust floating in the sunlight near the window seems respectfully still.

All this is disturbed halfway through the lesson, when Rachel and Maya come to the door, giggling and apologizing over each other for being late.

"Sorry—"

"We were just—"

"She was just—"

"Shut. Up." Everyone looks over to where Bradley Ruben is sitting, both hands resting calmly palms-down on his desk, glaring at the girls in the doorway. Rachel and Maya go quiet and slink into nearby seats, not daring to make eye contact with each other. Then Bradley picks up his pen and leans over his notebook, drawing something in the margin. Wisps of his hair fall into his eyes, and he sticks out his bottom lip and blows them away.

"All right, everyone. Let's continue," Mrs. Kansky says. She calls on Simon Herschenberg to read his testimonial, and everyone gives him their attention. Everyone except me. I can't stop thinking about how much I love Bradley Ruben, how brave he is for saying what he said, and how I wish I had a sad Holocaust story to tell, so he would know I'm not so different from him and all the others.

. . .

Yulia takes public transport home, so I walk up to the school buses by myself. It's a warm day for April and in the bus park some older kids get into a water fight. Walking past, I get splashed with water from someone's bottle. It rolls down my legs and into my socks. I look around but no one's looking at me.

"Let me take off my sweater first," one guy calls to another. "I'm all sweaty."

"Yeah, you smell like a Russki," a girl says, and people laugh.

There are twenty-nine school buses. I take number three. I stay close to the chain-link fence on my way down there. My right shoe squelches as I walk.

"Hi, Anya," the bus driver says as I climb on.

"Hi, John."

"Warm one, isn't it? Lucky I got this air conditioner working again. My missus told me this morning it might rain. Melbourne weather for you."

"Yes," I say.

"I'm just hoping it lasts till the weekend. Go Dogs!" His mustache lifts to reveal a grin, and he laughs. I try to laugh back but it just sounds nervous. I walk halfway up the aisle and take a seat.

Five minutes later, when the drivers turn on their engines, all the kids outside hurry to end their conversations. They hand back each other's Walkmans, kiss each other on the cheek, and yell "I'll call you!" as they rush to catch their buses.

People pile on. The oldest kids head toward the back, touching the top of every seat as they go. A younger girl sits next to me. She lifts the armrest, swings her legs into the aisle, and spends the whole ride talking to a girl in the seat opposite.

The drive from Burwood to Caulfield takes forty minutes. My stop is one of the last ones. John opens the door for me and waves goodbye as I step down onto the sidewalk.

"Bye, Anya. See ya tomorrow."

"Okay, John. Yes, thank you. Bye."

Our house is the only single-story place on the street. The front garden is overgrown with long grass and a wayward rhododendron bush that hasn't flowered in the two years we've been here. As I pull the rubbish bin from the curb through the gate, I hear the sound of "Hava Nagila" being thumped out on the piano. Inside, the house smells like frying fish.

"Hi," my mother calls from the living room when I pass. "There's sirniki in the kitchen if you're hungry."

"Okay," I say.

The young boy she's teaching doesn't look up from the keys.

In my room I throw my backpack on the floor and fall back flat onto the bed. On the ceiling above me there's a poster of Edward Furlong wearing a white undershirt and a scowl, torn from a magazine someone left on the bus last year. I roll over on my side and press my nose to the wall, breathing quietly as I remember. Bradley Ruben with his eyes on me. Bradley Ruben with his palms flat on the desk. Bradley Ruben with his fingers cupped around my breast, his tongue pushing its way into my mouth.

"No no. Like this, like this," I hear my mother say in the next room. I hold the pillow over my head to muffle the broken English coming through the wall, and the sound of a clumsy kid making the same mistakes over and over again.

I had barely spoken to any of the Australian boys until two weeks ago. It was a Monday afternoon, and I had climbed off the bus to find Bradley Ruben sitting on the sidewalk, leaning up against someone's fence and smoking a hand-rolled cigarette.

"Hey," he said as I walked by him. Then he picked a piece of tobacco thoughtfully off his tongue.

"Hi," I said, ducking my head down and pushing a strand of hair behind my ear.

"I was waiting for you." He picked up his bag and followed me. "You're good at chem, right?"

"Yes, I suppose, yes." My face felt hot and was, I was sure, as red as Gorbachev's.

"Well, I'm screwed for this lab report. Do you reckon you could help me? My house isn't far. Just off Orrong."

I knew my mother would worry but I went anyway. His house was enormous, one of only four on a dead-end street, and it was painted sky blue. Inside, everything was blue—the carpet, the banister, the frames around the family portraits in the foyer, even the backdrops in the photos themselves. He rushed to a switch and pressed a few buttons—"the alarm," he explained—and then we stood there, listening to the hush of the air-conditioning and a television playing somewhere in the house.

"Come up," he said at last. I followed him up the stairs.

His bedroom was the last one in a long corridor of closed doors. It was large and light, with a single bed beneath a framed poster of Kurt Cobain singing into a microphone with his eyes shut. A glass door led out to a balcony with a view of the swimming pool in the backyard. When I stood on my toes out there, I could see Port Phillip Bay on the horizon. The color of the water matched Bradley's house.

"Is nice," I said.

"It's all right." He shrugged. "This one's really big but I liked our old place better."

When we came back inside, Bradley shut the sliding door and pulled the blinds down. He went over to his bed and pressed some buttons on a remote control. He sat down and looked at me. "*I wanna die next to you, if you'll die too,*" a man's voice sang from the stereo. I wondered if I should get out my notes.

"Come here," Bradley said. I went and stood in front of him. He tugged at the bottom of my school dress so I bent my knees and knelt down. Up close he smelled like smoke but his mouth, when it kissed me, tasted like green apple Warheads. I kissed back, distracted by his hand, which was moving from my waist, up my side, and then under my arm. He pulled his face away then and wrinkled his nose.

"Is it true that in Russia it's so cold, you guys don't even use deodorant?"

"Yes," I said. "Russian winter is very cold."

He tilted his head to the left and I made the same adjustment, and we started kissing again. There was more tongue this time, and his hand was moving faster, over my collarbone and down my chest until it rested firmly, finally, on one of my breasts. I stopped breathing for a moment, certain that he would be disappointed with my size, that he would notice I didn't wear an underwire bra and would ask me to leave. But he didn't say a thing.

I don't know how long we stayed like that, kissing under Nirvana, with Bradley's sweat mixing with spit around my mouth, his hand moving from one breast to the other. My knees were sore from kneeling on the carpet, and my shoulders ached from my book-filled backpack, which I'd forgotten to take off. I had never touched a boy before, so I don't know how I knew exactly what to do next, when he unzipped his fly and lay back on the bed, his hands resting under his head.

Afterward, he pulled up his pants and said he had to study for his bar mitzvah.

"Did guys have barmis in Russia?" he asked me.

"Sometimes," I said. "Is very difficult though. Maybe dangerous."

"Crazy." He stood and opened his bedroom door. I went out into the hall. "Do you need me to walk you?"

I pictured the front of my house, with its paint faded and peeling off, the antenna that had fallen over and now hung from the roof, tapping my window on windy nights, and the sound of Rachmaninoff wafting out from behind my mother's lace curtains. "No, thank you, no," I said.

"Okay," he said. "Don't tell anyone."

"No."

He shut his bedroom door. I heard him walk across the room, and then the music got louder.

Downstairs I went the wrong way and ended up in the kitchen, a big, bright room with blue marble countertops and a pretty girl standing in the center. She was shorter than me, but she was wearing a twelfth-grade sweater, and even through that I could see her arms were as thin as a child's. Her eyes were brown like Bradley's but her hair was curlier, and her cheeks were long and gaunt.

"Are you Brad's tutor?" she asked, looking me up and down.

"No," I managed. "Just from school."

"Oh, okay." I stared at the ball of bone pushing against the skin of her wrist as she pulled open a cheese stick. "Want one?" she asked when she noticed me watching. "There's another box in the fridge."

"Oh, no," I said, walking backward out of the room. "Thank you."

As I rushed through the foyer, I knocked a porcelain bluebird off a table with my backpack. It fell on the carpet but didn't smash. I left it there and hurried out.

When I got home that day, the windows were closed and

the house was silent. I found my mother in the bathroom, sitting on the edge of the tub, leaning over with her head in her hands.

"Mama?" I said. She lifted her face, which was paler than I'd ever seen it, her eyes rimmed in pink.

"Where were you?" she asked in English. It sounded so strange I almost laughed. "I've been vomiting, and sick with worry," she said, this time in Russian.

"I was at a friend's house," I told her, glimpsing a slice of my reflection in the mirror above the sink. My ponytail was loose in its hair elastic and my right cheek was rosier than the left.

"Which friend?"

"Rachel Hoch," I lied. "A girl from school. She wanted help with homework."

"How was I supposed to know that? You've never been late before. I thought someone took you."

"Who would take me?" I asked. But she turned her face away and I understood, without knowing why, that I should shut the bathroom door behind me and go to my room.

My mother's student has gone home now, and my father is back from work. He's sitting at the table in the kitchen, his blond curls tight on his head, the armpits of his shirt wet with sweat.

"They call this autumn?" he says. "It's over eighty-five degrees out there. These people don't know autumn."

"You're telling me," my mother says from the sink. "The

postman was wearing shorts today. Tiny blue shorts with knee-high socks. It was almost obscene. I had to look away."

"Did you have that test?" my father asks me.

"Friday," I say.

"It's maths, isn't it?" my mother says. "You're good at those things."

"Yeah, if you study a little, you'll have no problem."

"Smart girl." My mother hands me a bowl of soup and puts one in front of my father. She sets a smaller portion on her own place mat, then goes back to the sink.

My mother is tall, a full head taller than my father, with a thin nose and light-blue eyes, and a waist so small she has to tie her apron straps around it twice. When she was my age, growing up in Russia, she thought one day she would be a famous concert pianist. My father as a boy, growing up just two towns away from her, dreamed of marrying the most beautiful girl in the world.

"At least one of us got our wish," my mother says bitterly whenever this topic comes up. Then my father always laughs, and she lets him pat her hand.

Back at the table now, she places a plate of fish and a kugel on the doily in the center, and takes her seat. "Well?" she says. "Eat." My father has already finished his soup and is reaching for the kugel, but I push my own bowl away. I get up and go to the fridge, holding the door open with my hand and sticking my head right deep inside where the air is cool and quiet. I close my eyes.

"What are you looking for, Anyishka?" my mother wants

to know. From where I am, her voice sounds far away. The fridge is full of jars and bowls of leftovers from other dinners, all covered neatly in aluminum foil.

"Why don't we throw some of this food away?" I click my tongue in irritation. "Don't we have any apples? Or cheese?"

"What? You're not hungry? My food's not good enough for you?"

"All those years going without," I hear my father say. I know without looking that he's slowly shaking his head. "Cordial instead of orange juice."

"And newspaper instead of toilet paper," my mother joins in.

"Uch, don't remind me," he says.

"Is that true?" I ask, standing up straight.

"You don't remember?" my mother asks. "For years our backsides were black from the ink. We left fingerprints on everything we touched."

"Wait one second," I say. "Let me get my notebook."

My father refuses to get a cordless phone. He says they're too expensive and that by the end of the 1990s, everyone who has a cordless phone will have brain tumors or ear cancer. So when Yulia calls after dinner, I have to pull the cord from the kitchen out into the hallway, past the bathroom, around the door frame where my mother marks my height in pencil once a month, and into my room.

"What are you doing?" she asks.

"Homework." I push the door shut and lean back against it, sliding down to the floor.

"Maths?"

"Jewish History."

"Can you believe that Bradley guy?"

"I know," I say. "Those Japs were silent for the rest of the lesson."

"And I thought Maya was his girlfriend."

"Really? Are you sure?"

"Why?" she asks. "Do you like him or something?"

"Who? Bradley? No. Why, do you?"

"No." We sit in silence for a moment.

"What's that noise?" I ask her.

"My mum's crying."

"Is your dad drinking?"

"No, she's watching *90210*. They're closing down the Peach Pit. She loves that crap."

"Hey, Yuli?"

"Yeah?"

"Are you planning to write a testimonial?"

"No, I'm doing the ESL questions, then I'll study for maths. And then I'm going to sleep to dream about Rachel Levine's face when she got told to shut up."

"It's Rachel Hoch," I say. "Rachel Hoch and Maya Levine."

"Who cares? Both their faces went pale. You could see it happening, even under the fake tan."

. . .

In school the next day, I feel so nervous I think I might be sick. After lunchtime, I go to the toilets, cover the seat with paper, and sit down. I take out my notes and read through them. A group of girls come in and stand by the sinks. Under the cubicle door, I can see their Airwalks and Clarks crowding around the mirror.

"I'm starving," one of them says.

"I know. This diet sucks."

"Apples and cheese were okay. But I could *not* do chicken for breakfast."

"We should go to McDonald's for nuggets after school."

"Totally!"

"I can't, I'm going shopping for my brother's barmi."

"Why don't you wear the dress you wore to my brother's barmi?"

"I can't. It's, like, too small and so Russian. Anyway, how do we even know the diet works?"

"Have you ever been to Israel? Those soldiers are, like, hot."

When the bell rings, I come out of the stall and wash my hands. One of the girls smiles at me in the mirror. It's the one from Bradley's kitchen.

"Hey," she says.

"Hi."

"You haven't come around again."

"No."

All the other girls are staring at me in the mirror now, too.

"I wouldn't take it personally," she says. "I mean, I love my brother, but he has pretty boring taste in girls. Maybe when he's older, he'll want someone, you know, a bit different."

"Okay," I say.

"Okay. See ya." She gives me a little wave in the mirror, and then she leads the other girls out of the bathroom.

"Who is that?" one of them whispers. I don't hear her answer.

Bradley Ruben is giving his testimonial when I get to class. He glances up when I come in, then looks back down at his notes.

"Sorry," I mutter. This is the first thing I've said to him since the day at his house.

"In January 1946, my grandfather found out that his first wife and daughter had perished in Majdanek. By May, my grandmother had received her own bad news. They got married the following year and by 1949 they were in Australia and my dad was born. Thank you." Bradley folds the piece of paper he's holding, and goes to his desk. It feels like we should clap but no one does.

"Right, thank you," says Mrs. Kansky from the back of the room. "Anyone else?" The class sits in silence. "No?" I hold my breath and imagine I'm a different person. Then I raise my hand.

It takes her a minute to see me. "Anya?" The class turns to look. I stand up, swaying slightly.

"What?" I hear Irina say under her breath. I push my chair back and move to the front of the room. My throat feels dry and chalky. Everyone is watching me now, except for Bradley Ruben, who is bent over his notebook, pen in hand, drawing something in the margin.

"After Jews were allowed from Russia in 1989, my mother, my father, and I lived in a flat in Vienna for eleven months, waiting for a visa for here. We were eight people in one small flat, all from Russia or Ukraine, and the toilet was often not working so were sometimes very sick." I hear a rustle in the room then. Someone coughs, or maybe laughs. I don't look up. "We had food given to us, not very much, but we made it so it could be enough. My mother in this time got pregnant two times. She had to have abortions because there was no moneys or room for babies."

"Anya," Mrs. Kansky says.

"Once, the abortion came wrong and my mother had an internal ha—ham—hemorrhage." I stutter over the word and when I finally get it out, Mrs. Kansky is by my side.

"Anya," she says again, her hand on my arm now, her bracelet cool against my skin. "This story is from more recent years. That's not what we're discussing this term." Her voice is quiet and she's looking right into my eyes. "Maybe you can tell it later in the year, but I think right now you should go and sit down."

So I do. There is nothing else to do so I go back to my seat and put my hands on my desk and stare at them. Yulia passes me a note but I don't feel like reading it. I leave it there, folded up next to my pencil case. And though the class continues, I hear nothing for the rest of the lesson but a low humming noise in my ears, like an airplane stuck in midair.

After school, Yulia walks with me to the buses. There are discarded chicken bones on the quadrangle and they crunch under our feet as we go. In the sports hall kids are arriving for detention, and on the oval the football players are already doing suicides. At the bus park, we stand outside the gate. Yulia lets me drink some of her chocolate Big M while the rest of the school files past.

"Why did you do that?" she asks me finally. "We never talk in Jewish History."

I shrug and just as I do, I feel a hand on my arm.

"Hey," Bradley says. He has a cigarette tucked behind his ear. For a second my heart feels like it's trying to escape my body. "Was that a true story?"

"From the class?" I say. "Yes."

"That's fucked up," he says. Then he breaks into a grin. "Sorry, I don't know why I'm laughing."

"Brad," calls Maya Levine. She's standing a few feet away with Rachel and Josh. "We're going to the shops. Are you coming?"

"Yep." He looks at me with a straight face, but then he looks over at Yulia and bursts out laughing again. "Sorry," he manages to say. Then he turns and jogs to catch up with the others.

"What an asshole," Yulia says. "I wish *his* mother had an abortion."

I stick my thumb through the hole in my sweater and squint into the afternoon sunlight. "You know what?" I say. "They're right. We do dress like Russians."

"What?" she says, although I know she heard me.

"And we stink." I turn to look at her. "It's disgusting. We stink."

She stands and looks at me for a long moment. Then she takes her drink out of my hand and walks away without a word, leaving me to face it all on my own, and all over again.

Chagall's Wife

had never before bumped into a teacher on the weekend.
But there he was, sitting at the counter in the window,
and I slowed down to take it all in: the face that looked
more relaxed than it usually did, the late breakfast in front
of him, the hardcover book in his hand with the library tag
on its spine. Through the glass I saw him slide something
off his fork with his mouth. I felt his eyes land on me the
second I took mine off him. I drew in a breath, and went
inside.

I took a seat next to the wall and sipped my juice through
a straw, flipping through every page of a magazine without
taking my eyes off his back. Dressed down for the weekend,
he was wearing a pair of faded black jeans and a khaki
jacket. His dark hair, usually as carefully arranged as his
desk, was ruffled on one side, as though he hadn't even

checked it before heading out that morning. When the waitress came to collect his plate, I saw her brush her arm against his as she reached over him. He looked up and smiled and said something before going back to his book.

Under the fluorescent lights in the toilets, I rubbed some gloss onto my lips. I yanked my hair out of its ponytail, ran my fingers through it, and arranged it over my shoulders. It was dirty blond, and dirty. I tied it back up. My jeans were good and new and tight, but the gray hoodie that showed a stripe of stomach kept going from dorky to cute and back again. I narrowed my eyes at my reflection. *Whatever you do,* I told myself, *don't mention tampons.*

"Mr. Ackerman."

"Sascha, hello."

"I saw you earlier, when I walked in."

"Ah, yes."

"You saw me, too. Why didn't you say hi?"

"I don't know. I suppose I thought you might have better things to do on a Saturday than chat to your boring old science teacher."

"You're not dorky." I lap-danced my eyes over his weekend stubble, the gray T-shirt, his right hand, which was tugging at the leather band of his wristwatch. "What are you drinking?"

"It's an affogato."

"What, like the vegetable?"

"No, it's a coffee drink. Kind of like an ice cream float for grown-ups."

"I see." I leaned one hand on my hip and sucked my bottom lip under the top one until it disappeared. Mr. Ackerman looked down to the floor, where one of my sneakers was standing firmly on top of the other. Then he looked around the café, at the other people sitting there, reading newspapers or quietly chatting, and back at me.

"Would you like to try one?"

I perched on the stool next to his and leaned my elbows in front of me. We kept our eyes on the street. It was early afternoon in the middle of autumn, and the sun was bright but stingy with its warmth. A woman walked past pushing an empty pram; she was talking on her mobile phone. Our silence was long and expectant, like the minutes between the snooze button and the return of the alarm.

"So," I spat out, "sorry about the tampons."

"Oh, don't worry about that," he said. "You've done your time."

Every year since seventh grade, a nurse had come to science class to talk about periods and menstruation. We were never warned beforehand; it was always just sprung on us at the beginning of the lesson. They'd schedule it for first term so the weather was still warm enough for the boys to go play sport with Mr. Ackerman on the oval, while the girls were forced to sit again through the same embarrassing question time; the same video with the same girls wearing 1980s hairstyles and fashion, back when it was really the 1980s and before it was cool again.

This year when the boys returned after the talk, Sam Geary and Sam Stewart had snatched the box of complimentary Tampax off my desk. I was too embarrassed to ask for it back. While Mr. Ackerman was out saying goodbye to the period lady, the boys had unwrapped the tampons, wet them under the tap, and thrown them up at the ceiling, where they'd stuck, the strings hanging down above us for the rest of the lesson like the stalactites we'd learned about the year before.

Later that afternoon, the tampons had dried up and started dropping, one by one, onto the floor and the heads and desks of Mr. Ackerman and his eighth-grade students. I wished I could have seen it. We were halfway through English class, and the boys were excused and the girls told to produce their tampon boxes right there and then. Of course, I was the only one who didn't have mine, so I got sent to Mr. Ackerman's office, where I stood in front of him and told him with a straight face that I had gotten my period that day and had used them all up already.

"All of them?" he'd asked.

"Two at a time," I'd said.

Unfortunately for me, Miss Nesbit, the swimming teacher, had been keeping track of our cycles so we couldn't use the same excuse every week. When consulted, she had divulged that I wasn't due for another fortnight. I wasn't about to snitch on the Sams, so I'd sat through detention every Thursday afternoon for a month.

When my drink came, I started eating the ice cream out of it with a teaspoon. Mr. Ackerman told me in his classroom voice to stir it in so it would sweeten the coffee. I left it to melt and reached for the sunglasses sitting next to his book and keys.

"Are these yours?" I asked, putting them on. They were too big for me. The arms reached way beyond my ears and I had to press the lenses to my face with my fingers to stop them falling off. The world looked blue from beneath those glasses, like science fiction. "They're so—blingy."

"I don't know about that." He smiled for the first time, his face stubbly, and blue now, too. "I've had those since I was at university. They're almost as old as you are."

I kept them on while I tasted my coffee. It was bitter and strong, and it made me cough so hard my throat stung. I pushed it aside. By the time we stood up to go, the ice cream had floated to the top and was sitting on the surface, solidifying.

Mr. Ackerman was shoving his wallet into his pocket when he came outside to where I waited on the curb. "Well, thanks for the company."

"Thanks for the coffee." I took a step closer. He looked

away from me, to the traffic in the street. "I didn't expect to see anyone I know hanging out on this side of town."

He looked down at me with a small smile. "I live on this side of town."

"Oh, really? With your wife?"

"No, with my parents. I'm just here temporarily. On Charles Street."

"Is that where you're going now, then? To your mum and dad's?"

"No, actually, I was planning to go over to the National Gallery."

"I could come," I said, lowering my voice, my eyes still on his. "I've got nowhere else to be."

On the tram, I sat down while he went to buy himself a ticket. When he came back, he stood across the aisle from me and tilted his head to look out the opposite window. I looked, too.

"Think it'll rain?" I asked without caring, and he shook his head.

"Nah," he said.

At a tram shelter outside, a few girls were laughing and backing away from another girl, who was sitting on the bench, pulling off her sweater. She was red-faced and laughing, too. *A bird probably shat on her,* I thought.

"Where are your friends today?" Mr. Ackerman looked over at me.

"Uh, Amy's at drama lessons. Nat's babysitting. Court-ney's at home, she's still got glandular."

"And your family? How come you're out by yourself?"

"My parents are in Portsea. We've got a place down there."

"Ah, yes," he said, as though he'd known that already. He had his sunglasses on now, so I couldn't see his eyes. More than half the seats around me were empty but he stood the whole way there, his arm reaching above his head, past the swaying handles, to hold on to the rail.

The security guard and I played the game: He pretended not to be checking me out while I pretended not to notice. My teacher went to the cloakroom, and I stopped at the first picture and checked my reflection in the gold frame. Why, I wondered, couldn't I have just drunk the stupid coffee?

"A monogamist." Mr. Ackerman had come up behind me.

"Sorry?"

"Chagall. He loved his wife very much." He leaned in close to the painting. "That's her up there, see? She's flying. And there he is, on the ground below, waiting for her to come down. Hoping to catch her. He put her in all his work."

He walked on to look at the next one and I watched him go. For a science teacher he seemed to know a lot about art. I, on the other hand, didn't feel like learning schoolish things on the weekend. I dragged myself from painting to painting, ignoring the essay-long inscription next to each one, staring at the colors till they blurred. I made inkblot tests of them all. Instead of a tableful of angels, I saw a close-up of a mouth with teeth falling out. I turned a juggling bird into a woman belly dancing. A bunch of doves in a tree became soggy tampons just hanging there.

But it was true what Mr. Ackerman had said, about the guy's wife. She was all over the place. First she lay draped naked over a tree of roses. Then she was dressed as a bride with a long veil, holding a baby in her arms. And later she wore a housedress, and the two of them floated together above the orange floor of their kitchen.

I finished the room quickly and wandered out to the foyer. That's where Mr. Ackerman found me fifteen minutes later, sitting on a cushioned bench with my legs tucked under me, staring at the floor and pressing the pad of my thumb up onto the roof of my open mouth. He sat down beside me.

"I don't get what he saw in her," I said. "I mean, she was nothing special, as far as I could see. She had no fashion sense whatsoever and she was probably double his size."

"Maybe Chagall liked substantially sized women," Mr. Ackerman said. He laughed when I rolled my eyes at him. "You've had enough, Miss Davies. You want to go home."

"I want to eat." I pulled myself to my feet. "I haven't had anything all day."

. . .

He knew a place in Southbank that was nice and quiet, with white tablecloths and waiters in half aprons. He furrowed his brow over his menu like he did in class when someone gave a wrong answer, and he chose my meal for me because I couldn't decide. Then he asked me what had brought me to the "wrong side of town." So I told him about the formal dress, and the sewing lady at my dad's factory who had put straps on a strapless gown, and how I wished I'd just gone to Chapel Street and bought something off the rack like all the other girls had, because now I didn't even think I should go to the formal because I'd probably be the only one in straps. He was silent through all this, looking around the room at the empty tables, the waiters chatting near the kitchen, then out the window at the river.

"What's wrong?" I asked.

"Oh. Nothing. It's just a little strange, I suppose, sitting here."

"Do you want to go to the food court?"

"No. I just—I haven't eaten out in a restaurant for a long time. But this is nice. This is fine." He looked at me. "You're hungry."

"I'm ravished," I said, and he nodded and smiled down into his bread plate.

Halfway through our risottos, I finally got up the nerve to ask him if he was married. He had been, he told me, for three years, but it was over now and he didn't say why.

For a while after the divorce, he told me, he had stopped

reading books. He couldn't sleep properly, either. For the longest time, he said, he would go to see movies, dramatic movies, and keep his eyes closed the whole way through. Just so he could be moved by the music. I asked him why he didn't just stay home and listen to songs in the dark, and he said he liked the ritual of buying the ticket, smiling at the popcorn sellers in their vests, and sitting among the couples and groups of kids who didn't bother turning off their phones before the main feature started. He said he liked the way the score kept up throughout a film, dipping and rising, like someone's chest as they lay sleeping. It was cathartic, he said.

"Like, calming?" I asked.

"No," he said. "More like healing."

"So now you read books again?"

"Yes, I've started to. And I guess I'm becoming more social."

I had waited through the last few hours for him to tell me something about himself, something personal like this, but now that it had happened, I didn't know how to respond.

As he talked, I found myself imagining the scene at home when I got back. The quiet that would greet me once I'd shut the big door behind me. The laughter of my sisters coming from somewhere in the back of the house. I saw myself going to the pantry and standing there, surveying the shelves full of lunchbox food: Le Snaks, fruit leathers, apple purees, and twelve-packs of Twisties. Leaving the kitchen without taking anything, I would sneak upstairs to my room unnoticed and lie on my bed, fully clothed, with my school-books open on the desk, Natalie Portman grinning down off the wall, and the duct on the ceiling slowly exhaling its heat into the room.

"Excuse me, sir, this card's been declined. Did you want me to try it again or use an alternative method of payment?" The waitress stood beside him with her hands behind her back. The two of them looked down at his card lying on the tablecloth.

"Uh, give me a second."

"Of course." She unclasped her hands but stayed where she was. Mr. Ackerman fumbled through his pockets.

"Shit," he murmured. I bit down on the inside of my lip. I shouldn't have eaten a main course, I thought, should have asked for a soup or salad. I shouldn't have said I was hungry in the first place.

"I have some money," I said. I took out a twenty and two fives, and handed them to him.

"Thanks, Sascha. I'll pay you back. I have the money, it's just in a different account and I have to transfer it."

When the waitress came with the change, neither of us touched the two-dollar coin on the plastic tray. The kitchen staff were loitering near their window, looking out at us. What are they thinking? I wondered. *She's too old to be his daughter,* probably, *and too young to be his sister.* I wondered what they'd finally decide.

· · ·

Outside, a chilly afternoon wind had started blowing, and the clouds over the city were threatening something worse. We walked among the Saturday shoppers, all searching the sky for a sign of what might come next. By the time we reached Collins Street, it was spitting, and I tried to lead him into a shoe shop.

"Don't worry," he told me. "It'll clear up any second." But a few blocks later, it had turned into a downpour, and the wind was so strong it was sucking people's umbrellas up into tulip shapes. "Here." He pulled me into a building and we stood inside the doorway, staring out at the water thrashing onto the road. We looked at each other, the rain streaming down our faces, and laughed.

We had walked into the foyer of an old-school theater. There were a few people sitting along the wall, reading or staring out at the rain, paying us no attention. There were posters behind them advertising films I'd never heard of, and the concession stand consisted of a basket of mixed-lolly bags, selling, the handwritten sign told us, for $1.50 each.

The woman at the box office was glaring at us, as though we should be paying for the privilege of taking refuge in her dingy little foyer. As though he agreed, Mr. Ackerman went over and asked when the next movie started.

"There's one just started at four," she told him. "Or the next one's at five thirty."

"Should we hide out till the rain stops?" he asked me, and they both watched me nodding.

"One adult and one child?" She coolly met his eyes.

"Student." We both reached for our wallets. "One adult and one student."

The movie was a foreign one, old and black-and-white, and as we sneaked in he whispered that he'd seen it before. The plot was nonexistent and there were no effects or celebrities, it was just people talking. I ignored the subtitles and studied the main girl, who had cropped hair and sold newspapers on the street. I wondered if he found her attractive. Probably, but why? I was yet to work out exactly what it was that guys found sexy in women, but I knew whatever it was, I had it. My body was still boyish and small and straight up and down, but I knew that it was interesting to men. Not necessarily the guys from school, but other men. I'd known this fact for two years now, since the day on the train.

I had felt them before I saw them, the man's eyes on me. I had been sitting across from him and his family and looking out the window behind them, at the back fences and side streets, and the lights being turned off in small office buildings. Then, with a snap like a rubber band, I felt the heat of his gaze, and shifted mine until we met.

It had been a Tuesday evening and I was twelve years old, heading home from school with my mind on homework and netball and *Survivor,* and then suddenly this man had found me, my reflection in the window, and held me there. His arm was thrown around his wife's shoulders and she fussed with the two small kids beside her.

"Don't do that!" She slapped the toddler's hand from its nose. The man smirked at me in the window and raised his eyebrows.

I don't know how long we sat like that for. My house was pretty close to school, so it couldn't have been longer than five minutes. But I knew as I sat there in my uniform, my nipples growing hard, my cheeks hot, the terrible secret passing between me and the stranger, that I was being admitted into a new world—that I was growing old or dying or changing or something. A sensation passed over me then, like insects crawling around on my back.

That was the first time. Since then, I had started a list in a notebook in my room of other things that gave me that sensation. Like 50 Cent videos on MTV. A car crash I saw happen on Glenferrie Road. An article I read about peacekeepers and refugees in Africa. Being on a tram without a ticket when the inspectors climbed on. The faces of people waiting outside nightclubs on weekends. A porn site I'd found open on my dad's computer when I was checking my email in his study one night. And standing in front of Mr. Ackerman in his office and lying to his stern face that I had been shoving tampons up into my vagina, two at a time.

And so today, walking down Smith Street, when I'd glanced up from the sidewalk and seen him sitting there in the window, looking both strange and familiar, like photos of my parents when they were young, I had felt it: the heat, the hardness, the insects. I had turned into the café without missing a beat, as though this were a movie and I was only just now being shown the script. I had had the sudden and full knowledge that there was a reason that I had been admitted into this new world; that here, today, later today, sometime, Mr. Ackerman was going to take this feeling to its real and necessary ending.

In the flicker and dark of the movie, I closed my eyes. There was no soundtrack but I listened to the up-and-down lilts of the language as though it were music. I leaned my head onto his shoulder. His jacket still held the cold of the rain and it smelled like outside when I breathed into it. Mr. Ackerman put his hand on my hair and stroked it. I felt dizzy and humid, like I was flying above myself in the dark. I imagined him standing below me like that painter guy, getting ready to catch me before I hit the ground.

"Mr. Ackerman," I whispered, my teeth against his jacket.

"Are you tired, Sascha?" His mouth found my ear and he took his eyes off the screen. "Or do you want to go somewhere else?"

The Withdrawal Method

"There's this story about a girl who goes to see her gynecologist," I tell the gynecologist. "She gets up early on the morning of, while her roommates are still sleeping, and goes for a run. When she comes home, she's all sweaty, but she doesn't have time to shower before her appointment. So she grabs a towel and wipes herself off. You know, down there."

"Uh-huh," says Dr. Hill as she holds the speculum against my thigh. "This might be a bit cold." She inserts it into me. It *is* a bit cold, and uncomfortable. I worry for a moment that there will be a sharp edge or angle on there that she doesn't know about. "Go on," she says. "So she wipes herself off—"

"Yeah. Then she goes to the gyno and takes off her pants, gets on the chair, spreads her—oh." I hold my breath as she cranks the thing open. It squeaks as it pushes against me.

"Lie back," she says. "Breathe. Concentrate on the bear." I press my head back into the chair and stare at the poster stuck to the ceiling above me, a photo print of a bear standing on a grassy hilltop. "That's it," she says, as she gets me wide open.

"So the girl spreads her legs, and the gyno comes in—it's a man—and he comes into the room, stands in front of her, looks between her legs, and says, 'Oh, I see you dressed up for me today.'"

Dr. Hill scrapes a cotton swab against my cervix. The discomfort feels real and far away, like someone yelling your name outside your front door while you're sleeping.

"And the deal is, the girl lives with this raver chick, and the towel she grabbed to wipe herself off was covered with the chick's face glitter. So the gyno thinks she's applied it especially for him."

"Urban legend," says Dr. Hill as she winds the speculum closed.

"Really?" I say, sitting up and leaning back on my elbows.

"Absolutely."

I inhale as she pulls the metal out of me. Inside I feel like I felt in eleventh grade, when Becky Addis and I got drunk in the park and she shoved her hand down my jeans and put her fingers inside me with fingernails that were too long.

"Vaginas don't sweat," says Dr. Hill. "Not inside anyway. I'll go to the lab and check on your other tests. Why don't you get dressed and meet me in my office."

. . .

I expect AIDS, because I had sex with this Irish guy who told me he'd gone to see prostitutes in Amsterdam. I expect herpes because this drummer Chris went down on me and I found a tube of Zovirax on the floor under his bed the next morning. I expect HPV because I saw a segment about it on *60 Minutes* last week. I expect chlamydia, gonorrhea, hep A, B, C because I'm a floozy whose back catalog of lovers should be organized with the Dewey decimal system. But I do not expect a fetus. And that's what it is.

"Do you know who the father is?" Dr. Hill asks me.

"Yes," I say.

"Was this something the two of you planned?"

"No," I say. "Complete accident."

"What precautions were you taking?"

"He was, uh, pulling out."

"The withdrawal method?" she asks. She shakes her head as I nod mine. "Very risky." She opens a desk drawer and takes out a pamphlet with a photo of a pensive-looking Asian girl on the front. Above her head it reads, so . . . YOU'RE PREGNANT.

"I don't need that," I say.

"Are you sure?" She holds the pamphlet toward me like a stubborn canvasser on a street corner.

"I know my options," I say. "I don't want the baby."

She puts her hands in her lap. "Well, then," she says. "I guess you're looking at adoption, or a termination."

"I want a termination," I tell her. "Is that still legal in this country?"

She leans back in her desk chair and sighs. "Thirty-five

years of fighting to maintain our rights and every second girl who sits in that chair asks me that question."

"I'm not American," I remind her. "How soon can I get this done?"

"Well—" She pushes the mouse across the mousepad to wake her computer. "It's too late to book you in somewhere today, and most places will be closed over the weekend."

She types something in and I look around her office. It's almost empty, except for the desk, the two chairs, the computer, a phone, and a poster on the wall telling me to ask my doctor about the IUD coil.

"What's the IUD coil?" I ask her.

"One thing at a time," she says. "I found an open appointment, on Monday at two thirty, at a center in South San Francisco. They offer a free and confidential counseling service onsite. I also suggest you talk this decision over with someone beforehand. A close friend or family member. The father, perhaps?" She looks in the drawer for another pamphlet.

Suddenly I'm aware of how alone I am in this city, how far away all my best friends and family are. Suddenly I'm wishing that my teenage experimentation with Becky Addis had taken; that she and I were now living together in a cottage on the coast of Brighton, clipping our fingernails as foreplay, flushing our contraceptive pills down the toilet, and laughing triumphantly at our risk-free lesbian life.

. . .

Being unexpectedly pregnant is like learning that someone you love has died. You remember, then you forget, then all of a sudden it dawns on you again. The brain separates the enormous shock into many minor shocks and doles them out at five-minute intervals. I walk to the BART station. I'm pregnant. I buy a ticket. I'm pregnant. I ride the train and get out at 24th Street. I'm pregnant. I buy a pack of cigarettes at the corner store. I give the woman seven dollars and she hands me coins. I'm pregnant. I go to see Luke at the Common Room.

"Hey, I'm pregnant."

"What?" He can't hear me. He's standing behind the espresso machine, his manager Katie is at the roaster, and Slow Club is crooning through the speakers. "Did you get my text messages?" he asks loudly.

"Probably not all of them," I say. "You filled up the memory on my phone so I couldn't receive new ones."

"Well, I wouldn't have to send so many if you just answered one." He doses into the portafilter and tamps it down. "What are you doing here anyway?" He slams the instrument harder than he needs to into the machine and positions a cup under the spouts. "I told you it makes me uncomfortable to see you."

Then we have the same fight we've been having for the last three weeks.

"I've been coming here since the first day I got to the city. Way before I even met you."

"Well, I was working here a year before you even arrived in the States."

"This café is one of the reasons I moved to this neighborhood."

"Well, there are other coffee shops in the Mission District."

"Why don't you work in one of them, then?"

"Are you fucking serious?" he says. "Low-fat latte for Allie," he calls out.

I'm pregnant, I think.

"Look," he says. "I still love you. If you don't want to be in contact with me, you can't come in here."

"Oh yeah?" I say. "If you're so in love with me, why did you change your MySpace status to single?"

"You're the one who said you wanted a clean break."

"And you took my band out of your top twelve."

"Americano for George. Why do you even care? Why are you even checking my MySpace?"

"It's bookmarked on my computer."

"So un-bookmark it."

"Fine," I say.

"Fine." He glares down at me over the row of glasses and mugs on top of the machine. I glare right back. "I created a new espresso blend," he says. "A Colombian microlot and a Cup of Excellence from Brazil. Ripe cherry acidity with a maple syrup finish. Really sweet."

"What's it called?"

"Straight Shooter. Wanna try it?"

"Sure."

. . .

On his break we go into the green bean room. I sit on a sack of Santa Isabel. He leans back on a stack of Bolivians. It's cooler in here than the rest of the café; the beans absorb the heat. *I'm pregnant,* I think, looking him up and down. But it's not the baby that's making my stomach churn. He's wearing his tight black jeans and a very low-necked white T-shirt, and an open gray-and-blue cowboy shirt with the sleeves rolled up. His hair is messy, his eyes bright blue, and he's got a few days' worth of stubble on his face. I can see three of his tattoos: the EKG squiggles over his heart, the vintage gun on his right wrist, and the numbered lines on the inside of his left arm:

1._____
2._____
3._____

"It's where I write my to-do list," he said last June on our first date, as we sat spinning right-to-left-and-back on barstools at the Dovre Club. Then he took out a pen and scrawled my name on all three lines, then again and again, all the way down his arm—CLAIRE CLAIRE CLAIRE CLAIRE— before dropping the biro on the floor and reaching for me. His teeth pressed against my lower lip drew blood, and when I climbed onto his lap and wrapped my legs around him, the bartender told us we had to leave. He rode with me on the handlebars of his fixed-gear to his apartment on Harrison, and I forgot we weren't using anything until he pulled out of me, wrapped a fist around himself, and came into his hand.

"Hey, thanks for not knocking me up," I said, reaching across the floor for my cigarettes.

"Of course," he said, wiping his palm on the sheet, on the part of the bed closest to the wall. "I'm nothing if not a gentleman."

Today, in here, the sight of him, both put-together and disheveled, and the smell, that deep, sweet, caramel scent of roasting coffee that sticks to his clothes, his skin, his hair—that scent that is so strongly linked to him in my mind that some mornings just walking past a Starbucks on my way to class and inhaling is enough to get me wet inside my underwear—it all almost makes me forget the fifth, sixth, and seventh months of our relationship. For a moment I want to turn and lock the door, and walk the few steps it would take for my hip bones to be pressed against his jeans. I want to stand on my tiptoes till my face can reach his face. And as if he's thinking the same thing, he clears his throat and says, "What are you wearing under that blazer?"

"Nothing."

"No skirt?"

"Nup."

"What about under the tights?" he asks.

I smile up at him.

Then he says, "Why are you dressed so sexy? Do you have a date? Are you seeing someone else already? Do I mean so little to you?" And I remember the fifth, sixth, and seventh months of our relationship. So I leave the door unlocked and try to breathe through my mouth. I stare at the floor, scattered with unroasted beans, and I tell him, "I'm pregnant."

The first thing he does is slap a palm to his forehead in a cartoonish gesture of shock that almost makes me laugh. His fingers are brown with coffee stains. "Is it mine?" he asks.

"What kind of a—" I try to look hurt and insulted like women do in the movies when men ask them this, but I can't maintain it for long. "Yes," I say. "You're the only person I've slept with since we broke up."

There's a knock on the door, and Katie pokes her head in. "Luke—oh hey, Claire—are you almost done in here? There's a line out the door and Jackie's pulling horrible shots. I want to put her back on the register."

"I'll be right out," he says. When she's gone, he turns to me and takes my hand. "Hey. When can we talk about this?"

"I've already decided. I'm not having it."

"Huh." He looks at the wall, pasted with flyers about workplace safety and the minimum wage in California. "Is there anything I can do?"

"You can pay for half the procedure."

"How much is that gonna be?"

"I think it costs two hundred and fifty dollars," I say. "But I might just be getting that from *Dirty Dancing*."

It's almost four o'clock and outside it's getting windy. The fog is rolling in to the north and the south, sparing our little bowl of a neighborhood, where it is always sunny. A block away from where I live on Shotwell Street, I run into Sean. He's got his laptop bag over his shoulder and he's wearing a fedora.

"Hey," he says. "I put you in my new book. You're the Scottish girl in the pop band. Chapter six."

"I'm English," I say. "Let's go. Rematch." I put out my hand and we grip each other's fingers and start moving our thumbs from side to side.

"One two three four," we say in unison. "I declare a thumb war."

"Okay, kiss," I say, pushing my thumb against his for a second. "Now, bow." We both bend our thumbs at the knuckle. "Into your corners, come out fighting." It doesn't take long for him to pin me, his thumb covering mine completely, and he takes his time counting up to knockout.

After he's won three rounds, he asks me, "When are we gonna go on a date?"

"I told you," I tell him. "I'm not attracted to you."

"Shut up," he says. "Seriously, when can we go out?"

"I don't see you in that way," I say. "All I can offer you is friendship."

"You're not scaring me," he says. "How about Wednesday?"

"I don't date writers," I say. "I really can't stand writers."

"Maybe Thursday's better?"

"Don't you people realize that nobody reads books anymore?"

"I want to go on a date with you. To SFMOMA. Next week."

"I can't next week," I say. "I'm having an abortion next week."

"Shut up," he says. "You look hot today. Meet me right here on Thursday at five."

"I won't be here," I say as he walks away.

"It's a date!"

My roommates are giggling in the living room when I get home. "Claire," Sophie calls out. "Can you come film us? We're trying to make a video response for YouTube."

She has her hair pulled back and is wearing a white onesie. She's sitting on Andrew's lap. I take the camera from her and stand across from them. When I press RECORD, Sophie starts gaga-ing like a baby. Andrew holds out his index finger and Sophie bites it.

"Ow, Charlie bit me," Andrew says in an attempt at an English accent. Sophie clamps down again. "Ouch ouch ouch. That really hurt, Charlie, and it's still hurting."

When they finish, I stop filming and they collapse with laughter.

"Let's do another take," says Sophie.

"Let's watch it first," says Andrew.

"Yeah yeah," says Sophie. "Claire, you wanna see the original?"

"No thanks." I hand her the camera. "I don't think babies are funny."

In my room, I find my phone card on the desk and follow

the automated prompts until I'm talking to my mother in London. It's nighttime there.

"Hiya," I say.

"Hiya," she says.

"I need to talk to you about something."

"Hold on, how do I get this thing on speakerphone? Meredith, can you do it? I can't find the button. I don't have my glasses. Can you see it?"

"Hi, Claire," says my brother Paul, when they've got it worked out.

"Hiya," says my sister Meredith.

"Hi, Claire Bear," says my father.

"Hi, Claire," says my ex-boyfriend Alistair.

"Hey," says my sister-in-law Wendy.

"Hello, sweetheart," says my grandmother.

"Hi, everyone," I say. "Wait, what's Alistair doing there?"

There's a long silence and I picture everyone sitting at the kitchen table, nervously eyeing one another, and rolling crumbs over the tablecloth with their fingers.

"Mum was supposed to tell you," says Meredith. "Al and I are together now."

"What?"

"I was planning to tell her in December when she comes to visit," my mother says.

"Oh my God," I say.

"Charlie!" I hear my roommates yelling in the other room. "Charlie, that really hurts!"

"What's the big deal?" my brother says. "I thought you were the one who broke it off."

"She was," Alistair says.

"Because I moved to America," I say.

"You said you were glad to be leaving him," Meredith says.

"Cheers for keeping the family secrets," I tell her.

"Why don't you meet a nice American boy?" my grandmother asks.

"I'm sorry," Meredith says. "I know it's really weird."

"It's worse than that," I say.

"But sometimes good people just find each other," she says.

"Let's talk about this when you come to visit," my father says. "They might not even be together by then."

"Dad!" says Meredith. "We will be. We definitely will be."

"I'm gonna go now," I say. "Bye, everyone. Bye, Nanna."

"Bye, sweetheart," my grandmother says. I hang up before anyone else can speak.

On Saturday morning I take BART under the Bay to visit James and Amanda in Berkeley. They've moved into a new house, wooden and cozy, with a deck overlooking a backyard full of trees. Amanda is pulling a frittata out of the oven when I arrive, and James is in the living room, mixing up mimosas. When I tell them about the baby, they exchange a glance.

"Well, if it was a boy, it'd be tall like Luke," Amanda says.

"And clingy and obsessive," James says.

"Just what the world needs," I say.

"How did this happen?" Amanda asks.

"I'm an idiot." Neither of them responds to this. I wonder what they'll say about it later, after I'm gone.

The three of us eat out on the deck and talk about our dissertations—a conversation that inevitably devolves into complaints about our meager stipends, the user-unfriendliness of EndNote, and the unavailability of our supervisors.

"Do you ever think that our relationships with our supervisors are like parent–child relationships?" Amanda says, shaking hot sauce onto her eggs. "We start out feeling completely dependent on them. We don't do anything without getting their opinion or permission."

"Then they let us down," James says.

"Then we realize they're not perfect." Amanda puts her bare foot on James's lap and he covers it with his hand. "And that they have other children to deal with, too. So we resent them, and decide we don't need them, and we strike out on our own."

"Yeah, but I made out with mine," I say. "So how does that fit into the analogy?"

"Jesus," James says. "Professor Fursten? Really?"

"Is that bad?"

"When do you find time to work, with all this stuff going on?"

"On the holidays. Everyone goes home to their families. I stay in the city and work my ass off."

"That's probably ten days a year," James says.

"When do you two work?"

"Monday to Friday," says Amanda. "Nine to five."

"Wow, you guys are such grown-ups," I say. "Do you want a baby?"

"I don't think so." She shakes her head. "At least not one of our own."

"Maybe we'll adopt one day," says James.

"No, I mean, do you want *this* baby? I can have it and then hand it over."

They laugh. "I definitely don't want a kid right now," Amanda says.

"Neither do I," James says.

"Me neither," I say. "First I need a calmer life. Maybe get married like you guys."

"You think marriage is a calmer way of life?" James asks.

"It's when the terrifying shit really begins," Amanda says.

"What you need is a *quieter* life," James says. "So you can process all the craziness."

"Maybe you should move to Berkeley," Amanda says. "Come be our neighbor."

"I'd love to," I say. "But there's a whole city to conquer over there. San Francisco is trying to kick my ass, and I can't let it get the better of me."

A screen door slams in a neighboring yard and a woman calls to someone to bring her a sweater. Amanda starts humming what sounds like an M. Ward song. James pats her foot in three–four time. I look out at the fig tree, heavy with fruit, and I try to imagine a life in which monogamy didn't feel like a locked cell in which I always start wishing my cell mate would get released early for good behavior.

"You guys are so lucky," I say. "You have each other and you want each other."

"It's true," Amanda says. "We're lucky, but you know it's not perfect. We're both in the same department. We're competing for funding, and we're always busy and stressed out at the same time."

"Yeah, but at least you understand each other's work. You can read each other's papers."

"Uh-huh," James says. "Try sleeping next to the person who just correctly informed you that your entire thesis topic is flawed and untenable and you've just wasted two whole years of research."

"So what you're saying is, I should give Professor Fursten a call?" I stand up and start clearing dishes.

"Don't do that," James tells me. "We'll do it. You're in a delicate condition."

"Oh don't, that's awful," Amanda says, smiling at me apologetically.

When it's time to leave, they stand on the front porch and wave goodbye.

"There she goes," Amanda says. "See you soon."

"Come back bearing stories," James calls after me.

Back in the city, I stop in at the Common Room. Luke is roasting, pouring beans from a bucket into the hopper of the Probat.

"What's cooking?" I ask him.

"Fucking decaf," he says. "I'm glad you stopped by. I wanted to tell you: I think this baby is the best thing that could have happened to us."

"What are you talking about?"

"Think about it," he says. "I pulled out hundreds of times when we were together, and it worked fine. Then the one time we have sex after the breakup, and *bam*"—he slams his fist into his palm—"we make a kid."

"All that means," I say, "is that we're both fertile."

"No, no." He turns back to the roaster, pulls out the trier, holds it under his nose, and smells the beans. They're the color of wet sand. He puts it back. "This baby means more than that. It's a sign that we're supposed to be together."

"But I'm not keeping it," I say.

"That's even more reason to be together. An abortion is a big deal. I want to be there for you, in whatever way I can."

"Well, right now I'd love a Gibraltar."

He turns down the gas on the roaster and goes behind the bar. I take a seat at a nearby table. All around me, people are sitting with coffee cups, staring into laptop screens. The girl at the table in front of me has a sticker of a peach stuck over her Apple logo. The guy to my left is working on a Word file titled *Start-Up: A Memoir.*

"Do I know you?" he says when he sees me looking. He has black curly hair and straight white American teeth.

"No," I say, "I just thought I'd save you some time by telling you not to bother writing that memoir. Nobody reads books anymore."

"This isn't a book," he says. "It's my senior thesis." He leans back in his chair. "So what's that accent? New Zealand?"

When Luke comes back, he puts the drink on the table and walks away. I take it and follow him over to the roaster. He checks on the beans again, then pushes a lever. The beans shower out of the drum and into the cooling tray.

"Thanks for the drink," I say, sipping it. He doesn't answer me. "What's going on?"

"Nothing," he says. "Who's that guy?"

"Some kid. College kid."

"And you feel perfectly okay about flirting with him while I'm over there making you a beverage?"

"I would feel okay about that, if that's what I was doing."

"There are plenty of other coffee shops in San Francisco you can go to."

"Why don't you work in one of them, then?"

"Are you kidding? This is my workplace. And you're ruining it for me, emotionally. Would you mind leaving now? I have stuff to do."

"Fine," I say.

"Fine."

Halfway down the block, I run into Andrew. He's got his skateboard under his arm and he's talking on his phone. "Wait one second," he says to the person he's speaking to. He holds his phone facedown on his chest and asks me, "So when are we gonna go on a date?"

"We're not," I tell him. "You're my roommate."

"Does that mean Sophie's off-limits, too?"

When I get to Amnesia, Lars is sitting on the edge of the stage, bent over with his face in his hands. "Dude," I say, sitting next to him. "What a shitty week." It's only then that I notice his ear is all scraped up and bloody. When he looks at me, I see he has a black eye, and a big gash at his hairline. There's a hole in his T-shirt the size of a pancake.

"Bike accident," he says.

"Whoa," I say.

"Beer," he says.

"Got it."

The bartender is a tall redhead guy with a face that's more sideburns than skin, and a mustache that would make Dalí swoon. He nods when I order, and pulls me a pint.

"Seven bucks," he says, placing it in front of me.

"I'm in the band," I say.

"I know. Seven bucks."

"Don't we get drink tickets?"

"Last time you were in here, you made out with my girlfriend. That'll be seven bucks."

"Fine." I get out the money and put it on the bar. "I'm not tipping, though." He shrugs and takes the bills. I pick up the drink and say, "Why are you being so weird about it? It's girl-on-girl. Aren't guys supposed to be into that?"

"This isn't fucking Los Angeles," he says.

I go back to the stage and give the glass to Lars, who takes a couple of sips and then chugs the rest down. He leans his head on my shoulder. "I was turning left, man, and this guy in a taxi slammed straight into me."

"Did he have right-of-way?"

"Yeah."

"Did you have lights on?"

"No."

"That bastard."

"I think I may have chipped a molar."

"I'm pregnant."

"Man." He sits up and glares at me. "You're always one-upping me."

The bar is almost empty, but an hour after we've sound-checked, there are about twenty people there; at least four of them have come to see us. Lars has graduated to a bottle of Knob Creek I bought at the corner store across the street. He takes a slug as we climb onto the stage, then passes it to me. I take it with my non-tambourine hand and hold it up at the bartender in a gesture of cheers. He sticks up his middle finger.

"Hey, thanks for coming out tonight. We're Betty Cooper's Revenge," says Lars, who has, I now realize, developed a bit of a lisp from the accident. "I fell off my bicycle today and Claire is pregnant. Now you're all caught up. Let's play some tunes."

He starts in with the opening chords of "Mood Ring."

"If any of you record this and put it online," I say into my microphone, "I will track you down and—add you to our email list." Then I put the bottle to my lips and drink.

"Mmm, baby loves bourbon," Lars says, smirking at me.

"He's a lousy lay, ladies," I say. "Believe me, I tried him out. And that was before the concussion. One. Two. A-one two—" I hit the tambourine hard against my palm and shake it.

"Honey baby, you're a tall drink of water," Lars sings. *"I'm kind of regretting that restraining order."* His falsetto is so pretty. I close my eyes. *"Please take it slow, don't get carried away. Let's drive through the desert and get married today."*

After the set, we stand at the end of the bar, finishing the bottle, until the guy from Coed Dorm comes and screams at us to get our shit off the stage so they can play. I'm sloppy on my feet now and I drop my triangle wand as I'm shoving the percussion gear into my bag. I think about bending down to look for it in the half dark, but I need to use the bathroom, so I decide I'll just play it with my house key from now on.

When I get to the ladies' room, there's a line outside. "Hey," says the girl in front of me. She's wearing dangly earrings. "Great show."

"Hey, thanks," I say. She smiles at me and I wonder if I should make out with her.

"You're pregnant, right?" says the girl in front of her. "You can go ahead of me."

"Oh, cheers." I move to the front of the line and try the bathroom door. It's locked. The girl who gave me her spot is wearing little black shorts and tall brown boots. I wonder if I should make out with *her.*

"Do you date anyone who works here?" I ask her. She looks confused.

"The men's room is free," says a guy coming out of the men's room. "You can use it."

The bathroom, like every public bathroom in this town, is disgusting. The floors are wet, the door handle is sticky, the graffiti isn't funny, and there's no toilet seat. I half sit, half stand, pull my dress up, clutch it in a bunch, and hope for the best.

When I come out, the same guy is still standing there. He has blond floppy hair and wide-set blue eyes and he's probably attractive but he's not my type. Tan pants, lace-up Vans, a short-sleeved pale blue button-down shirt, and a big fat silver ring on his thumb.

"I think your friend should go to the emergency room," he says.

"Who?" I look around until I see Lars sitting at the bar with a girl who waits tables at Suppenküche. She's holding a handful of ice to his forehead and it's dribbling down his face as it melts. He's trying to catch the droplets with his tongue. "Look at those reflexes," I say. "He's fine."

"Are you really pregnant?" the guy asks.

"Yep," I say, "for a limited time only."

He holds his hand out and introduces himself as Anton. He asks what I'm doing in the States, and I say I'm doing a PhD in cinema studies, and we get into a conversation about

Wes Anderson and Paul Thomas Anderson, and the difference between childish cinema and the cinema of childhood.
Then my stomach rumbles and it takes me a minute to work
out that it's not alcohol or attraction or my unwanted pregnancy that's doing it. I just haven't eaten since breakfast.

"Hey, where do you live?" I ask.

"Just on Seventeenth. Whoa, are you okay?"

I reach out and grab hold of the wall beside me. "Do you
have any food there?"

His bike is an eight-speed with brakes and a brand name,
and tires that wouldn't look out of place on an army jeep.
He rolls it between us as we walk. When we get to his building, he says it's too heavy to carry up the stairs, and he takes
his time locking it up in the downstairs hallway. "You've got
nothing to worry about," I say. "You could leave that thing
lying out on the pavement all night and no one would take
it."

He looks down at his bike and gives a small, sad shrug.
"I'd take it," he says.

The apartment is standard San Francisco Victorian: a
long narrow hallway with bedrooms and a bathroom coming off it, and a living room and a kitchen in the very back.
Anton's probably about twenty-four and I'm expecting
ramen noodles or leftover Chinese takeaway, but what he
brings out is a plate with five different cheeses on it, a bowl
of hummus ("homemade," he says), and crackers imported

from Sweden. He sits opposite me and watches while I eat. "I've seen you before," he says. "At the Common Room. You go out with that tall dirty guy."

"Not anymore," I say.

"Huh." He looks down at the table and smiles. This is when I should probably say something—*I'm not looking for anything,* or *I don't want to date right now,* or *We should just be friends.* Or maybe it's some nonverbal cue I'm supposed to give: lean away, seem bored and uninterested, don't make eye contact while smiling. But those things don't come naturally to me. So I do what I always do when I meet a new guy: I tell him about all my troubles with the other guys.

"He went away to Honduras to visit a coffee farm, right, and he sent me a text message saying he was spending the last two days on Roatán. We're writing back and forth, and it's all really fun, so I say, 'I'm glad you're having a break. You need a holiday. Go get laid and be safe.' And then he sends me this barrage of vitriolic—"

"He's still in love with you," Anton says. "He doesn't want to hear some buddyish suggestion like that. You're the only one he wants to sleep with."

"I guess." I cut off a piece of blue Brie and pull it from the knife with my fingers. "But then there's my thesis supervisor, who's so smart and I could talk to him forever, but when we kissed, there was nothing there. I couldn't believe it. On paper, we're so right for each other. So I kissed him a few other times just to make sure."

"And?"

"And nothing. Even his smell. You know how they say if you're attracted to someone's scent, it means they have a different immune system from yours? So then your babies would have really strong immune systems. With my supervisor, I'm not attracted to his scent at all. I can barely smell anything, and when I can, I don't find it sexy. I think it's because we're both descendants of Eastern European Jews. We're from the same tribe."

"You both have the old Ashkenazi immune system?" he says.

"Exactly. So then there's this guy back home—" I tell him the story of my sister and my ex-boyfriend, and I expect him to be appalled and horrified, but all he says is, "Do you still have feelings for this guy?"

"No. But what's that got to do with it?"

"Do you like him at all? Like, as a person?"

"Al? Yeah, he's lovely. Super sweet guy."

"Well, then maybe you should get out of their way."

"What? I can't do that. It's too weird. You don't get how weird it is."

I'm halfway through the next story and have eaten most of the hummus when one of Anton's roommates comes home. A skinny guy with a side part, and a red bandanna tied around his neck. "What's up?" he says. "We're having a surprise party for Calorie at the playground in Dolores Park. Wanna join?"

"You have a friend called Calorie?" I ask.

There are voices in the hallway, and the lights go off in

the living room. The fairy lights rimming the ceiling come on, and suddenly there are about ten people in there, sitting, standing, talking. One guy has a radio strapped to his back with what looks like a seatbelt. It's playing a Cut Copy song.

"Who are these people?" I ask, standing up as two girls in leg warmers rush into the kitchen with a foil-covered baking dish that holds, it is soon revealed, a birthday cake for Calorie. Whose name is spelled with an *o-r-y*.

"They're moped people," says Anton. Then, "Wanna go up on the roof? I have wine."

We go through an alcove full of bicycles and skateboards, out the back door and up some stairs, past the back door of the apartment above, and up another flight till we reach the bottom of a ladder. "Are you scared of heights?" he asks, handing me the bottle. He turns and grabs hold of a rung. I look up the ladder to the awning of the roof and beyond it, to a few city stars.

"I'm not scared of heights," I tell him, "I'd just rather not fall."

The roof is big and flat, and we sit right in the middle—Twin Peaks before us, the park to our left, the skyline and bridges behind our backs. The wine is full-bodied and tastes like grapes. Luke, I know, would taste other things in it—stone fruit or Meyer lemon cake or red Jolly Ranchers—things I would never have thought of but, when he identified them, would realize were there.

"So," Anton says.

"So," I say.

"So why do you think these guys are into you?" He takes a swig and passes the bottle.

"It's probably just the accent."

"It can't just be that," he says. "Maybe it's the Winona Ryder thing. You look a bit like her in the nineties."

"Wow, I do? Like, which one? *Heathers* Winona or *Little Women* Winona?"

"Um, I think *Beetlejuice* Winona."

"What? That's not a good thing. No one's trying to date *Beetlejuice* Winona. Except Beetlejuice."

"Oh," he says, "then I don't know what it is. You don't even have big tits."

"Small mercies," I say. "What's that noise?"

"Mopeds."

We go to the edge of the roof and look over, and he's right. A crowd of people on mopeds are revving on the sidewalk. They're all wearing helmets and jeans and it's difficult to tell who's who. I make out a pair of purple leg warmers on one person. A red bandanna on another. Then they all follow one another in a U-turn and ride up the street in a mess of effete urbanism. They turn left onto Dolores Street and head for the park.

"So this abortion thing is a big deal," Anton says, once they've disappeared.

"Nah. This abortion is the most practical and organized thing in my life. It's the only thing I'm certain I want."

"Still, it's like an operation. Operations suck."

"Yeah," I say. "I guess they do."

We sit back down. The roar of the moped motors turns into a high-pitched buzz as they get farther away. Then it gets quiet. I think about my cigarettes. I left them downstairs in my bag. I lie back, ignoring the gravel digging into me, and picture myself at the clinic on Monday, lying on an operating table, with blood coming out of my—where? With medical instruments lying about that look like—what? I realize I don't know anything about the procedure I'm going to have, and that seems scarier than knowing every tiny detail about it.

"Let's stop talking about me," I say to Anton, feeling suddenly short of breath. "Let's talk about you. Let's talk about everything there is to know about you. Like, what do you do?"

"I'm a graphic designer," he says. "And I paint."

"Sounds great," I say. The tightness in my chest gets worse. "Do you have a girlfriend?"

"No. I just broke up with a woman about four months ago."

"Cool," I say. "Can I sleep over?"

"Uh—" He smiles an embarrassed smile and looks up at the radio tower on the hill. "I don't think that's a good idea."

"Please," I say. "We don't have to do anything. We can just sleep."

"I just met you," he says. "I don't know you."

"I'm nice," I say, grabbing his hand and squeezing.

"You're smashed," he says. "It wouldn't feel right. Why don't I just walk you home?"

. . .

When I wake early the next morning, it's still dark outside my window, and I feel like something has gone horribly wrong. I sit up and rack my brain for a minute before I remember: I'm pregnant.

"What's going on?" someone says.

"Jesus."

Luke is lying beside me, one hand under his head, the other one lying flat on his bare chest.

"How did you get here?"

"I rode my bike," he says.

"Who let you in?"

"You did. You drunk-dialed and told me to come over. I asked if we were gonna talk about the baby and you said yes. But when I got here, you kept telling me to shut up. You had other ideas."

"Shut up," I say. I find my phone on the floor by the bed and scroll down to the outgoing calls section. And there it is: *(Don't call) Luke 1:38 a.m.*

"That's my name in your phone?" he asks.

"It's a joke," I say, lying back down. He props himself up on his elbow and looks at me. His face is just a few centimeters from mine.

"Anyway," he says, "I was happy you called."

"How do you do that?" I ask him. "How do you smell like coffee first thing in the morning?"

"I didn't shower yesterday," he says. Then I lift my face

and kiss him because, for some reason, right now I can't think of a single sentence that is sexier than that one.

I fall asleep and when I wake again, the sun is rising over Potrero Hill. I slip out of bed, go to my desk, open my laptop, and stare at the last words I wrote, over a week ago: *The enduring namelessness of the protagonists of* Hiroshima Mon Amour *underscores the fragmentation and anonymity that, Resnais holds, are universally characteristic of the postwar experience.* I read it over three times. Then I think, *God, I'm a wanker.*

I look around for my cigarettes. I find an unopened pack in my bag, along with my percussion instruments and a pile of pamphlets that Dr. Hill gave me. The one on top has a picture on it of a Latina girl who looks both solemn and confident. Above her head it reads, ABORTION: WHAT YOU NEED TO KNOW.

By the time Luke wakes up at eight thirty, I've read through all of them, and am showered and dressed. "Shit," he says, climbing out of the bed. "I have a staff cupping at nine."

I stare at his crotch as he pulls his jeans up his legs, and I say, "This was an isolated incident."

"Uh-huh," he says. "Sure."

Mission Street is almost deserted. There's a prostitute talking on her phone on the corner of 21st Street, and a couple of dealers standing outside the Beauty Bar. None of them pays any attention to the two of us: Luke on the seat of his fixed-gear, pedaling, and me on the handlebars, giving directions. "Keep going," I tell him. "Okay, move a little to the left. Now there's a stop sign coming up in about half a block." Either it's too early for this, or I'm still drunk from last night, or maybe it's the first signs of morning sickness, but I feel every pothole and every piece of rubbish we ride over like it's a punch to the abdomen. I almost scream when he runs a red light at 19th Street. When he turns left onto 17th, we narrowly avoid a collision with a girl riding a beach cruiser in the other direction.

"You don't look so hot," he says when I hop off the bike outside Anton's place.

"Yeah," I say. "That was rough. You have to change your gear ratio or something."

"Who lives here?" he asks, looking up at the building.

"Uh, this girl Calory," I say. "You don't know her. Thanks for the lift."

When I ring the doorbell, Anton's roommate opens it, wearing just his boxer shorts. He rubs his eye with the palm of his hand, walks down the hallway, bangs on a closed door, and then goes into the next room. When Anton comes out, he's wearing just his boxers as well. He's not as skinny as Luke and he has less chest hair and no tattoos, but what strikes me is how similar all these guys look when they're half undressed.

"Hi," I say. "My name's Claire. I don't know if you remember me but we met last night at the bar."

"You do look familiar," he says. "Betty's Revenge, right?"

"Yep, founding member."

He doesn't ask me in so I cross my arms and lean against the door frame. "So I was reading up about this abortion stuff. And there's this website run by a really nice woman in Georgia called Loretta who'll pay for a girl like me to have an ultrasound of my baby. Just to help me make the decision."

"That's sweet of her," he says in a croaky voice. He has sleep goop caught in the corners of both eyes.

"So I was wondering if you're interested in a road trip?"

He stares at me and yawns at the same time. "Are you serious?"

"No. Actually, I need someone to pick me up from the clinic tomorrow. I'm not allowed to leave by myself. I guess I was wondering—"

He looks like he doesn't want to do it. But then he says he'll do it.

"Thank you," I say. "You're the only person I know who wouldn't judge me, or try to sleep with me, or tell me to keep the baby."

"Jesus," he says. "I can't wait to meet your friends."

And I can't help it: The future reference makes me happy. "Do you want to go get a coffee or something?" I ask him.

"No," he says. "I'm going back to bed."

It's a Sunday morning and Valencia Street is quiet. There are a few couples walking together, with rolled-up newspapers under their arms or with babies in prams, but the road is empty and the sidewalks are mostly vacant. I realize I can walk slower and look around a lot more when I'm not expecting to bump into someone I know. I walk the two blocks to Amnesia, and the next four to the Common Room. Then I cross the street, cut over to Shotwell, and let myself into my apartment.

I go to my room, take out my phone card, and call the number on the back. I punch in my PIN and dial the number of my sister's flat in London. It rings, and I wait for her to pick up. It is late in the day where she is. I am excited to speak to her. I am excited to tell her that I'm happy she has found love.

Warm-Ups

Yesterday was my thirteenth birthday. When I woke up, my grandmother was still asleep in her bed across the room. My dad was awake. I could hear him in the shower, whistling. I was caught between two feelings: I wanted to curl over and fall back asleep, and I wanted to climb out of bed and see what the world looked like now that I was a teenager.

I turned onto my side, covered my ear with the blanket, and thought about Dimitri. I tried to picture his face in my mind. This is the weird thing—I can clearly imagine anyone's face, except if it's a boy who has a crush on me. Once somebody has saved me a seat in English class, or teased me in a way that means he likes me, I can't keep his image in my head for a second. I can remember pieces of him—the color of his eyes, or a shirt he wore—but I can't create a whole picture from those parts.

Dimitri is cute. He has straight hair the color of Licorice (my cat), and green eyes that look their best when he smiles. He's one of three boys who have definitely shown interest in me this term—the others are Anatoly and Vlad—but I like him best because he's mysterious but not too mysterious. He definitely compliments me (like, about my hairstyles or the things I say in class) but he doesn't fall all over himself like some sappy, desperate idiot (Vlad).

I had just started to conjure Dimitri's face in my mind, especially the way he looked last week when I told him I wasn't sure I had time for a boyfriend, when I realized that my dad was whistling the tune to "Happy Birthday." My feet hit the floorboards and I ran to the bathroom without putting socks on, even though it's January and has been snowing for almost a month.

"Papa," I called through the door. "Do I get a present this year?"

"I'm no surprise-ruiner. You'll have to wait till your mother's up."

"But what am I supposed to do in the meantime?"

"Go back to sleep?"

"Ugh! Impossible."

Lately I've been quarrelsome with my parents. I try to be good but it's hard when they sometimes treat me like an adult, and sometimes treat me like a child, just based on whatever happens to suit them at the time.

I decided to do handstands in the hallway, kicking my feet up and seeing how long I could hold myself upside down before flinging over into a bridge. Then I kicked my feet up again. I was half doing it to stay warm and half doing it in the hope that the sound of my feet thumping on the floor might wake my mother.

"Kira, stop with the noise," my father said on his way out of the bathroom.

"Is that the birthday girl?" my mother called.

I ran into their room. She was propped up on her pillow, her eyes puffy, the lids a smudgy blue with the residue of yesterday's eye shadow. I kissed her on the cheek and she tugged on my ear. I usually hate it when she does that but I didn't say anything; I was waiting for my present and didn't want to start a fight. Then she said, "Look under the bed."

I got on my hands and knees. Licorice was under there, snoozing on the floor among the dust balls. I shooed him away. There was a small white paper bag sitting there and, inside that, a carton the size of a jewelry box. My dad came and sat on the bed. They both watched me run my fingernail along the edges to break the sticky-tape seal.

"Oh my gosh." Inside the box was a digital camera. It was a metallic navy-blue color, 6.0 megapixels with a zoom and LCD screen. "How did you—" I looked from my mum to my dad and back again. They seemed tired, but they were smiling.

"It's to take with you to America," my mother said then.

"What do you mean, America?" I knew my voice was getting loud but I couldn't help it. "I thought the answer was no?"

"Coach Zhukov came to speak to us last week." My mother looked at my father.

"He said it's the opportunity of a lifetime," he said. "He's convinced us to let you go."

I know I had just become a teenager but I could not stop myself from squealing like a little kid. I stood and started jumping up and down on their bed. It made them laugh. A minute later my grandmother was in the doorway, rubbing her eyes and asking what the noise and commotion was about. Then the neighbors' babies started crying—the one next door as well as the one upstairs—but I was too excited to feel guilty.

I am a gymnast. I have wanted to be a gymnast my whole life. I have been taking classes since I was four years old but my first real lucky break came last October, when my father read an article in the paper about Mr. Zhukov, a gym coach and choreographer who had just moved here from St. Petersburg, where he had his own gymnastics academy. He was planning to start one here in Vladivostok.

My mother called and arranged for me to audition. On the day, she wanted to come with me, but I wouldn't let her. It's embarrassing, being escorted around by your mum when you're old enough to look after yourself. It was a group audition and there were probably fifty girls stretching their legs in the foyer of the church hall. I watched one girl practicing her punch-front salto, taking off from two feet and then pulling them into a tight tuck before she rolled. Another girl hand-walked past me.

"Those beam shoes are too small for you," she said when her face was next to my feet.

"I know. They're really old," I said. "I'll probably do my routine barefoot."

She turned herself right-side up. "I'm Anastasya," she said. "I'm best on the floor."

"Kira. I prefer the beam." I couldn't help wondering how she did well at anything gymnastic. She was the tallest girl there and, with her round hips, big breasts, and long legs, she had the body of a model rather than an athlete. I felt like a child standing next to her, with my skinny legs and flat chest, wearing the same leotard I've been using since I was eleven. When Coach Zhukov's assistant came out and called for everyone's attention, Anastasya took my hand and squeezed it.

"I'm shitting myself," she said.

The assistant's name was Xenia. She was plump and smiley and middle-aged, and she used the same color maroon to dye her hair as my mum. She explained that we would each perform a routine on the apparatus of our choice. She read the list of compulsories. For the balance beam, it was a 180-degree split and a 360 turn, plus a clean mount and dismount. Easy-peasy, I thought. We went into the hall and chalked our hands.

Coach Zhukov was less intimidating than I expected. He had strawberry-blond hair with bits of red in his beard, and a squinty look behind his glasses. He was taller and bulkier than the average gymnast, but just as graceful when he moved around. He seemed more like a dad than a coach; he had a kind word of praise or encouragement for everyone.

"All right!" he said as I began my routine with a flic-flac then lowered myself into a straddle split. I held my legs straight out to the sides as I somersaulted, and then raised myself onto the beam for a handstand. "Nice transition," I heard him say. I turned my hands on the beam, pirouetting around with my legs in the air. I felt calm and happy, the way my dad always describes me on the beam: *You look so at home up there, they should be charging you rent.*

I lowered myself into bridge position, and then flung my legs up and over, willing my feet to find their way back onto the beam, one in front of the other. Once upright, I raised my arms and stood in place for a moment, evening my breath, before flinging myself into a double back, and off onto the mat.

It was a clean landing. I smiled like there was a crowd and a TV camera, and a bunch of nodding judges taking notes. But really there was just the scattered sound of light applause. That's when I knew I'd done well. The better you do in gymnastics, the less your competitors clap for you.

A girl in a black leotard prepared to mount the beam and I went and sat with the others. "That was great." Anastasya tapped my shoulder. "I saw him pull your form and photo out of his folder. I think you're gonna get in."

"Who knows?" I said, shrugging, but I hoped she was right.

"Will you stay to watch me?" she asked. "I'm worrying my tits off."

She started out strong in her floor routine with a double front handspring, but she stumbled badly on the landing. Coach Zhukov smiled and said, "It's always good to get the stumble out of the way at the beginning." She blushed, moved back to the corner of the mat, and started again. After she was done, she came and sat next to me. "I'm finished," she whispered.

"You never know," I said.

She shot me an insulted look, like we had been best friends for years and I owed her the truth. "Come on," she said. "I wouldn't let myself in after that performance." At the end of the afternoon, though, my name was on the acceptance list, and so was hers.

Coach Zhukov said we would have to clear our calendars for him, and he wasn't joking. Practice started the next week, three evenings after school and all day Sunday. It was exhausting. I had to go to bed right after I did my homework every night. I fell behind on socializing with my friends. I had to miss out on my first best friend Lara's birthday, when she took some girls from school to see *Pirates of the Caribbean,* and at my second best friend Raya's slumber party I had to go to sleep way before the others did so I could get up early the next day. I barely had time to flirt with the boys in my class anymore. If one of them wanted to talk to me alone, he had to walk me to practice after school.

"You're no fun, Kira," Dimitri said one day in November. He was walking beside me, with his hands in the pockets of his jeans. "All you care about is gymnastics." He kicked his feet into a pile of leaves on the sidewalk.

"What would you prefer? One of those dumb girls who can't think about anything besides which boys like them?"

He curled the top corner of his lip up in disgust.

"That's what I thought," I said. "Wait until you see me compete in the regionals at the end of term. Then you'll see where all my spare time's been going."

I started to set my alarm clock ten minutes early in the morning, so I could lie in bed and picture myself competing. Every morning, the daydream got more elaborate; one day I would be wearing a sparkly turquoise ensemble like Alina Kabaeva in Athens, the next day I would be perfecting difficult routines I'd been messing up in practice: back handsprings from corner to corner on the floor, or a double-twist dismount from the beam.

Dimitri was always in the fantasy, too. I couldn't picture his face, of course, but I could see all the kids from school he'd be sitting with. He would jump to his feet as soon as I'd finished and clap louder than anybody, louder than my parents even. Later, after I'd been awarded a perfect ten, he'd meet me outside the locker rooms and the shake in his voice would tell me that he was so impressed with me, it scared him a little.

"It's still me," I'd say, and he'd laugh. Then, I imagined,

he'd kiss me. At first the kissing was tame—a quick brush of his lips on mine—but one morning I imagined he kissed me and opened his mouth. I saw him put his palm out and hold my cheek while he showed me how to kiss with tongues. I lay on my side and slid my hands, palms together, up the outside of my pajama pants and between my thighs. It felt nice, lying there. I decided that if he came to watch me in the regionals, I really would let him kiss me, and maybe even be my boyfriend.

But one Monday afternoon in December, after two months of solid practice, Coach Zhukov sat us all down and told us that we would have to postpone our participation in the regionals until the following round. We all looked at one another and groaned.

"What the hell?" Anastasya muttered beside me.

"I've already got my costume," a girl called from the back.

"I know you're all upset," said Coach Zhukov. He was sitting on a chair, with his forearms on his legs, leaning forward to talk to us. "But I promise there's a good reason. I've been invited to give a talk at a conference. It's in America and it's called 'The Global Gymnast.' Colin, the director, called me last week and asked me to give a presentation about competitive gymnastics in the new Russia." He sat up straight in his chair and beamed at us. "Now the exciting part. He's asked me, also, to bring a small group of students to present something in the showcase section of the conference. So a few of you, I hope, are going to come with me to the USA and perform."

We all burst into speech simultaneously, like guests at a surprise party. Who would get to go? How would he decide? "It's totally gonna be you," Anastasya said. "You're one of his favorites."

"No way, I'm sure it'll be you," I said, but I didn't really mean it. She was a good gymnast but not outstanding and, at sixteen, she was too old now to even think about serious professional competition.

"Girls, girls, quiet down," Coach Zhukov said. "I'll cure you of your curiosity. I wanted to make this decision right away, before we break for Christmas, so we can start the preparations in time. So, after a difficult weekend of deliberation, and some discussion with Xenia, I have come up with a list of four. Four girls."

He said all the usual stuff about how it had been a hard decision and we were all deserving, in a perfect world we could all go, blah blah. And then he took a piece of paper from his pocket, unfolded it, and cleared his throat. "I'd like these girls to come to the front of the room," he said. My heart was beating so hard in my chest I felt like a cartoon character with a crush. "Vera." A fourteen-year-old girl called Vera with blond hair down her back got up and stood next to his chair. Her face was borscht red and she had a crazy grin on her face. "Ehma." Ehma stood up. She was a pretty brown-eyed girl, stupid as anything, but she could twirl with a ribbon like it was a limb she'd been born with. Then he said my name. "Kira."

"Yes?" I said. I thought he wanted to tell me something

or ask me for a favor. I didn't think he was actually calling my name to go to America.

"Told you so," said Anastasya, pushing me in the back until I stood up and went to the front of the group. I felt so dazey. It was cold in the room and I was just wearing my leotard, but suddenly I felt warm, like I was bundled up in a winter coat with a hat on top.

"And, last, Anastasya," Coach Zhukov said, and my tall friend came and stood beside me.

"No way," I said.

"I know," she whispered. "I'm not even good enough."

"You are so." I took her hand and squeezed it.

The rest of the girls sat cross-legged on the floor, staring up at us. I could tell they felt awful. I would have hated me if I hadn't been me, standing there at the front of the room beside the teacher and the other chosen girls.

"Okay, everyone, let's begin our warm-ups as usual. Xenia, please start the tape." Coach Zhukov turned to us and smiled. "Well done, girls. Now I have some forms for you to take home to your parents."

The coach said that both Ehma and Anastasya would do floor routines, Vera would be on the uneven bars, and I would be on the balance beam. He said we could choose our own music, and straight away I knew which song I wanted to use: "Ya Soshla S Uma" by t.A.T.u. (I love t.A.T.u.)

We set to work practicing but I couldn't concentrate on anything for more than three seconds at a time. That's how long it took my mind to wander back to one thought: I am going to America. It was my second lucky break.

My excitement lasted the two hours of practice and the twenty-minute trolleybus ride home. It ended a minute after I'd come into the kitchen and put the forms on the table, where my parents and grandmother were sitting down for dinner.

"You can't go," my dad said. "You know we can't afford it. We can barely afford the lessons."

"Coach Zhukov said the conference people pay for our tickets."

"All the way to America," my mother said, spreading margarine onto a piece of bread. "For a three-minute gymnastics routine."

"It's not even a competition," my father said.

"The coach said it's good exposure," I told them.

My parents looked at each other and tried to make a silent decision.

"Please!" I said. "When else will I get to go to America? For gymnastics!"

"In the middle of the school year."

"I can ask the teachers for extra homework so I won't fall behind. It's just six days. Look, the form says."

My mother dipped her bread in her ukha and took a bite. She pulled the form toward her. I watched her face soften as she read what Coach Zhukov had written about the conference.

"San Diego," she said.

"Yes," I said, silently willing her to keep reading. "California."

"It's sunny there all year round," my father said.

"Really?" I took my coat and scarf off and hung them by the front door, instead of throwing them in a pile on the floor like I usually do, like my mother hates.

"Even in winter," he said.

My grandmother, who had stayed silent the entire time, finished eating and dropped her spoon into her bowl with a clink. "A twelve-year-old girl," she said, nodding while she talked, "alone in a foreign country with some teacher you hardly know." She stood up and pushed her chair back. "You'd have to be crazy."

"I'm almost thirteen," I said loudly as she left the room. But my father's face told me all I needed to know about my chances of getting to California.

"Your grandmother's right," my dad said. "You're too young."

"It's not fair." I started to cry.

"Here." My mother pushed a bowl across the table toward me.

"And don't tell me that thing about life not being fair."

"Well, it's true," my father said.

"Maybe it is," I said. "But it's more fair for adults than it is for kids. At least you get to decide what you can do."

"Eat something," my mother said.

"What's the point? If I can't go to America, I'd rather starve and die."

My birthday party becomes my farewell party. All my friends attend but instead of giving me birthday gifts, like stickers or candies, they give me going-away presents. My first best friend Lara arrives first with a mauve satiny eye mask to wear on the airplane while I sleep. Manya, a girl from my class who my mother always makes me invite to my parties, gets me a Pokémon watch with the price sticker still on it. It cost eighty-five rubles. It stops working two minutes after I take it out of the packet and put it on my wrist. I don't care; I haven't liked Pokémon since fifth grade. Anastasya comes without a present. She's saving her money for America, so she can buy Rollerblades there. My second best friend Raya brings me a diary with a glittery airplane on the cover, a silver pencil attached by a ribbon, and a lock with two little keys dangling from it.

"You have to tell us everything when you get back," she says. "This will help you keep a record."

"Give the other key to Orlando Bloom when you meet him." My first best friend Lara winks at me.

"He's English," Raya tells her.

"They all live there," Lara says.

The boys come late and stand all together by the television. The girls are squeezed onto the sofa or sitting on the floor in front of it. My mother comes out of the kitchen with the radio and puts it on the side table.

"Mingle," she whispers on her way out of the room.

"Why don't they?" I whisper back.

"*I'm yours,*" Polina Gagarina sings from the speakers.

I get up and go over to the boys. There are five of them, all leaning back against the wall.

"Happy birthday," Anatoly mumbles.

"Yeah," says Vlad. He runs a hand back over his wet-gelled hair, then he looks down at his fingers (now all sticky and gross) and shoves them into the pocket of his jacket.

"Thanks for coming," I say. I smile at Igor and Slava, and go over to Dimitri.

"You look pretty," he says.

"Thanks," I say, twirling the Pokémon watch around my wrist. "Um, so do you." The other boys laugh. I roll my eyes and go back to the sofa.

"Who's that?" Anastasya asks.

I shrug a shoulder. "Some guy from school."

"He has a crush on her."

"He's cute."

"Yeah, but Kira's saving herself until she gets to America and meets Johnny Depp," my first best friend Lara says.

"He's French," my second best friend Raya says.

"They all live there."

Ten minutes later my parents bring out a birthday pie, with SAFE TRAVELS carved into the crust. My grandmother, the maker of the pie, doesn't come out of our bedroom for the entire party.

Coach Zhukov and Xenia had come to see my parents when I was at school one day. They told them I was the best gymnast in the group, and a performance at the conference would raise my profile in the world of international gymnastics. They told them about the people who would be in

San Diego watching me perform—world-class coaches, the president of USA Gymnastics, and senior American gymnasts like Shannon Miller and Carly Patterson. As for us being alone in a foreign country, Xenia promised she would be there at all times. She would accompany us girls everywhere and stay in the same hotel room.

They gave my parents the name and details of a government official who could get me a passport quickly. They said they needn't worry about the cost of the trip. The conference would pay for the basics and, if they wanted to give me spending money, Coach Zhukov could refund them the rest of the term's tuition. My parents signed the permission slips and in-case-of-emergencies, and Coach Zhukov wrote them a check. That's how they paid for the digital camera, with a memory card inside it that can hold two hundred photos.

I take pictures of everything. I take one of Licorice up on his hind legs at the windowsill, trying to swat a moth with his paw. I take one of my father smiling at the kitchen table, my mother beside him, lighting a cigarette. I take one of the upstairs neighbor with her baby in the stairwell, its mouth wide open in a scream. I take some self-portraits: one of my feet on the kitchen floor, wearing one red sock, one navy one; one of myself in the mirror, balancing on my left leg with my right one straight out in a half split; one of the inside of my mouth, the back teeth crowded together like schoolkids on the trolleybus. I take one of my grandmother sitting on the edge of her bed in the morning, halfway through a yawn.

"Look, Baba." I turn the camera around and show her the picture on the screen.

"Great," she says. "It's not bad enough that I have to get old and ugly, now I have to watch it happen on a little television."

"It's not a television, it's a camera."

"Well, watch that you don't get it stolen in America. Those cities are full of thugs and thieves."

"That's just New York," I tell her. "I'm going to California."

The day before I leave is a Sunday but practice has been canceled until we get back. My mum helps me pack my bag in the morning: clothes in the main section, shoes in the front pocket, my ticket and brand-new passport in a secret zippered compartment inside.

After lunch, Dimitri calls and asks if I have time to see him. We arrange to meet at Café VIP downtown. I take the bus there, looking out the window at the apartment buildings rising up beside every street, a light shining behind almost every curtain. I wonder if people in San Diego ever have to turn on their lights in the middle of the day. I imagine big houses with all their windows and doors open, letting the sunshine and warm breeze come in and tickle the legs of the people who live there, who will all be wearing shorts or mini skirts and have bare sandy feet.

When I get to the café, Dimitri is waiting outside, wearing a leather jacket that's too long for him. Inside, he buys us each a mug of hot cocoa. We sit at a table next to the front window and talk about America. He says his cousin went there once and told him that the candies are made with sugar-free sugar. And all the women have bodies like the girls on *Baywatch*. And if you look a black guy directly in the eyes he'll kill you.

"He's in jail now, though," he says. "Here in Vladivostok. He killed his landlady and her boyfriend."

"Oh my gosh," I say.

"Yeah, him and some Chechens were selling guns out of his flat and when his landlady found out, she reported them to the police. He went to prison for four years and when he got out, he hunted her down."

"And shot her?" I ask.

"No, I think he did it with a knife. He's back inside now. You can have my marshmallow if you like."

Later, when we leave the café, a wind has started up and the street is empty. I blow warm air into my gloves, then hold my hands over my ears.

"So." Dimitri buttons his jacket up to the collar. "Do you think you want to be my girlfriend?" He sniffs and spits into the gutter.

"I don't know," I say, watching his saliva freeze up on the ice. "I might meet someone in America."

"You're only going for a week," he says.

"I know. But it can happen quickly. Ever heard of—" I try to find the English expression. "Love at first sight?"

"Yes," he says. "Yes, I have." He takes a step toward me and puts his hand on my cheek. The kiss is just as I'd pictured it in bed every morning for weeks: our mouths slightly opened, his tongue skimming my upper lip, my lower lip, then finding the tip of my tongue before he pulls away. He takes his hand back and stares into my face for a minute. "Let me know when you get back, Kira," he says. Then he turns and leaves.

He's half a block away when I realize I didn't get a photo of him. "Hey, Dimitri?" I call. "Dimitri!" The wind snatches my voice away, and he doesn't hear me. I get my camera out and take a photo of his back, walking away from me on the icy street. It won't help me conjure up his face when I'm in America, but it's better than nothing at all.

That night, I can't sleep and neither can my grandmother. I listen to her bed ticking under her as she turns over. Finally I ask, "Baba, can I get into bed with you for a while?"

"Come on, then," she says.

I cross the room and snuggle against her back. I wonder if she misses my grandfather, but instead I ask, "Will you miss me?"

"You and your acrobatics all over the flat. How could I miss that? We'll have some peace around here for a while."

I don't say anything and she sighs.

"I remember when your grandfather and I left Kurilsk for Vladivostok. I was pregnant with your father and I didn't know when I'd see my parents or my brothers and sisters again. Leaving behind an old place for a new one is like dying. Traveling is like a little death."

"I'm only going for six days," I remind her.

"I know," she says into the wall. "But when you come back, you'll be a woman of the world. You'll have been to a country your parents and grandparents have never been. You'll be more of a grown-up than a child."

I put my arms around her and feel her belly heaving in and out. When I fall asleep I dream that I am lying on a balance beam. I have to curl over on my side and stay very still in order to not fall off. I keep waiting for the judges to disqualify me for going over time, but they don't say anything.

All the mothers cry at the airport but none of us four girls does. It's been almost a month since we found out we'd been chosen, and we are ready to go. I hug my mother, then my father, then my mother wants to hug me again. She tugs on my ear and I don't complain, because she's sad and I don't want to make her sadder.

"Don't forget to take care of Licorice," I say, "and give him treats."

"We won't forget," my mum promises. "Don't forget to call us when you get there. Please make sure she calls," she tells Coach Zhukov.

"Of course," he says. "I've got all the parents' details." I hand him my camera and I stand between my parents as he takes a picture of the three of us. I look at the photo on the screen. My dad has his eyes closed in it, so I delete it. Then he takes a picture of the four of us girls: Vera, Ehma, Anastasya, and me. And then it's time to go. I hug my parents again and wait for Anastasya to finish saying goodbye to her father, a tall man with a mustache and no wedding ring on. We walk to the door, and turn and wave. Then we head toward security.

I have never been on an airplane before. I get a window seat, right near the engine, and the stewardess gives me earplugs to wear if it gets too noisy. Anastasya, Ehma, and I are seated in a row of three. Vera and the adults are a few rows behind us. The sun is setting as we take off. Anastasya grabs my left hand and Ehma's right hand. She sits back and closes her eyes. "I'm crapping my heart out," she says.

Anastasya watches *Along Came Polly*. Ehma and I watch *50 First Dates*. The English is too hard for me to follow without subtitles so I listen to the music stations. There are twenty of them. There's jazz, classical, rock 'n' roll, opera, and even a European pop station. I listen to that one for a while and then they start to play "Ya Soshla S Uma." It's definitely t.A.T.u. singing but the words are in English, and it's called "All the Things She Said." I can't believe it! I turn to tell the others but they're both asleep, their heads leaning against each other. I listen to the song and go through my beam routine in my head. Handstand into double salto into a one-handed straddle split.

I fall asleep without realizing it, and wake up hours later

with a dry mouth. The airplane is dark now except for a few people's individual lights on overhead. Anastasya and Ehma are still asleep. They don't even wake up when I push past them to go to the bathroom.

On my way to the back of the plane, I have to step over Coach Zhukov's right foot, which is stretched out into the aisle. When I look up, I see that the three of them—Coach Zhukov, Xenia, and Vera—are all sleeping. I also notice that Coach Zhukov's hand is resting in his assistant's lap. I wonder if it's an accident, or if they're actually boyfriend–girlfriend and have kept it a secret all along.

In America there are advertisements in the airport for alcohol, banks, and Hawaii. In America, there are moving walkways in the airport, and everyone I see has a small suitcase on wheels. None of them seems to have checked in bags. They roll their hand luggage to the exit and out into the night.

We're all exhausted. We've been through airports in Moscow and Anchorage, and we girls are half asleep on our feet. We shuffle after Coach Zhukov and Xenia. The coach holds our passports and tickets, and takes them up to the customs officer when he's called. The officer looks at our passports, then over at us. He says something to Coach Zhukov and both men laugh.

"He thought you were all my daughters," he tells us as we head for the baggage claim area, and we giggle.

"Papa, where are our bags?" Anastasya says.

"Yeah, Papa, where do we go next?" I ask.

"Come along, daughters," he says. "It's this way." We laugh again.

Outside, the first thing I notice is that there are yellow cabs lined up at the curb, just like the ones in the movies. The second thing I notice is the weather. It's windy and chilly. I worry for a moment that I didn't bring the right outfits with me. I decide I can wear my leotard under my clothes if I get too cold.

The conference has sent a driver to pick us up. He's standing next to a white sedan, holding a sign with Coach Zhukov's name printed on it. Xenia helps us load our bags into the trunk while the coach speaks to the driver.

"Xenia and I will follow you in a cab," Coach Zhukov tells us as we climb in. "He knows where to go for the hotel. See you there in a few minutes, girls."

The driver is wearing a blue-and-yellow baseball cap and a leather jacket that reminds me of Dimitri. His skin is the color of Enrique Iglesias's. (I love Enrique Iglesias.) As we drive away, I tell the other girls, "I saw Coach Zhukov touching Xenia's leg."

"I saw that, too!" says Vera. "They were holding hands."

"No way."

"Uh-huh."

The road from the airport to the hotel is a highway. There is a motel and a billboard for a radio station. Anastasya, in the passenger seat, turns to the driver and asks, "Do we travel by the animal zoo?" The rest of us giggle at the sound of her speaking English. The driver glances over and shakes his head. It's not clear whether he understands her or not. I stare at the people in the cars driving past. I see a blond girl in her twenties driving a jeep car. And a black couple in a station wagon with a baby sleeping in a baby seat in the back.

We see the San Diego skyline just before we turn off at the exit.

"Just like on September eleventh," Ehma says.

"That was in New York," Vera tells her.

"Yeah, but it easily could have happened here," Ehma says.

"No, it couldn't."

"What do you know?"

"Idiot."

They're still arguing about it when the driver pulls over to the curb and stops the car. We're parked on a wide city street that's empty except for a few open cigarette shops and bars. The driver gets out and goes around to open the trunk. When we climb out of the car, there's a man standing on the sidewalk, holding a mobile phone. He is tanned with bleached hair, and he's wearing jeans and a tight white shirt.

"Russia?" he says in English, looking right at me.

"Uh, hello?" I try.

"You're all from Russia?" he says.

We look at one another. "Yes."

He goes over to the driver, who places the last of our luggage on the sidewalk and then hands him a big white envelope. The blond man opens it and looks inside. He gives the driver some cash (just like the money they use on TV), and turns to us.

"Come in," he says, tilting his head toward the building we're standing in front of. We all look away, down the block. A couple of cars approach and pass us, but neither one is a taxi.

"Coach," I try in English. "We waiting, Mr. Zhukov."

"Oh right, he'll come. He's on his way," he says.

"You are Mr. Colin?" Ehma says.

"Uh-huh." He nods. "Yep. Come on in."

The hotel room is up four flights of stairs and is less glamorous than I had imagined. It isn't all that different from our flat in Vladivostok, really—a living room, two bedrooms, a bathroom, hallway, and a kitchen. But in this flat, there is no sofa in the living room, just white plastic chairs; no bases under the beds, just mattresses on the floor; no mother, father, or grandmother waiting for us in the kitchen, just a woman wearing glasses and a floral wraparound dress. She smiles at us, and even though I don't know her, I'm happy to see her.

"My wife," Colin says. The woman says hello and puts two paper bags on the table.

"Take a seat," she says. "I brought you McDonald's."

We grin at one another as we sit down. Colin's wife opens the bags and passes around hamburgers, chicken nuggets, and fries. I unwrap my burger, take a bite of it, and keep grinning as I chew. I've had McDonald's before, but never the real McDonald's, in the country where it was invented.

While the four of us eat, Colin sits across the table and empties his envelope. Our passports are there, along with our original audition photos and the consent forms our parents signed. He opens each passport, looks at its owner, and then hands it to his wife, who slides it back into the envelope. When he opens Vera's she giggles and says, "Is me, short hairs."

He looks at her and says, "We'll hang on to them, just to be safe. Do any of you have cellphones?" None of us does.

"The coach," I say. "And Xenia?"

"He'll come," he says. "Tomorrow."

"Tomorrow is perform?" Anastasya asks.

"No," Colin's wife says. "The performance has actually been canceled."

"No," I say, hoping it's just my English skills failing me, and she doesn't mean what I think she does. "Can't be."

"Yes, I'm sorry, but you arrived too late and the gymnastics has been canceled." Her face is stern behind her glasses.

"She doesn't know what she's talking about," Anastasya says in Russian.

"You'll all have to pay us back for your tickets and expenses," Colin says. They both stand up. "We'll be here tomorrow."

"It can't be right," Ehma says after they've gone, dipping the last of her fries in the honey mustard sauce. "The coach will know more. He'll explain it to us."

"He probably doesn't even know yet," Anastasya says, with a bite of burger in her mouth. "He's probably busy on the street, kissing his girlfriend, fat Xenia." The four of us laugh.

We wander into the living room. There's no TV and nothing to do so we flop down onto the linoleum and do our stretches, practice our routines. I'm in a front split with my nose to my knee when Anastasya goes into the hallway and comes back, saying the front door is locked.

We all go to check and it's true, the door is locked, and we can't find a key anywhere in the apartment. What we do find is a condom wrapper next to one of the mattresses.

"Are you sure that's what it is?" Ehma asks, examining the little black pouch with its corner ripped away.

"Definite," Anastasya says. "I've seen them in my dad's room."

In the bathroom we find a hair scrunchie on the sink, a towel hanging on a hook behind the door, and a camisole draped over the edge of the tub. It's pale pink and lacy. "Cotton nylon blend," Vera reads off the label. "Made in the Philippines." She flings it at me and I screech. It lands on my shoulder and I throw it at Ehma, who ducks aside. I grab it again and chase her into the kitchen.

"Here, here." I throw the camisole to Anastasya, who dangles it in Ehma's face before tossing it at Vera.

"Yuck."

"Gross!"

After an hour, we're sleepy and we decide to go to bed. I

share a mattress with Anastasya, and the others sleep in the room next door. I put my head on the pillow, lie on my side, and pull the blanket up over my ear.

"I hate this hotel," Anastasya says. "I don't even think this is a hotel."

"Let's not stay here tomorrow night. Let's ask the coach if we can move somewhere else."

"Good idea."

In the other room, one of the girls coughs, and then it's quiet.

After a few minutes, Anastasya says, "If those people expect me to pay them back for the ticket, they're crazy. There's no way my dad can afford that."

"Same here."

"I hate those people."

"Same here."

Soon her breathing gets slow and throaty. I try to sleep, too, but I'm cold. The covers are more like a bedspread than a blanket. The window looks out onto an air shaft, and there's a gap between the frame and the sill where the air's coming in. I lie there for a while and then I get up, go into the hallway, and do two cartwheels to warm myself up. I come back into the bedroom and unzip my bag. My leotard and leggings are folded on the top. Under those is my diary. I unlock it and open it to the first page.

Dear Diary, I write with the little silver pencil. *California is freezing, brrr. I can't wait till the sun comes up.*

I take out my digital camera and flip through the photos.

Licorice, Mama, Papa, neighbor. Self-portraits, Baba, Dimitri's back. Group photo at airport.

"Where's Ehma and Vera?" Anastasya asks, suddenly sitting up.

"Sleeping. In the other room."

"Oh. Is it morning yet?" She turns to the window.

"No, it's still night."

She lies back down and falls asleep again.

Licorice, Mama, Papa, neighbor. Self-portraits, Baba, Dimitri's back. Group photo at airport. Dimitri's back, group photo at airport. Dimitri's back, group photo at airport.

Sometime before dawn, I realize that I don't have a picture of Coach Zhukov. I decide it's the first thing I'll make him do when he comes to find us.

"Smile for the camera," I'll say, capturing him in my viewfinder. "And I won't tell my parents about what went wrong."

Same Old Same As

Dr. Carvden had been using the word *abuse* for months before Ramona said it for the first time.

"It just makes me feel gross," Ramona told her. "Like I'm damaged goods."

"You're not the damaged one," the therapist said. "You're someone else's victim. This isn't your shameful secret, it's his."

It was the end of the session and, as usual, Ramona didn't want to pull herself up out of the chair and leave.

"I feel like I'm an adult in here and a kid in the rest of the world," she said as the older woman wrote out a receipt. "I feel like in here, we're grown-ups or equals or friends."

"You could think of me as a friend you see once a week," Dr. Carvden suggested. "Someone who lives far away, or goes to a different school. I'm still right here for you, though."

. . .

Outside in the car her mother was listening to a talk-radio show about books. *If the author intended me to fall in love with the character, she wouldn't have named him Brick,* an irate caller from Brisbane was saying as Ramona climbed in.

"How was therapy?" her mum asked, the way other mothers of ninth-grade girls might ask, *How was play rehearsal?* or, *How was athletics?*

"Okay," Ramona said, buckling up as her mother put the car in drive. "We talked about school, and the accident again."

"Oh, that's good," her mother said. "Good to talk about those things."

"She said I'm getting over the PTSD from the accident."

"God, you'd think someone would let me in. What are they in such a rush for, anyway? To get to a red light?"

Ramona looked straight through the windshield at the painted lines on the road. "And then we talked about the sexual abuse that happened after the accident. Remember? When I had to take baths, and Tony used to come in and dry me afterward? That really sucked."

There, she had said it. The word—two syllables, five letters long—that Dr. Carvden had been using to her face every week for three months now. There, she had used it, in front of her mother, who was watching the road, pulling in and out of lanes on Bell Street, extending her index finger to press down the turn signal without taking her hands off the wheel. Her mother, whose idea it had been for Ramona to see a therapist after an electric heater had caught fire last June and burned a red splotch into her leg, causing her to have nightmares for weeks, and to compulsively check every electrical outlet in the house before she left for school each morning. Her mother, who, when driving her to her first session with Dr. Carvden, had joked, "I'm glad you've agreed to talk to someone, but therapy can do funny things to people. Just remember: You haven't been abducted by aliens, you weren't Marilyn Monroe in a past life, and you never had a drunk old uncle with wandering hands." Her mother, who was silent the whole way home, until they pulled into the driveway, the second story of the house blotting out the gold of the setting sun, when she stopped the car and said, "Well, then. I hope everyone's going to be happy with spag bol for dinner. I didn't have time to get to Safeway because I had to go get Steve from swimming practice, drop him at home, and then turn around to come get you. There's nothing in the house. Nothing. Just a packet of spaghetti, and some mince meat in deep freeze."

Steve was asleep in front of a rerun of *M*A*S*H* when Ramona came into the living room. He was lying on the couch with one arm behind his head, still wearing his glasses, and Ramona leaned over to take the remote control from his hand.

His eyes flicked open. "Hey. What are you doing?"

"Nothing." She aimed the remote at the TV. "I just want to see if *The Simpsons* is on."

"I was watching something."

"You were sleeping."

Steve sat up and pressed his glasses to his face. "I was watching *M*A*S*H*." He was raising his voice and Ramona, aware of their proximity to the kitchen, knew it wasn't worth the risk of attracting their mother's attention. She handed him the remote, and he changed it back to Channel Seven.

"Why are you watching that, anyway?" Ramona sank down onto the other couch. "I thought you were a pacifist."

"I am." Steve lay back and yawned. "Can you fuck off and leave me alone?"

Ramona felt an itchy sensation in her eyes and a whole batch of tears mobilizing behind her sinuses. "Don't talk to me like that," she said, her voice cracking on the word "talk." Steve turned his head to look at her. "I've had a really fucked-up day, okay? I basically failed an algebra test. Plus, Tony sexually abused me last year."

"What are you talking about?"

"I think Mum knew about it, too. Unconsciously anyway. That's why she was talking about sending me away to boarding school."

"You were begging her to send you to boarding school."

She shrugged. "Whatever."

Steve looked at the remote in his hand and then flung it across the room toward her. It hit the seatback and fell onto the couch next to her thigh. He stood up. "You're really fucked up, you know that? Watch the bloody *Simpsons,* then."

"Thanks," Ramona said brightly as he left the room. She pulled herself off the couch and took his spot in front of the TV, where the seat cushions were still warm and flat from his weight.

Her mum had made dinner. Later Tony would wash the dishes. It was Ramona's job to dry them and put them away, Steve's job to set the table before the meal, and Lockie, the youngest, had to carry the plates of food from the stove, where their mother was dishing out, to the table, where the others were already waiting, hungry and quiet.

Lockie was the only one talking, chatting on about a project he was doing for school, a "roots project," which had him drawing up a family tree that went back four generations and including whatever basic biographical details he could find.

"How come you don't know where Dad's father was during the war?" he asked as their mother sat down.

"Your dad never talked about that sort of thing with him. Apparently your Uncle Rob asked about the war once and your grandfather got out the wooden spoon. It was the only time he ever did it."

"What spoon?"

"It means he bashed him," Steve explained to Lockie. He

sucked up a piece of spaghetti until it disappeared through his pursed lips.

"Steve!" their mother said.

"Well, it's true."

"So there's a history of abuse in our family," Ramona said.

"What history?" Lockie asked.

"Haven't you heard? Tony abused me last year."

"Shut the fuck up, Ramona," Steve said.

"Steve," their mother said.

"She's a liar," Steve said.

"She's in therapy," their mother said. "Now, pass the salad."

Tony sat next to their mum, looking tired and worn out as usual, putting food in his mouth, then twisting more spaghetti around his fork before he had finished chewing that mouthful.

"Can I put this in my roots project?" Lockie asked.

"Sure," Ramona told him.

"No," her mum said. "Ramona, everyone at this table has had a hard day. You're not the only one alive in the world, you know."

Steve smirked as the toe of his shoe found her ankle under the table.

"Ow," she said. "He kicked me. Mum! Tony." Their mother tossed the salad and said nothing. Tony, his head still bowed over his bowl, raised his eyes briefly to look at Ramona, then turned back to his food. Tears filled her eyes and the table blurred as she pushed her bowl away. "Can I be excused?" she asked.

"Yes," her mother said.

Ramona ran up the stairs, crying, but secretly pleased that she wouldn't have to dry the dishes that night.

In her room, she opened her laptop, hoping to find Kirsty or Minyung or one of the popular girls online. Instead it was just Danielle and Skye, chatting about the turkey slap incident on *Big Brother*.

That girls a whore, Danielle wrote.

Yeah they always say they forget theres cameras but as if u rlly would

Totally

Hows therapi? ;), Skye asked her.

Ok. Now Im depressed

Y?

Ramona typed her answer and hesitated before pressing ENTER. *I found out I was sexually abused*

R u serious? Like raped or something?

No but kinda like that

By who?

My stepdad

That sux!

Dont say anything

Omg I never would

Me neither :)

Are u still gonna have ur slumber party?

I dunno

. . .

By the time she got to school the next day, most of the girls in her year already knew.

"Hey," they all said. "Are you okay?"

They gathered around her locker, watching her pull out her books. This was exactly how they'd been two years earlier when Amber's mother had died of leukemia: a crowd of mourners with big sorrowful eyes, who stood around exchanging hugs and sad meaningful expressions.

It was like that all day. Even the girls who didn't know what had happened could sense a shift occurring in the social structure at Kenley Girls. Seats were being switched, and notes passed in class, and everyone knew for certain that Ramona MacKenzie was riding the elevator to a new floor in the tower of popularity.

In PE, Mrs. Parker started the lesson by telling the girls to run two laps around the oval. Ramona raised her hand.

"I'm not feeling well. Is it okay if I sit out?" The teacher extended an arm toward her, her palm opened expectantly. "What?" Ramona asked.

"Where's your doctor's note? You either bring me a note or you run with the others."

"But Miss." Minyung stepped forward. "She isn't feeling well."

"Yeah," Kirsty agreed, one hand on her hip. "She's got personal problems."

"Yeah," some other girls joined in.

"You can't make her run."

"She's having family issues."

"Yeah, Miss! It's not fair."

"Fine, fine." Mrs. Parker held up her clipboard. "No one has to do laps today. Okay? But I want you all on the volleyball court in thirty seconds. Ready? Thirty, twenty-nine—" The teacher blew her whistle and the girls scrambled toward the court.

"Thanks," Ramona said as Kirsty came up to run beside her.

"No worries." Kirsty held her tongue over her braces as she smiled. "I mean, you didn't, like, go through horrible abuse to have a cow like Parker force you to do something you don't want to."

"Totally."

The volleyball courts came into view and Ramona realized that, for the first time ever, she was going to be picked first for someone's team.

At lunchtime, a few of the girls kept watch behind the gym while Ramona crouched beneath the windows and called Adil on her mobile.

"Hey," he said. He'd picked up after one ring. "I was just thinking about you."

"Oh really?" she said, as quietly as she could. "Do tell?"

"I don't know." He sounded embarrassed, and Ramona could picture him kicking at something on the ground, a small, almost undetectable smile on his lips. "I guess I was just thinking about how nice it was to, like, hold hands with you at the movies the other night. I mean, I know my fingers were all greasy from the popcorn, but you were terribly gracious about not complaining and, you know, letting me have my way with your fingers in the dark on the armrest for a few minutes."

"Well," she said, "maybe I did complain about it. Just not to you. Maybe I complained about it to my friends."

"Yeah, you see I thought of that, but I've got it covered. I asked my sources and they told me you were appalled by the shoes I was wearing and the fact that I had to ask you to lend me fifty cents for my ticket. But none of them said anything about popcorn or butter or hand-holding at all."

"And these sources of yours. How do you know they're not working for me?"

He laughed. "Oh no, I've checked them out thoroughly. Rorschach tests, lie detectors. They're very reliable sources."

"Hmm, I see."

"Ramona. Ramona!" Minyung had come around the edge of the building and was whispering to her. "Come on."

"Shit," Ramona said, moving toward Minyung with her head tilted down and out of view of any sport teachers. "I have to go. But wanna see me later?"

"Sure," Adil said. "Should I meet you there?"

"No. I'll come to you. Gottagobye." She flipped her phone shut, dropped it into the pocket of her blazer, and followed Minyung around the corner. But what she saw there was not what she had expected; what she saw was not a teacher coming to bust girls using mobile phones on school grounds, but a group of six or seven girls with Kirsty at its center, and in Kirsty's hands a cupcake covered in pink icing with a fat red candle sticking out the top.

"We just wanted you to know we're thinking about you," Kirsty said.

"Yeah," said Amber, her curls nodding in concurrence. The bell rang for the end of lunch but none of the girls moved.

"And we know it's not your birthday or anything," said Kirsty, "but we thought you might want to make a wish. For the start of a new life without anything weird or, you know, gross in it."

"Thank you so much." Ramona smiled. She felt like she'd won an award and her speech was being televised. "Um, I don't even know what I'd wish for. With such good friends like you guys."

"Aww," Hayley said, "we love you, too."

All the girls stood in a circle around Kirsty, who raised the candle to Ramona's face and said, "Yeah!" when she blew it out. She handed Ramona the cupcake as the second bell rang, then grabbed her free hand as they rushed toward the main school building.

"I can't believe you got molested," Kirsty said as she stopped in front of her locker, out of breath. "I feel so bad for you."

"Thanks." Ramona spun the dial on her combination

lock. She felt so happy she didn't even care that she was on her way to a double period of maths.

Dowling Boys finished fifteen minutes after Kenley, so Ramona was waiting out front when the guys started coming through the gates. Adil kissed her on the cheek when he found her.

"Hey," he said.

"Hey. Hey Jules." She reached over and gave Adil's best friend an awkward hug, one arm around the back of his neck. He was red-faced when she pulled away.

"Miss MacKenzie," he said. "What are you doing here? Didn't know you were moonlighting as a safety monitor."

"Yeah, LOLsies," she said. Jules could be a smartass but, Ramona had noticed, he never looked her in the eyes when he spoke to her.

"Should we go?" Adil put an arm around her, and the three of them headed to the station.

On the train, the guys talked about something that had happened at school. A substitute teacher had told the class about a brief stint he'd done in a Malaysian jail for drug possession. He'd ignored the teacher's lesson plan and answered their questions for the entire period.

"He didn't even ask us not to tell the principal or the other teachers or anything," Jules said. "Some people have a death wish, I guess."

Adil shrugged. "Maybe he just trusts us."

Jules got off at Clifton Hill, and Ramona and Adil rode on together.

"How was your day?" he asked as they stepped onto the platform at Northcote. "Anything special happen?"

"Nothing at all." She shook her head. "Same old same as."

His mum was in the living room, spoon-feeding baby Zahra, when they came in.

"Hey, guys." She smiled up at them. "Please don't tell me you're hungry. All I've got in the fridge is baby food and baby formula. Don's gonna do a shop on his way home."

"I'm fine," Ramona told her, stroking baby Zahra's head. It felt like a warm coconut.

"Me too," Adil said.

"You're never not hungry." His mum laughed. "Take heed, Ramona. He has two settings: starving and ravenous. Just pray he's grown out of this stage before you two get married."

"Umi!" he said. "You're gonna scare her off. It was hard enough just getting her number."

Ramona smiled at Adil's mum, then followed him to his room. Once inside, she closed the door, raised her hands up to his shoulders, and pushed him against the wall, standing on tiptoe until she could reach his mouth with hers.

"Geez, girl," he said. "You gonna at least let me get my jacket off first?" He pulled it off and they lay down. Adil had a double bed—Ramona still had her old single—and she loved the feeling of being able to open her legs and still have both feet on the mattress.

Adil was her second boyfriend, and not as big as her first. They'd been sleeping together for a month now but she still wasn't used to the difference. She lay there, arched her back, and concentrated on his scent. He worked weekends boxing pastries at his uncle's bakery, and she could swear he smelled like cinnamon all through the week.

"Oh God," she whispered after a few minutes. "I love that."

"Wait. Wait." He stopped moving and closed his eyes in concentration. She held herself as still as she could. A slick of his hair was stuck to his forehead and she brushed it aside with a finger. "Wait," he said. She pulled her hand away. After another minute he opened his eyes and nodded. "Okay."

He leaned his forearms on either side of her head and started to move again. "Can you say something?" Ramona whispered.

"Like what?"

"I dunno. Something sexy."

"You're so sexy and beautiful," he said. "You feel so good. And warm."

"No!" Ramona scrunched up her nose.

"What?"

"Just, warm isn't a sexy temperature."

"Sorry," he said. "I guess I'm just not that into talking during."

Ramona turned her head and looked at his wristwatch, then at the fish swimming around in the aquarium on his desk. His closet door was open a crack and inside she could see something—a backpack or a pile of clothes—and she looked at it for a while. Then she squinted her eyes almost shut and pretended the object was Jules—Jules crouched on the floor of the wardrobe watching them fucking, Jules waiting for them to finish so he could have his turn with her. He was jealous, she imagined, crazy jealous, and also a bit ashamed, but mostly he was just turned on. And ready to have her as soon as his best friend was done.

"Oh my God," she said, turning to face Adil, who was watching her, his eyes wide above her. "Oh my God," she said again, her head falling back.

"Yeah," he said. "Yeah, me too."

"Your mother called," Dr. Carvden told her the following week. "She mentioned what's been happening at home. She and Tony are very upset. They think I'm putting ideas in your head. She said they're considering discontinuing your therapy."

"They can't do that," Ramona said.

"Well, they're the ones paying for our sessions."

Ramona stared at the tissue box on the table next to her. Last week it had been silver with pink and blue dots on it. This week there was a new one sitting there, green flowers on a peach background. A lot of people must cry in here, she thought. She had never cried in the therapist's presence and she wondered if there was something wrong with her because she hadn't. For a moment she considered forcing herself to produce a few tears, just so Dr. Carvden might like her more, just to be like the other clients. But then the therapist said, "I do hope they'll continue to let us work together," and Ramona realized that she must like her already.

"Did I do the right thing?" Ramona asked. "By telling."

"That's not my call to make, Ramona."

"So, you think I shouldn't have said anything?"

"I would support you, no matter what you decided," Dr. Carvden said. "It's your experience to share, or not share, as you see fit."

Ramona waited for her to say something more, but she didn't. The therapist's response was like an algebra problem that was so hard, it seemed to have no answer.

Her mother made shepherd's pie for dinner that night. Afterward, Tony stood at the kitchen sink, washing dishes and passing them to Ramona, who dried them with a tea towel and put them away. Behind them, her mother sat at the kitchen table with Lockie and helped him with his schoolwork.

"No, darling, Scotland has no *u* in it," she told him.

"Oh, I thought it was called Scoutland." Lockie leaned over the page, his tongue pressing into his lower lip as he fixed his mistake.

"So," Tony said. He was using the rough side of a sponge to work at the mashed potato stuck to the bottom of a pot.

"Your mum thinks this whole thing has to do with boarding school."

"It doesn't," Ramona said.

"It's just too expensive," her mother said from the table.

"We'd have to cut right back," Tony said. "Stop paying your mobile bill. And your psychologist. You'd have to get a job over the summer holidays."

"I don't want to go to boarding school anymore," Ramona said. "I like it at Kenley."

"Since when?" her mum asked.

"Since recently."

"That's great news, hon."

"What's Steve's middle name?" Lockie asked.

"Frank," their mother said. "F-R-A—"

Tony rinsed out the pot and placed it on the dish rack. Ramona picked it up.

"Well, if this isn't about boarding school, I don't know what it is you want."

"I didn't say I want anything."

"It's not very nice having someone make up stories about you and go around telling them," he said. "I'll tell you that much."

"That's not what I'm doing."

"I just don't understand where this is coming from. I thought we were sending you to the psychologist to talk about what happened with the heater."

"We are talking about that. But we're talking about other stuff, too."

"All right. Well." Tony squeezed out the sponge and

dropped it into the empty sink. He sounded annoyed but when he turned to face her, his forehead was all creased up, as though it pained him to look at her. "I hope she can help you, Ramona."

"Thanks, Tony. Me too."

"Because your mum and I are upset, but we're also extremely worried about you."

"Don't be."

It was hard to keep looking at him. His sad droopy eyes, the dark patches beneath them. He looked like he actually was worrying about her, like he thought she was doing this specifically to hurt him and he couldn't understand why.

He turned to her mother. "I'm all done here, love. Think I'll head out for a bit."

"Where you going?"

"Just for a drive."

"Can I come?" Lockie asked.

"I don't think so, mate." Tony left the kitchen. Out in the hallway, there was the sound of keys, and then the front door shutting behind him.

Ramona's mother smiled over at her. "I'm glad you two had that talk. Now maybe things can return to normal around here."

"I'd hardly call it a talk."

"Well, you know Tony. He tries."

Ramona did know Tony. She remembered a joke someone had made at the wedding, about how the longest sentence he'd ever spoken was "Will you marry me?"

"I've finished most of the dishes," Ramona said. "Can I leave the rest?"

"Can you just dry them and put them away?" her mum said. "A full rack of dishes is the last thing I need to deal with first thing in the morning." She stood up and ruffled Lockie's hair. "Come on, you," she said. "Let's get you changed and into bed."

All the girls except Minyung came to Ramona's slumber party on Saturday night. They ate pizza in the living room and watched *Napoleon Dynamite* on DVD. Most of them knew it by heart. Every time someone walked past to the kitchen, the girls turned their heads to see if it was Tony. But he didn't appear—he'd gone for a drive as he had most nights that week—and the only person who came by was Steve, who stuck his finger up at Ramona and said hi to the other girls.

"Hi," they said, looking at one another to check if anyone was flirting with him. Nobody was.

After they'd watched the special features, Kirsty said, "Let's go to Ramona's room." The girls followed her upstairs, where Kirsty shut Ramona's door and told everyone to sit in a circle on the floor. She switched the light off and turned on a torch. "The reason Minyung isn't here," she said, sitting down, "is because she told her mum about Ramona being molested, and her mum wouldn't let her come. Here." She handed the torch to Ramona. "Hold this under your face and tell us exactly what happened with you and Tony."

"I don't know," Ramona said. The girls were all sitting cross-legged, watching her. "He'd, like, rub me down. He never touched me with his hands. He always used the towel."

"Did he, like, use his fingers?" Skye's eyes were shiny in the low light.

"Not right inside," Ramona said, the heat from the torch warming her chin. "But almost. Like outside, in between."

Kirsty reached out and took the torch from Ramona. She held it under her face and looked around the circle. "Once, a few years ago, I was at the movies with my mum, and this guy sitting two seats away from us had these running shorts on, you know? They were all pushed up to his thighs and his dick was hanging out of them. I saw it as soon as we sat down but it took my mum a few minutes to notice. Then straight away she grabbed my hand and pulled me into another row, far away. I thought it was a mistake, and the guy didn't know. But my mum told me later that the guy was a sicko and he was doing it on purpose."

"Hey, that happened to me once!" Hayley said.

"You can't talk unless you have the torch," Kirsty said.

Hayley took it from her and began to speak. "That happened to me once, in Princes Park. I was waiting with my sister for our brother to finish footy practice, and this guy was sitting near us under a tree and he was hanging out of his shorts. We didn't move. It was weird. Jodie wanted to leave but I felt like it would be mean to the guy. Like he'd be angry or something. Or maybe he'd follow us."

"Yeah." Skye reached for the torch. "Like sometimes on a crowded tram, a guy will pass me and I'll feel him brush up against my bum. But I can't do anything about it because, like, who would I tell? And anyway, it's impossible to know if he did it on purpose or not."

Amber was next. "When I was going out with that guy Tyler last year, he made me give him blow jobs all the time. Like every time we were together. We'd be kissing and stuff, and then he'd put his hand on my head and push me down there."

"This isn't about me," Danielle said, "but my cousin Marnie was raped once. It was by a guy she was going out with but they hadn't done it before, and that's how she lost her virginity."

"I once saw a prostitute doing it doggy-style in an alleyway in St. Kilda. The guy was just, like, a business guy in a suit."

"My brother downloads this porn with these guys being really mean to women, calling them bitches and forcing them to do stuff. I don't think his girlfriend knows about it."

"About a month ago—" Kirsty was whispering now. The torch batteries were dying and the light was dimmer than before. "Me and Jeremy got really stoned with some of his friends. We were all in his room watching a movie and he pulled his pants down under the blanket and I gave him a hand job. And the others could see what was going on under there and they didn't say anything. I felt weird about it but I kept going. For, like, ages. Maybe it was because he was stoned, but he didn't come." She looked at Ramona. "One of the guys in the room was Adil." Just then the torch flickered and the bedroom door creaked open.

"Aaaah!" All the girls screamed.

"Girls?" Ramona's mother stood in the doorway with a plate in her hands.

"God, you scared us," said Skye.

"Yeah," said Kirsty. "We thought you were a man coming to get us."

"Don't be silly," said Ramona's mum. "It's just me. I thought you might like some Anzac biscuits."

"What's happening?" Steve appeared behind her in the doorway, craning his neck to try to see into the room.

"None of your business," their mother said. "Good night, girls. Don't forget to brush your teeth. There's quite a bit of sugar in those." She pushed Steve away from the doorway and turned on the light in Ramona's room before she closed the door.

In assembly Monday morning, during the singing of the national anthem, Amber put her hand to her forehead and collapsed into the aisle. The teachers found an empty bottle of liquid laxative in her bag. They called her father and sent her to the nurse's office. At first recess, the girls stood in the corridor exchanging hugs. When Ramona asked if anyone could come keep watch for her behind the gym, they shook their heads and went off to visit Amber, with an oversized get-well card they'd made in art class.

"Hi," Ramona whispered when Adil picked up. "I was just thinking about you."

"Really?" he asked. "Is that why you called?"

"No, that's got nothing to do with it."

He took a moment to answer. "Sure. Umm. You know, Jules's sister is in eleventh grade. She goes to Kenley."

"I didn't know that."

"Yeah, she, um. She told him the rumor about you and what happened, with Tony. Is it true?"

Ramona fidgeted with the zip on her uniform. "Yeah."

"Like, when did it happen?"

"Last year, when my leg was bandaged. Before I met you."

"Man. I want to kill him. Could I kill him? I guess I can't kill him." There was another silence and then he asked, "So, do you want to talk about it?"

"I thought we were talking about it."

"Did he do that thing to your leg, too?"

"No," she said. "That was the heater."

"Well, if you don't want to, you know, have sex with me anymore, that's okay. I mean, I think I'd feel bad about it. If I hurt you or something."

Ramona rolled her eyes. "Whatever," she said. She wished he were there so he could see her roll her eyes. "Hey, Kirsty told me you were at Jeremy's place once when they were fooling around in his bed."

"Oh yeah," Adil said. "Yeah, I remember that. It was weird."

"Why? Were you turned on by it or something?"

"No," he said, "oh my God, no. I just felt, I don't know, sorry for her, I guess. It was embarrassing."

"Ramona MacKenzie." Ramona looked up to see Mrs. Parker coming toward her. For a second she thought about running. "Hand over that phone immediately." The teacher put her hand out. "And come with me. The principal's looking for you."

The phone had rung twice by the time they got to the principal's door. Mrs. Parker didn't know how to turn it off, so she handed it to Ramona and instructed her to do so.

"Can I just tell the person that I can't talk?"

"No," Mrs. Parker said. "No phone use on school property. Isn't that right, Principal Valetti?" The principal's door swung open and Ramona could see into her office: to the principal's desk and filing cabinet, to the armchair, the coffee table, and the couch on which sat, Ramona could see now, her mother.

"Come in, Ramona," Principal Valetti said. "Have a seat."

"Hi, honey," her mother said. Seeing her there in the middle of the day made Ramona feel like she was back in kindergarten; like it was her birthday and her mum had brought an ice cream cake for the class to share.

The principal thanked Mrs. Parker and shut the door. No one spoke. Then Ramona heard someone clear their throat and a voice came from the other side of the room.

"Ramona?" the voice said. "This is Mary. I've just been talking to your mother and your principal about what's been going on." It took Ramona a moment to see the phone on the principal's desk, and to place the voice on the speaker as Dr. Carvden's. She'd never known her as Mary before.

"These are very serious allegations, Ramona," Principal Valetti said. "You're lucky Minyung's mother called me and not the police, or family services. Now, I'm in a difficult position here." Principal Valetti looked over at Ramona's mother, then back at her. "Under mandatory reporting rules, I'm obligated to notify the authorities. But I want to hear from you before I proceed."

"What do you want to hear from me?" Ramona asked.

"Once I report this, it's out of my hands," the principal said.

"Then what'll happen?"

"Well, first child protection would be notified. And they would do their own assessment. The worst-case scenario might be that you're taken away from your mother and stepfather. Your siblings might be as well."

"That would be the *very* worst case," Dr. Carvden said. "And, I imagine, not very likely."

Ramona's mother was leaning on the armrest of the couch. She had her eyes closed and her thumb and forefinger pushed into her eyelids like she did when she was stuck in a traffic jam, or when Ramona and Steve were fighting and she couldn't make them stop.

"It's also possible you'd be taken out of Kenley," the principal went on. "And sent to another school, somewhere else."

"I don't want you to report it," Ramona said, her voice straining around a fast-forming lump in her throat. "There's nothing to report. I don't need child protection. I take it back."

Principal Valetti nodded very slowly but no one said anything.

"I take it back. I lied. Please don't get me in trouble."

Her mother started to cry. "Why did she do this?" she asked. "Is it the PTSD?"

"I don't know," Principal Valetti said. "There's been an awful lot of drama with the ninth-grade girls recently. I can't explain it. Mary, do you want to field this one?"

"Well—" Dr. Carvden exhaled. Ramona knew the therapist was making a decision. "Maybe Ramona perceived something as a boundary cross and it wasn't. Maybe Tony was just trying to help but, in doing so, made Ramona feel uncomfortable. There are a lot of mixed messages out there for young women these days. Scare tactics, even. It's very confusing for them. Ramona and I will continue to discuss this in our therapy sessions, but I have to get going now. My next client has arrived."

When the meeting was over, Ramona walked her mum to the car. As they neared her English classroom she hoped the other girls would be looking out the door, so they could see the two of them there together, and wonder what was going on. But they were all leaning over their exercise books, writing, and none of them noticed as they passed.

"Thank goodness that's over," her mother said when they got to the car park. "I didn't enjoy that one iota."

"Am I in trouble?"

"Honestly? I haven't got a clue what to do with you anymore. You've put me in a terrible position. Do you realize that? Now whenever I come back here, for parent–teacher or sports day or to pick you up, all the other parents and teachers are going to be staring at me like I'm a terrible mother. Like I'm married to some kind of monster, instead of to sweet old Tony, who's working nonstop to help me pay for everything and raise you kids. Do you understand?"

"I wouldn't worry about it. In, like, two weeks, no one will even remember any of this happened."

"I hope not." Her mother opened the car door and tossed her handbag onto the backseat. "Now I have to go pick up Steve's new goggles from the optometrist's, rush over to drop off these cake pans at Rob and Lynne's, get Lockie from soccer, and come home and make dinner. Jesus, what a day."

"Can I come with you?" Ramona asked. "I can help. I don't have any important classes this afternoon."

"No, just stay here," her mother said, getting into the car. "For once can you just stick to the rules and do what you're supposed to do?"

. . .

Before therapy on Wednesday, Ramona saw one of Dr. Carvden's other clients. Ramona was sitting in the waiting room, staring at the poster on the wall of a marathon runner, below whom was printed the word ENDURANCE, when Dr. Carvden's door opened and a man walked out. He was in his twenties, with light-brown hair and glasses, and he kept his hands in his pockets and his gaze on the floor all the way to the exit. Ramona wondered what Dr. Carvden did in the ten minutes between the man's session and her own.

"You were put on the spot," the therapist said, once Ramona had come into her office and taken the seat opposite hers. "And I'm so sorry about that. But I'm glad your principal won't report this. I'm glad you told them you take it back."

"You said it wasn't my shameful secret."

The therapist nodded and used her left foot to pull the heel of her right shoe off. "That's right, I did say that. It isn't your secret. You can keep fighting this if you want, and I'll support you if you do. But I don't think the best thing for you right now is for child protection to get involved, or for you and your stepdad to be dragged through the family court system. I'm thinking about you, Ramona, and your healing process. I hope you understand that, and we can keep working together."

There was silence after that, several minutes of it. Ramona sat very still and listened to some kids playing in a nearby yard. She thought about how Dr. Carvden had said she wasn't damaged. Did she really believe that? Or was that what therapists were trained to tell abused people, so they could try to get on with their lives; to give them the illusion that they might be just like everyone else one day, even though they obviously wouldn't.

"I haven't told Adil I'm seeing you," she said finally.

Dr. Carvden shifted slightly in her seat. "Well, that's not unusual. You're pretty early on in the relationship. Maybe one day you'll feel comfortable telling him."

"I think I'm gonna break up with him," Ramona said.

"Why?"

"I'm just not into him."

"What do you think it is that he can't provide?"

"He's just too normal, too nice. It's boring."

"How long have you felt like this?"

Ramona shrugged. "Since the beginning, I guess."

"So why have you stayed with him?"

"I wasn't that popular in first term. He was probably one of the only guys I could get."

"Is that the only reason? Because he was accessible?"

"I don't know. I guess I feel like I *should* be into him. He's cute and funny and fun to talk to. He's so nice, he doesn't even know there's bad things in the world. I'm scared that if I can't be attracted to someone like him, there must be something really wrong with me."

"Well, you could try being attracted," Dr. Carvden said, sneaking a look at the clock on the side table by Ramona's elbow. "If you really want to, I think it's certainly possible. You could try being in the moment. Concentrating on the details of what's going on. Thinking about all the things you like about him. It might not work right away, but after a while you might find you can appreciate the excitement in the even-keeled."

When Ramona came outside after the session, the station wagon was parked in the driveway, with Tony in the driver's seat. She slid in next to him and put on her seatbelt.

"Your mother had to cook," he told her. "I said I'd come get you."

"Okay."

He put the car in reverse and backed out into the road. A couple of approaching drivers honked at him. He sped up to stay ahead of them.

"Geez," Ramona said. He was driving faster than he ever did when the family was in the car. Ramona wondered if this was what he did when he went out at night, sped around with the windows down, pretending he had nowhere to be.

"Your mother's very upset about the lying," he said. "She thought about grounding you, but she's decided just to put it behind us. If I were you, I'd watch my behavior from now on. You've put her through a lot."

"Uh-huh," Ramona said.

"What does that mean?" Tony looked at her.

"It means I know."

Ramona leaned her elbow on the sill and stared out the

window, at the park whizzing by, then the hospital, hoping they could sit in silence for the rest of the ride. But a minute later, Tony cleared his throat and said, "Remember my sister Leanne? You met her at the wedding."

"Yeah." Ramona pictured the skinny woman with the frizzy hair and sparkly black dress.

"When we were kids," Tony said, "she must have been ten or eleven, she was playing in the front yard when a neighbor walked past. He came into the garden and tried to—interfere with her."

Ramona turned from the window and stared at him. "What did she do?"

"She yelled bloody murder. She screamed and scratched him. She said every obscenity she could think of, then ran inside. He never came back. I think he might have moved away. At least, we never saw the man she described."

Tony changed lanes without a head-check, and turned through a yellow light onto Moreland Road.

"Geez," Ramona said again.

"What I'm saying," he said, "is you never had to put up with anything you didn't want to. I was just trying to help you out during a difficult time. If you didn't want my help, you could have said so."

Ramona didn't know what to say. She wondered what Dr. Carvden would tell her to do now. They had never discussed the possibility of a conversation like this.

"That's good that the guy never came back," she said finally.

Tony nodded. "It is good." He reached over and turned

on the radio, pressing the buttons without looking at them. *I've sat on my veranda and watched them knocking over every rubbish bin on the street, one after the next,* a caller was telling a radio host. *I'm sure they're doing it on purpose, and that's our tax dollars.* Ramona wished they could switch to an FM station with music, but she settled back into her seat and listened, glad the conversation was over.

Steve was setting the table when they got home, and Lockie was in the living room, drawing a big tree on the cover of his project. "Where's Mum?" Ramona asked. They both ignored her.

She found her mother in the laundry, tossing clothes into the washing machine.

"How was therapy?" she asked.

"It was okay." Ramona watched her mum turn a pair of Lockie's jeans inside out before dropping them in and reaching for the detergent. "But actually, I don't think I need to go back."

"Why? I thought you liked it."

"I did. But my leg's all better now, and I haven't turned off an electrical switch in ages. Except for at the normal times, when you're supposed to turn them off."

"That's great, hon."

"It's costing you guys a lot of money and I think I'm cured now."

Her mum closed the machine and turned the dial. "Did you discuss this with Dr. Carvden?"

"No."

"Why don't you talk it over with her at your next appointment? See if she thinks you're ready."

Ramona wanted to roll her eyes and say, *Do I have to?*, but she stopped herself and nodded. "Yeah, okay," she said.

Ramona skipped dinner that night. She went straight to her room and thought about calling Adil, or chatting with some girls online. But she didn't feel like doing either. Homework was out of the question, so she turned the light off and climbed into bed.

Under the covers, she put her hands inside her school tights and tried to bring a story or scenario to mind that would set something alight in her. She tried to think about Adil and the smell of cinnamon. When that didn't work, she tried to picture herself as Kirsty giving Jeremy a hand job in a room full of boys. Then she was a prostitute in an alleyway with a businessman behind her and a wad of cash in her fist. And then Camilla on *Big Brother*, being held down and humiliated in front of the entire country.

And then she was herself, some sleepy winter morning last year, still in the bath when the door opened. She was rinsing conditioner out of her hair, her fingers pushing hard at her scalp, and wishing she could go away to boarding school. She was turning off the tap and stepping out with his help, raising her arms and inching her legs apart when he told her to. She tried to think of something to say but found she couldn't locate a single word inside her head. She just stood there, shivering dumbly, as water fell onto the bath-mat, one drop and then another, for what felt like forever.

Downstairs, she heard dishes clattering. Her clock said nine fifteen when she opened her eyes. Soon *Rove Live* would be starting and everyone would be sitting down to-gether to watch it. Steve would laugh at all the *What the . . . ?* jokes, Lockie would beg to be able to stay up past his bed-time, and Tony and her mother would look at each other and say, *Okay but just this once.*

The kitchen was empty when Ramona came in. There was a wok, some bowls, and a pile of chopsticks sitting on the drying rack. Her mother must have made stir-fry for dinner. "Please?" she heard Lockie saying in the next room. "I never get to see till the end." Ramona dried every dish and utensil and put it away in the cupboard or drawer where it belonged. Then she turned off the light, went into the liv-ing room, curled up on the couch with her family, and watched TV.

The Pretty One

There is a new boy in the neighborhood. Working at the gourmet ice cream place and bar-backing at the Make Out Room. He has a Japanese bike and a scar on his forearm and he always keeps a little notebook in the back pocket of his jeans. Gray ones. Tight. He has curly hair with a fringe that sweeps across his forehead and the eyelashes of a pretty girl. That's what everyone calls him: the pretty one.

I go to a reading at the Make Out. I don't know why. I see him there, moving across the room with pint glasses stacked a meter high, leaned up against his shoulder. The girl at the door is watching him, too. I hold out my money until she notices me.

Sean finds me at the bar. "Thanks for coming," he says. "It's nice to have groupies."

"There's a warehouse party in the Bayview," I tell him. "I can only stay for half an hour."

"I'll be on late," he says. "And I'm reading the part about you."

"Enthusiastic exclamation," I say without smiling. I order a dirty martini. Sean pays for it with a sweaty drink ticket. "Well, in that case," I tell the bartender, "I'll have two."

"A humble you're welcome," Sean says. He hands over another ticket and joins the crowd in front of the stage.

The place is filled with the literary strain of hipster: girls in bright T-shirts with jeans worn through at the back from sitting on desk chairs all day, and guys in plaid shirts they bought new, hiding bristly faces behind square-rims. Everyone has tattoos of text. Kundera and Eliot and others I don't recognize—big blocks of words inked in cursive and Helvetica and Arabic script, crawling down calves, forearms, upper backs. The girl on stage has a big old DADDY tattooed in blue on her ankle.

"The only. Thing. To fear," she reads from a chapbook. "Is tears. Themselves."

"Can I get another?" I ask the bartender. This time I pay for myself.

One after the next, they get up there, hands shaking, smiling at the microphone, prefacing with, "This is from this new thing I'm working on." Some of it is probably really good but we're in a bar, and the only bits that people pay attention to are funny or about sex.

"I wanted. To sleep. With him," reads a tiny girl with a big blond Afro. "But I had. Thrush."

The next time I order a martini it comes dry. "Can I get

this dirty?" I call to the bartender, but it's intermission and the kids have him slammed. "Excuse me!"

I leave my glass where it is, stumble down off my stool, and sneak back behind the bar. I crouch down and open the door of the fridge. Behind me I can hear people calling for Anchor Steams and PBRs. The only things in here are half a jar of maraschino cherries, an open carton of milk, and a stick of celery sitting in a glass of water.

"What are you doing?" Black Converse, tight gray jeans, a yellow T-shirt inside out, and a bunch of curly brown hair pushed to the side of his forehead. I stay where I am.

"I'm looking for something."

"What?"

"Olive juice."

He crouches down next to me, leans an elbow on the fridge door, and smiles. "Well, we haven't properly met yet, but thanks, I'm flattered."

I wait for some smart reply to come to me, something drink-related or cherry-related or a play on the word *dirty*. But he's looking right at me and he's so damn pretty, I blank. I stand up, slide past him, and run away, back around the bar.

"Hey, that's my martini," I tell some guy who's holding an empty toothpick between his teeth.

"I didn't drink any," he says. "I just got hungry."

The bar-back is turned away now, slicing lemons on a chopping board. *I didn't say "olive juice." I said "elephant shoe."* That's what I should have said to him. But it's too late now to get the upper hand. My heart feels panicky and un-familiar. I turn to the toothpick guy and, in a shaky voice, I say, "Why aren't we kissing?"

He takes the stick out of his mouth. "I don't know."

It's a weird kiss, more high school than grad school. He has his mouth so wide open, I can't even find his upper lip. And he's tentative and soft, like he might actually like me one day, and want to go on a date and tell me about growing up different in rural Michigan. *Oh, that's why,* I want to say when I pull away. But suddenly I remember how it feels to like somebody, and I feel sorry for this guy, teetering in this same rocky boat called love-at-first-sight, so I take a sip of my drink and kiss him again. In the background I hear Sean laughing into the microphone. "This is from this new thing I wrote." The guy's glasses push up against my face. I put my hand on the back of his head.

"She was good at beginnings. Good at the flirtation and the small talk and the straight talk and the glow. But after that, I saw her flinch and protect herself. Guy after guy became a first date, a second date, and then an ex. I waited for her to settle down, waited for her to want to settle down with me. 'You can't be pregnant at fifty,' I told her. All she said was 'Neither can you.'"

"That was great," I tell Sean later, after the toothpick guy's gone home with my number scrawled illegibly next to the Frank O'Hara on his right biceps. "But that character is nothing like me."

"That's the golden rule of fiction," Sean says. "Give a girl big tits, and she'll forgive all the awful stuff you write about her."

"Oh." I perk up. "I've got big tits in the story?"

"You weren't even listening." He shakes his head. "You were too busy making out with that guy to even clap at the end."

"I was clicking my fingers under the bar," I say. "Like in the olden days."

The bar-back is leaning over, wiping down tables, and it's only a matter of minutes before he gets to where we are. I stand up and sling my bag over my shoulder. "Hey, what do you know about that guy?"

"The pretty one?" Sean says. "His name's Sylus. Or Sy, I guess."

"Le sigh," I say. "Is he single?"

"I think so."

"How can that be?"

"He's young. I think, like, nineteen or something."

"How can he work at a bar, then?"

"He doesn't drink," Sean says. "You guys would be awful together."

I take off. I don't go to the party in the Bayview and I don't even feel like riding my bike. I walk it next to me, whacking my ankle on the pedal every few steps, and carry it up the stairs when I get home. Sophie is listening to Lykke Li in her room, but I don't feel like knocking and going in to chat. I close my door, kick off my shoes, and get into bed fully clothed. I don't feel like a nightcap, don't feel like brushing my teeth, getting undressed, falling asleep, or looking at porn. I just want to lie still and think about him all night and all day. I do that for about three minutes. Then I open my laptop and change my Facebook status to *abstinent until further notice.*

What's going on? a few people write on my wall.

Holy shit, I think I'm waiting for someone, I write back.

No one responds. They probably have no idea what to say to that, or maybe they just all fell asleep.

I get a taste for ice cream. I go to the shop at all times of day, trying to get a sense of when his shifts are, tipping big, sitting on the bench out front because I'm too nervous to say more to him than just my order.

"I liked it better when you dated baristas," Lars says one morning when I drag him there for a scoop of Secret Breakfast: ice cream, cornflakes, and bourbon. "You had all this energy back then, and you smoked more. Now you're just gonna get all fat and American, and I'll have to kick you out of the band 'cause you won't be cute anymore."

"But I'm getting it in a cup, not a cone," I protest. On the other side of the window, Sy has his hand up his shirt. He's scratching his chest and yawning. I turn back to Lars. "Do you think he's too young for me?" (Last year, on our way to a gig in the East Bay, Lars pulled up at a petrol station to buy a birthday card for the girl he was dating, and came back to the car pissed that they only had a *Happy 17th* card on the stand. "She'll just think it's funny," I said. "No, she won't," he said. "She'll think I'm a forgetful dick." Then he leaned on the steering wheel, crossed out the 7, and replaced it with a 6.)

"I think *you're* too young for him," he says now. "You revert to this weird preverbal state around him."

I laugh. "It's true because it's funny." I sit back and let the cornflakes go soggy on my tongue before I swallow them. The sun is out even though it's San Francisco in June. There is a tree right in front of us, with all its leaves bristling on it like goosebumps: a little miracle on Harrison Street that I never noticed before because I was too busy worrying that the wind was messing up my hair on my way to the shop.

"Isn't this gorgeous?" I say, leaning back against the glass. "Isn't it just fucking gorgeous in this town? Aren't we so lucky to live here?"

Lars shifts away and turns to stare at me. I smile and shrug and take a lick of my breakfast, and all he says is, "Ew."

I tell everyone about my new crush. I call friends in England and wake them up to talk about it.

"Babe," their boyfriends say, "who's calling so late?"

"How long have you been seeing him?" they all want to know.

"Well." I try to calculate. "If you add up all the interactions we've had, the time is probably equivalent to about half a date."

I tell all my friends and people I meet at parties, and I find it a legitimate enough excuse to use on other guys who ask me out. I tell every pretty, skinny, younger, single, straight girl I know, and half of them seem to know who I'm talking about.

"That guy?" says a girl at the Bike Kitchen who comes over to borrow a pedal wrench. "That guy's got hell of eyelashes."

"He's too young for you," I say.

I tell my Cinema 101 summer-school students at the end of class one day, after I've switched off *Annie Hall* and turned on the lights. They stop packing away their books and sit there blinking at me.

"Any questions?" I ask. "About Woody Allen's view of romantic love versus passionate love? Or about my new crush?"

They're silent for a moment and then Chelsea raises her hand—Chelsea from Santa Fe, who said on the first day of class that her favorite movies are the classics, like *Point Break*.

"I'm just confused," she says when I call on her. "I guess we all thought you were kind of, I don't know, old and married and settled or something." The other girls in the class nod. The boys sit there with their legs out straight, staring at their shoes.

"I'm not old," I say. "I'm twenty-seven." It takes a second of silence for me to realize that to them it's the same thing.

I go to tell my ex-boyfriend at the Common Room. A girl stops me on the corner of Valencia and 21st to ask me if I want to save the world.

"I'm a member in England," I say. That's the line I use for everything.

"No, we're a local group," she says. "We're lobbying the mayor to provide more community garden space in the city, so people can grow their own organic produce and eat locally."

"I mainly eat ice cream," I tell her.

"That can't be good for you."

"Well, I kind of like the guy who works at the ice cream place."

"Oh, okay." She looks up the street; waiting, I guess, for a more viable petition-signing candidate to come along.

"So I keep dropping in, you know. And I probably look like such an idiot."

"Uh-huh," she says.

"The guy's probably scared of me by now."

"Yeah," she says. "I better get back to work, so—"

Inside the café Luke is steaming milk. "Hey," I say. "Those street canvassers are so annoying."

"Yeah," he says, but he has other things on his mind. "I can't work out if I want to get rid of sugar altogether, or just charge people extra for it. Coffee's a fruit. It should taste sweet enough on its own."

"Uh-huh," I say. "Can I ask you the most inappropriate favor since the time I told you to make out with that French guy in front of me?"

"Did I do that?" he asks.

"No. You called him 'freedom douche' and you didn't

speak to me for three days. But can I talk to you about the boy I like?"

"Claire Claire Claire," he says. But he listens as I describe the guy, as do Jackie at the register and Alex, who's pulling the shots.

"Is it tall americano?" asks Jackie.

"I think it's double macchiato," Luke says. I tell them about the scar on his forearm, and they all agree he gets pour-overs to go.

"So what do I do?" I ask. "You hospitality people are so lucky. You stand here all day while a parade of cute people come in to flirt with you. The rest of us have to schlep around town just to get a little noticed."

"Speaking of," Luke says, looking over at a girl waiting in line, wearing leggings and a purple hoodie. "It's yoga girl."

"Hey, that's not fair," I tell him. "You can't date anyone before I do. You have to stay obsessively in love with me until I move on and feel secure with somebody else."

"You better ask this guy out, then," Luke says, handing me the other half of a shot to taste. "They say it takes a week for every month you dated someone to get over them. According to that schedule, I'll be done with you by August."

I go to the Make Out Room before open. "Hey," I say. He's sweeping the floor behind the bar and I wonder what it says in that little notebook in his pocket. He never seems to carry a pen.

"Hey." He leans the broom against the sink and comes over.

"My name's Claire," I say. "I've been taking a poll in the neighborhood and an overwhelming majority of respondents think you should ask me out."

He looks down at his hands and I think he's embarrassed, but then he looks right up at me and says, "Why don't you just ask me out?"

"Because you're the guy," I say.

"But you're older than me," he says.

"But you're the pretty one." We're at an impasse. He picks up the broom and starts sweeping again.

"Fine," he says, when he gets to the end of the bar. "Would you, Claire, like to go on a date with me sometime, and *not* drink alcohol, and *not* go for ice cream, and maybe even get out of the neighborhood and go somewhere else?"

"Why, I'd love to," I say. "Let's meet at the bar across the street tomorrow at eight."

So we go drinking. Well, I go drinking, and he sits next to me and watches. It turns out he does drink on occasion, but right now he's on a cleansing diet. All he's allowed to ingest is a mixture of lemon juice, water, maple syrup, and cayenne pepper. He pulls a jar of it out of his messenger bag, twists the lid off, and takes a gulp. He hands it to me to try.

"This'd be better with tequila," I say. "Should I get us some shots?"

"No," he says, hugging the jar to his chest. "Don't corrupt me."

After I've had two whiskeys with beer backs he says he thinks I should stop drinking for the night.

"But we're having fun," I tell him.

"I know," he says. "But we're getting to know each other and I don't want you to do anything you'd regret." (This reminds me of the time I saw Beirut play at the Great American Music Hall. It was their first tour, they were all still teenagers, and afterward I saw the guitarist having a smoke out front. "That was amazing," I said. "It made me wanna run away and join a gypsy band." "Hey, man, be careful," he said. "Don't run away from your problems.")

"Wow," says Sy. "You saw Beirut on their first tour ever?"

We walk over to my place on Shotwell, and we sit on the front steps while I smoke a cigarette. "You shouldn't smoke so much," he says. I'm kind of annoyed by all the paternal advice, but then I get this horrid thought that maybe he's thinking about the future, and our children, and how sad they'd all be if I got lung cancer and died. And then the second horrid thought comes: This idea of a future together pleases me. I butt the thing out and we sit there looking at each other. Then he puts his finger on my lips. "I really want to kiss you," he says. I look at him. I can't stop looking at him. "But I also wanna save it."

A week later, his cleanse is over. I go to his house on Bryant and we sit out on the fire escape and drink vodka with homemade lemonade and mint. His roommates go in and out of the kitchen, I can see them through the window.

When they finally turn the light off, I tilt over until my cheek touches his shoulder. I feel him tense up, and I wonder if he's changed his mind about me, but then he reaches over and takes my hand.

He looks down into the darkness. "It's hard to see it right now, but there's a whole garden down there."

"Really?" I lean forward, stick my face through the bars, and try to see something.

"Yeah, there are succulents and lavender and the most amazing bougainvillea. Plus a whole vegetable patch. Spinach, beets, cucumbers. All kinds of herbs."

"Did you plant it?"

"A lot of it. My parents own a nursery in Amherst. When I moved out here, I drove across the country with a suitcase in the trunk, and a backseat full of cuttings and seeds and bulbs. I had to drive super fast so things wouldn't wilt or die on the way. Then I had to search Craigslist for a place with a backyard."

Should it be like this? Should I feel intimidated by a nineteen-year-old? Shouldn't I be thinking about what's going to happen next: whether or not we're going to kiss this time, whether he likes me as much as I like him, whether or not the fog is doing crimpy things to my hair? Right now I don't care about any of that. I close my eyes and push my nose into his neck and he doesn't complain about it being cold. He squeezes my fingers between his and says, "I have no idea why you're in California and not in England, but I'm really glad you're here."

We stay out there for a while. We must get pretty drunk

because by the time we go to his room, we both fall into his bed in our clothes and pass out. When I wake up later, we're kissing. He puts his hand on my lower back and pulls me against him. We kiss some more. I roll on top of him, then he rolls on top of me. Then I take off all my clothes and he pulls off his T-shirt. His body is long and skinny with no hair on his chest. There's a tattoo over his heart but it's too dark in the room to make out what it is. When I go to put my hand inside his jeans, he pulls it away and puts it, palm flat, over his face.

"Let me guess," I whisper, "you want to save it."

"No," he whispers back. "I just have my period." He laughs and scrapes his teeth against my palm.

I roll away, onto my back, and try to slow my breath. After a few minutes he asks if I'm okay.

"I'm fine," I say. "My body's just going crazy right now. I'm trying to calm it. Maybe I should think about something else. The new Arsenal away uniform? Or my nanna?"

"Just pretend you're a little kid and you don't know about physical things yet," he suggests.

"Wait a second." I sit straight up and look at him. "Are you that kid? Are you still—a virgin?"

He props himself up on his elbows. "No," he says. "I'm nineteen."

"You kids today," I say. "Starting so young. Was it at a rainbow party? Or were you just sexting at recess?"

"Where did you meet your first boyfriend?" he asks. "In an IRC chat room? What was his A/S/L?"

The boy can hustle.

"Come on," he says now, tugging my arm.

"Where are we going?"

"To brush our teeth."

"No way." I flop down and push my face into the pillow. "I'm too tired."

"Come on. You'll be happy in the morning that you did it."

"Don't you know you get a free pass on brushing your teeth when you're drunk? Same as washing off your makeup. And, anyway, I don't have my toothbrush here."

"Don't worry about that," he says. "You can use mine."

He leans over and kisses me on the mouth, and I slowly get to my feet.

We're hanging out. Which comes before dating, which comes before seeing each other, which comes before being in a relationship. But I'm pretty sure it's happening. Every few nights we meet up and talk about going to see a band or catching a movie downtown or cooking something at one of our houses or introducing each other to our friends. Then we go drinking. And because he's pretty and I actually like him, I drink to get drunk.

"Don't you want to remember this beginning bit clearly?" my friend James asks me one day on campus, when I meet him for lunch wearing big hangover sunglasses to block out the Berkeley light. "You're getting to know him, you're learning about each other. Don't you want to have the memory of that later on?"

"He makes me too nervous," I say. "The only way I can talk to him at all is by getting totally drunkified."

We are getting to know each other, sort of. Some nights I'll ask him a question and he'll swear I've asked it before.

"An older sister and a younger brother," he says. "Remember? You said you have a cousin whose name is Harriet, too."

"Oh yeah," I say. "I wonder what she's up to."

I apply too many layers of lipstick in smudgy bathroom mirrors between rounds, and I feel like I'm being super sharp and funny because he laughs at most things I say. When we leave a place at two, he holds my hand on the walk home, steadying me as I jump between cracks in the sidewalk.

Sleepovers happen at his place because I'm embarrassed about how messy my room is. His bed is always neatly made with its white blanket and gray pillows, and it seems like he does laundry three times a week.

"I hope you can meet my mom sometime," he says one night when we're looking at photos on his computer. "You guys would get along."

"I feel like I have already," I say.

He likes to sleep naked and he likes me to sleep naked. On days when he gets up at five in the morning to go churn the new flavors, I make him turn on the light so I can see what he's wearing. Then I roll over and fall back asleep.

Late mornings, when I get up, always involve a sort of piecing-together of what happened the night before. One day there are soggy tissues on the bedside table.

"Did I cry last night?" I ask him that night over tacos and horchata.

"Yeah, you were missing your family. And then you said you were scared about what's gonna happen after you finish your PhD. And then you cried about your ex, and how horrible the breakup was."

"Well, I guess we covered all bases in one go," I say, scraping the jicama to the edge of my plate.

"And you, uh, you told me about the abortion," he says, looking at me and lowering his voice. "I was sorry to hear about that. I cried a bit then, too."

"Well—we don't have to worry about that anymore," I say. "I'm on the pill. It's not gonna happen again."

Another morning I wake up with a bad taste in my mouth. "You threw up," he says, pushing the hair out of my eyes. "This might seem forward but I'm getting you a toothbrush to keep here. You puked your little heart out, then wrestled mine from me and insisted on using it."

"I'm sorry," I say. I hide my face in his underarm and groan. "I have hangover head."

"That's the worst," he says.

"Yeah, wait till you're in your late twenties. It doesn't just disappear at ten A.M. It sticks around all day till you hit the bars again that night."

Another morning I wake up with a clear head but feeling

like something terrible happened the night before. He's not next to me in the bed. I find him in the kitchen making breakfast, a bowl of torn-up bread and soft-boiled eggs all mushed together. We eat on the couch in the living room. Then he carries my bike down the stairs and kisses me goodbye at the front door, and I think: I love him.

"Just so you know," he says. "You told me you love me last night."

"No, I didn't," I say, then I get on my bike and ride away.

Halfway home, I stop and get out my phone to text him. *It doesn't count when you're drunk,* I write. *And anyway, I think boys are gross.*

It is two excruciating hours before he writes back. I hate dating people with real jobs. The answer, when it comes, says *Uh-huh, whatever you say.*

I swear to myself that I won't say it again until he does, but the next night I say it again. The morning after that, I wake up before him and whisper it in French to the croissant tattooed on his chest. After that I say it all the time. I can't stop saying it. We're watching a movie, or we're lying in the park, and it just comes out.

"Oh my God." I cover my mouth with both hands. "I didn't mean to do that. Why do I keep doing that? Just ignore that."

"I ignored it last time," he says. "But this time I'm paying attention."

I have other thoughts, too—embarrassing thoughts. Like I want to call him my boyfriend, and I want to add him to the "favorites" section in my phone. I want to take him back to the UK to see the house I grew up in, and sleep next to him in my old bedroom. I want to make him, God help me, a mixtape.

He finally says it back to me, on the Fourth of July. We've ridden our bikes to the Embarcadero to see the fireworks above the bay and missed them by a minute. He shouts it to me over the voices of people pushing past us, excited to get to their cars and go home. I'm not sure if he's saying it because he means it, or because I'm bummed about not seeing the fireworks. But at the end of the night, in his room, in his bed, he says it again, all breathless and sleepy.

I say, "The week it's gonna take me to get over this past month is gonna be the worst week ever of my life."

He says, "Maybe you'll never have to."

He has a best friend. A short guy with blond curly hair and black plugs in his ears. His name is Connor. The three of us go to the Irish pub on Sy's day off. I've walked past the place every day for years, but I've never been in. We all order beer. They get pulled-pork sandwiches and chat about people they know back home.

"Did you hear Charles and Kelly are getting married?" Connor says, chewing on a garlic fry.

"Uh-huh," says Sy. "I told him a month ago that he should move out here. He was having anxiety attacks, and he said he didn't know what to do with his life."

"This is a great place to find out what you wanna do."

"Uh-huh."

"And now he's getting married."

"I know."

"Crazy, dude."

Connor is secretly seeing three different girls and he tells us that two of them showed up at the Homestead the night before. "I played it good," he says. "I bounced between the two of them until Leila said she was really sorry, but she was super tired and had to go home. Then I took Jamie back to my place."

"Nice," says Sy. The waitress comes and takes orders for the next round, and leaves again.

"Dude," says Connor, "this place only hires sevens."

Sy is watching the Giants game playing on the TV behind the bar, but he turns back long enough to say, "Dude, not true."

"Why does it have to be a number system?" I say. "It's kind of insulting. Why can't you just have a color grade? Like, one girl's turquoise, another one's magenta."

"You're a Mission nine and a Marina seven. Okay?" says Connor. "Happy now?" I don't know what to say to that. I haven't hung out with guys who talk like this since I was an undergrad and, besides, I am kind of happy with my rating.

The next night, I meet the rest of his friends from home. We go to Connor's place on 25th Street, where a bunch of them are playing a card game with coins. They're a hippieish group, with long dready hair and piercings in their eyebrows, lips, noses. The guys are sitting in a circle on the floor, gambling with quarters, and the girls are on the bed, humming along to the bluegrass playing from a laptop. I play two games with the guys and come in third both times. None of them asks me my name.

I defect to the bed. The girls are all talking about Gay Pride, and how it's gonna be awesome, and they hear there's lots of nudity, and should they go to the park or watch the parade downtown?

"Hey, they should also have a gay shame parade," I say. "Where gay people dress up like they're trying to pass as straight, and everyone else stands on the sidelines dressed like disapproving parents, shaking their heads."

They all stop smiling and just look at me. I can actually see chewing gum stuck in a clump to one girl's molar.

"She's joking," Sy says from the floor, and everyone relaxes a little.

"When did you all move here?" I ask them.

"A few months ago," they say.

One of them asks where I'm from. "Cool," she says when I tell her. "I'm going to Spain for my junior year abroad."

"Hey," says a skinny emo girl with a short fringe. "Did you hear about Charles and Kelly?"

"Uh-huh," says a redhead girl. I recognize her from behind the counter at Aquarius Records. "We're all going back for the wedding at the end of September."

"Dude," says Connor, throwing his cards into the center of the circle of guys. "I can't believe it. So close. So fucking close."

Sy hasn't eaten dinner so we leave after a couple of hours. He buys a bag of cheese popcorn from a corner store on Mission Street. He eats it in handfuls on the ride back to his place, dropping pieces onto the road along the way.

"Your friends are cool," I say.

"You think so?" he says. "I wasn't sure."

"Well, they're kind of young," I say. "There wasn't a load of stuff to talk to them about."

"Yeah," he says. "They can be pretty first-level. But I don't really mind that. I just enjoy their company, and accept them for who they are." He keeps one hand on his handlebars, leans his head back, and pours the rest of the popcorn into his mouth.

"Those have so much MSG in them," I say. "You're gonna be up all night."

"Nuh-uh," he says, shoving the empty bag into his back pocket. "I always sleep well when you're with me."

The next week, my friends Nick and Rafael are having a dinner party at their place in Oakland. We take BART over to the Lake Merritt stop, carrying a six-pack of IPA and a carton of salt-and-pepper ice cream from his shop.

Nick answers the door and leads us into the kitchen, where everyone is sitting around, drinking gin and tonics. "Hey," Rafael says, "maybe you have an opinion on this. We were talking about whether *A Woman Under the Influence* would be better or worse if you didn't know Gena Row-lands was married to Cassavetes in real life. Thoughts?"

"Well, their mums are in it, too," I say. "To me that's much more—" Sy has his hands in his pockets and is look-ing around the kitchen. I catch myself. "Wait, can we not talk about film right away? Let the layperson think we're actually fascinating people with diverse interests. For at least five minutes."

"I'm not a layperson," Sy says, putting his arm around me and waving at the group. "I'm her boyfriend."

Dinner is homemade pasta with a pesto sauce, and half-way through the meal, the conversation turns back to Cas-savetes. Sy is quiet the whole time, concentrating on his food. When he's done with that, he leans back in his chair until his belly button is exposed, and yawns. Later, his phone rings in his pocket. He has to stand up to get to it because his jeans are so tight. It's his dad, he says, and he goes into the living room to talk. Everyone else turns to me.

"We like him," Amanda says. The others nod.

"How do you know you all like him?" I ask. "You haven't discussed it. I've been sitting here the whole time."

"He's a much more comfortable person than Luke," James says.

"What does that mean?" I ask.

"And he's so pretty," Amanda says.

"So pretty." All the guys agree.

"Is he prettier than me?" I ask. They all look at one an-other.

"Well, you're cute," Nick says, "but he's just—everything."

"You're both very pretty," Amanda says.

"Do you wanna make out with him?" I ask Nick.

"Can I make out with him?" he asks Rafael.

"I thought we said only during birthday week," Rafael says.

Nick shakes his head. He looks down at his plate. "I can't make out with him."

"Hey, lady, what are you, pimping me out?" Sy comes back into the kitchen and snaps his phone shut.

"Trying to," I say, "but no takers."

"Wait," he tells the others. "You haven't even tasted my ice cream yet."

Later, the two of us walk back to the station together. "Sorry if that was boring," I say.

"It wasn't at all," he says. "They're really nice. I mean, there's definitely a nerd factor there. But I had a good time. It was relaxing. The pasta was good."

I reach out and put my hand inside the pocket of his hoodie. He puts his hand in there, too, and covers mine with his.

"Are we there yet?" I ask, bumping his leg with my hip.

"Not even nearly," he says.

We go to a party at the Common Room. It's a welcome-back thing for a guy called Calvin, who moved out to Brooklyn to work for Café Grumpy a year ago, and just got back. Everyone's doing KGB shots. In England we call it Russian Co-caine. You dip a lemon slice in sugar on one side and ground coffee on the other. Then you drink a shot of vodka and eat the lemon, coffee-side down. I do six.

There are probably a hundred people in there when Cal-vin gets up on the bar, all wobbly on his feet. "Man," he says, "it's good to be back." Everyone cheers. Someone passes him a bottle of Maker's and he takes a gulp. "In New York, there are hella babes." Everyone screams. "But it's good to see you ugly fuckers again."

People are wasted by this point. I go to find Sy and he's talking to a girl with Princess Leia braids in her hair. When I come up, she walks away. He puts a hand on my arm.

"Why aren't we kissing?" I ask him.

"I dunno. I feel kind of uncomfortable being affectionate around your ex."

"Luke?" I say. "Don't worry, he's fine with it."

"Maybe," he says. "When someone introduced us, he shook my hand and called me 2.0."

"He's just jealous," I say.

"Exactly."

Everywhere around us people are making out with each other. Unlikely couples, like Pete from Bi-Rite and Violet the documentary filmmaker who is, as far as I know, a radi-cal lesbian documentary filmmaker.

Calvin calls me over and pours some Maker's into a cup for me. "What news of New York?" I ask him.

"Man, there's like a portal from here to Brooklyn," he

says. "Everyone dresses the same, listens to the same tunes. You run into people from here all the time. It's crazytown."

When I look around, Princess Leia is talking to Sy again, doing a little dance that makes him laugh.

"But the weather," Calvin says. "The weather is shitty as fuck. You know how people always say that September eleventh was the most perfect summer day? They keep saying that because they have, like, three nice days a year. They were all kinda pissed that the terrorists ruined one of them."

When I turn again, Sy and the girl are heading out the front door. "Hey," says Calvin. "I picked up a little blow habit in New York. And I picked up a little blow when I got back. Wanna have a key party?"

"Uh, I'm a member in England," I say.

I'm halfway to the door when I see Katie the manager locking it.

"I need to get outside," I tell her.

"The cops came and I told them I'd lock the door so no more people could get in."

"I have to." I fumble with the lock until it turns, and I push the door open.

The street is quiet, the sounds of the party muffled behind glass. Sy is sitting on someone's front steps by himself, smoking a joint.

"What are you doing?" I ask.

"Just getting some fresh air."

"Where did that girl go?"

"What girl? Oh, I don't know. I guess she went home."

"Did you make out with her?"

He looks at me like I'm crazy. "No," he says.

"I don't care if you did," I tell him. "Just be honest about it."

"I didn't do anything with her. I'm in love with this other lady."

"I don't believe you. And I don't even care. You can do whatever you want."

Now he looks terrified. "Claire," he says.

"I don't care. I don't really even live here, anyway."

He stands up and flicks the rest of his joint into the gutter. "I'm going home," he says. He walks away.

Back inside, Calvin is behind the bar, pulling shots. "Come here," he says. "I'll show you how."

I go around and stand beside him. He shows me how to hold the portafilter under the grinder. I tamp it so unevenly that I have to throw the coffee out and start again. This time it's better, and I get it into the machine and watch it drip into the demitasse. Then I taste it. It's disgusting.

"Flavor notes?" he asks me.

"Uh, capers?" I say. "Salt-and-vinegar chips?"

He takes the cup out of my hand. "More like tears," he says. Then he asks, "Can we kiss now, please?"

"No," I say. "I have a boyfriend." I picture Sy's back as he walked away from me down the street.

"Well, can I touch your ass?"

"Uh, sure."

He grabs my butt and squeezes. "Nice," he says.

"Thanks."

Luke comes over and leans his elbows on the other side of the counter. "Did you screw up?" he asks.

I pout and nod.

"Why don't you go find him and make things better?"

"I will," I say, "whenever Calvin lets go of my butt."

At two, I walk over to Sy's and call his phone. He's still awake. I follow him inside, watching his left foot turn in slightly as he climbs the stairs. In his room, he sits on the desk chair and I collapse onto his bed.

"What is it?" he asks me. "Do you think you don't deserve to be loved or something?"

"I was just wastified," I say. He doesn't answer. I try again. "Everyone was drunk and making out and you wouldn't kiss me and it made me insecure and I saw you leave with that girl and I got jealous."

"I didn't leave with her," he says, his voice cracking on the word "leave." I want to make a joke about his age and puberty but it's not that moment. He swivels in his chair and turns to face the window. The lights on the Twin Peaks tower are blinking. I close my eyes and put my hands on my forehead.

"Listen," I say. "I think I just have to open myself to the possibility that things are going to be okay with you and me. That it won't end ugly like the rest."

He turns and looks at me.

"I promise promise this won't happen again."

"Okay," he says.

He comes and lies down and I shuffle over until we're close. His hair smells like smoke. We don't sleep together that night, but still I feel like things are going to be okay.

Another night, though, it happens again. We're at a wine tasting in Hayes Valley with a bunch of his friends. When we get on our bikes to leave, he speeds ahead of me with the others and leaves me trying to catch up. I'm pedaling fast but soon they're almost out of sight. Eventually Connor comes back to find me. "You okay, old lady?" he asks.

"Yeah." I laugh. "I'm thinking of switching to ultra-lights."

Sy is waiting for us alone at the lights opposite Zeitgeist. I ride up and tell him, "Everyone's nicer to me than you are."

"What are you talking about?" he asks.

"You don't even want me here."

"I'm sorry. My friends were in a rush, I thought you were right behind me."

"I don't even care." I glare at him. "You can do what you want."

"There's something wrong with you," he says. He sits back on his bike and rides away.

We make up again, but it's not the same between us. When I show up at his workplaces to visit him, he flashes me this big fake smile and talks about how tired he is—"I'm dying," he says—and how he doesn't have the energy to go out that night. When other people come in, he gives them his real smile. Even when we do hang out, for breakfast at the St. Francis or sandwiches at Pal's, I can't get him to talk about anything. He's receding, right across the table from me. On nights that we sleep together, I pull my underwear on afterward, and he doesn't even protest.

One morning, after he's left for work, I can't get back to sleep. I turn on his computer and check my email. Then I scroll through his Internet history, to see if there are naked pictures or movies of girls in there. But there's no porn, just a bunch of Craigslist missed connections ads. *Women for Men, Café du Nord Bluegrass Night,* is one that he looked at. *Women for Men, Make Out Room Saturday,* says another. They're all about him. They're all looking for "the pretty one." I close the laptop and I realize, anything at all can be porn.

Amanda rents a City CarShare car, picks me up, and takes me for a hike in Marin. We climb a grassy hill and sit and look at the ocean and the cars curling their way south on Highway 1, down to Santa Cruz or Los Angeles. All I can think is, I want to get away.

"So big deal, you got drunk and freaked out," Amanda says. "When I first met James I freaked out constantly. Even now I still do, like, once a month."

"And what does he do?"

"He asks me what's really going on. Then he says, 'Shut up, you *know* I love you,' and I feel calm again. I mean, what girls our age haven't had a couple bad relationships that still fuck them up?"

"Girls our age," I repeat.

"Listen," she says on the car ride back. "This guy's young. The fights probably brought stuff up that he's too scared to deal with. You need to give him time to process. He'll come back to you when he's ready."

We round a bend in the road and the city comes into view, silver and small and covered in fog.

"Do you ever think the fog might be divine punishment for all of us here?" I ask. "For being so liberal and gay?"

"Listen to you." She looks over at me. "Have you ever been shut out by a guy before?"

"Only once. When I was sixteen."

"Well, not much has changed since then," she says. "Except for cellphones and caller ID. You can't call all day and hang up as soon as he answers."

"I hadn't thought about that," I say. "Hey—"

"Forget it," she says, before I have time to ask. "You're not borrowing my phone."

We cross the bridge and drive on to my house. "Remember," Amanda says as we hug goodbye. "Give him some space."

So I do. I give him the whole afternoon at work, and then I call. We meet up at Toronado and sit at the bar, drinking beers and eating vegan sausages and sauerkraut from next door. I tell him about Amanda and James. I promise I will try not to lose it again but, if I do, I need him to just be calm.

"Yeah," he says, wiping the ketchup from the corner of his lip. "I can't do that."

I tell myself not to end it, but then I say, "Well, I guess we have to leave it at that."

"Yeah," he says, looking down. "I guess it's that."

I give him the rest of my food and we sit and drink our beers. "Just so you know," I tell him, "even though this is an amicable ending, I'm gonna have major separation anxiety when we leave. I'm probably not gonna want to let you go. And I'll probably try to convince you to take me home."

He laughs like I'm not serious.

We finish our drinks and head outside, and it all goes to script. He kisses me goodbye and I say his name in the quietest voice.

"Yeah?"

"Can I come home with you?" I ask.

"Claire."

"I've never broken up with someone and not slept with them after."

"I don't do that," he says. "The more I wanted to do that, the less likely I would be to actually do it."

He turns to go. "Sy," I say again.

"What?"

"It's just that—" I look down at my shoes and I feel tiny small. "I used to look at your tattoos and think I would still be looking at them when I was old."

"I know," he says, nodding. He puts his hand on my shoulder and squeezes. "My tattoos thought the same thing."

. . .

So it's over. But to me, it's not really. I call him the next day. I tell him that what I'm asking is something really simple, and I'm sure we can work it out.

"I need baby steps," he says.

"What does that mean?"

"It means you stress me out, and I need some time away."

The next day I call him again. I tell him I'm heartbroken and I miss him, and if we can just get back together it'll be okay.

"Stop thinking about it so much," he says. I hear a car horn in the background and I realize he's riding his bike. "You have too much time on your hands."

"So you're not thinking about it?" I ask.

"I'm trying not to. I'm keeping busy." He's slightly out of breath. "I mean, I went to yoga yesterday and I thought about it for the first five minutes. It felt good to, like, meditate on it."

"Can we meet up for a sec?" I ask.

"I'm late for work," he says.

"You're never late for work."

"Exactly. Stop calling so much. Give me a minute to miss you."

When I ring him later that night, he doesn't answer, and he doesn't call me back.

I shut myself in my room and look at his Facebook obsessively, but he hasn't updated it in days. I block him on gchat. Then I unblock him. I do this twice more. It doesn't make a difference; he's never online. I write three heartbreaking heartbreak songs on my keyboard and play them for Lars at our next rehearsal.

"These are terrible," he says, letting go of his guitar and letting it hang around his neck.

"Wait," I say, playing the opening notes to "Let Me Sleep Over and I'll Let You Sleep." "Just listen to this one."

"I'm suspending you from the band," he says.

"What? You can't do that."

He lifts his guitar over his head and kicks open his case. "Come back when you're happy," he says. "This is a pop band. And you're way too miserable to keep up the tempo."

That night, I call Sean. "Hey, who's the tattoo artist who does the text on all your friends?"

"Why, you gonna get one?"

"Thinking about it."

"What's it gonna say?"

For a second I'm embarrassed, but then I tell him. "'He's gone, he's gone, he's gone.' It's Junot Díaz."

"Hello, overreactor," he says. "Yeah, I know who it is. But that line is about the character's dead brother. You can't use it for some guy. How about 'he's young, he's young, he's young'?" he suggests. "Or how about you let me come over?"

"I don't think so."

"Come on. Don't mess with your body in a permanent way. Just do something temporary and self-destructive."

"I don't know."

"Come on," he says. "What would Junot want you to do?"

Half an hour later, he's in my living room. My roommates aren't home so we do it on the couch. I try my hardest not to think about Sy and his bed, but eventually that seems harder than thinking about it, so I just do. Halfway through, I realize I'm going to cry as soon as it's over. When Sean finishes, I start.

"Wow," he says, "do you always cry after you come?" But I didn't come, and that makes me cry harder. I want to curl up fetally, but he's squashing against me, so I stop sobbing long enough to ask him to leave.

"Are you sure?" he asks. I nod.

When he gets to the door, I say, "Please don't write about this."

"Why not?" He lifts his laptop bag onto his shoulder.

"Because maybe I want to."

"You're gonna start writing fiction now?"

"Maybe," I say. "Isn't that what all the miserable people do?"

I'm losing weight and my roommates are worried. They take me to the Knockout for sugary cocktails to fatten me up. On the walk over there, I can't concentrate on what they're saying. I scan the street, looking for him. I look into every restaurant, every store, hoping to see curly hair, a white hoodie, an orange hoodie, a green one. I look at parking meters and street signs, searching for his locked-up bike. Then I realize he might have gotten a new one, as a breakup present to himself, so I look at every single bike on every single street.

At the bar, we order Manhattans and the bartender makes them strong. We grab a table and I scour the room looking for him, but they can be strict about IDs here; he probably couldn't get in if he wanted to. I check out all the guys. Though they dress like they're my type, none of them is as pretty as him, and I can't bring myself to work up an attraction. The only pretty people are the girls. I'm on an extra play at the pinball machine when one of them taps me on the shoulder. "I like your dress," she says. She has pink lipstick on, and dark brown eyes, and her hair is dyed so blond it looks white.

"Thanks," I say.

An hour later she pulls me into the photo booth and shoves quarters into the slot. In the first picture we're laughing. In the second one we have frowns, and fingers above our top lips like mustaches. In the third and fourth ones, we're kissing. She puts her hand inside my bra, then pulls it out. "Oh my God," she says. She peeks out around the curtain and turns back to me. "My boyfriend's out there somewhere."

"Don't worry," I tell her. "If it happens in a photo booth, it doesn't count."

Late that night, alone in my room in desperation, I Google *messy breakup*. An advice website for teen girls comes up. I examine the thing for any signs of hidden Christian fundamentalism but it looks legit. The website tells me, and the brokenhearted teenage girls of the world, to look at what we've done, to apologize and tell the boys we've been tormenting that we forgive them for anything they did, and would like to do whatever it takes to start again. *Wait a few days to call him,* the anonymous writer tells us. *Guy time is different from girl time.*

He meets me at Dolores Park the next day. We know too many people there, so we walk over to Precita. We sit on the grass in the sun and his phone keeps ringing. He looks at the screen but doesn't answer it.

"I fucked up," I tell him. "I came into the relationship with all this vestigial insecurity and fear. Now I know I didn't need to feel those things with you. I should have trusted you more. I should have known you were going into this with good intentions, and had good intentions all along."

The wind is blowing but his hair somehow stays where it is. He has his sunglasses on but I can tell he's not looking at me.

"Well," he says finally. "It must feel good to have a new perspective." I wait for him to say something else, but that's it. All this talk about baby steps and giving him a minute, and he's only used the time to run farther and faster away.

"I'm gonna wait till you're twenty-seven," I say. "And if you're not back in love with me by then, I'll move on and find somebody else. You have eight years."

He clears his throat. "I think you should move on now. That's what I'm doing. I just want something lighthearted and easy and fun. I don't want to work on this. It's not worth it to me."

He's gone, he's gone, he's gone.

And then a little miracle happens. Nick and Rafael go to Burning Man to shoot a horror movie, and say I can house-sit their place for two weeks. I pack a bag and move over to the East Bay, where I can't look for him, and my roommates can't cheer me up, and I can finally wallow in peace. I go off my birth control pills. I stop drinking alcohol and stop drinking coffee. I smoke a cigarette about every ten min-utes, and watch every Kate Winslet movie they have in their collection. I replay the bit in *Sense and Sensibility* where she throws herself onto her bed, miserable over some pretty guy, and I tell myself I'll never end up like that. Then I throw myself onto the bed. I only eat what Nick and Rafael left behind in the fridge: cottage cheese, blackberries, almond butter, and chocolate chips.

On my third day there, I get out my laptop and look at my dissertation. I read through the first few chapters. Then I tear myself out of the house, go to the library on campus, pile books around me, and start to write. The work is the only thing that keeps my mind busy and away from him. I write, and write, and I ignore my spelling mistakes and scrambled footnotes. I write two chapters in ten days, and at the end of it I realize that the one thing the teen website didn't advise the girls is that you also have to forgive your-self.

I call my sister in England, and pray that my ex-boyfriend doesn't answer.

"Yes," Meredith says when I say hello. "Me and Alistair are still together."

"Good," I say.

"Really?"

"I'll give him a huge hug when I see him next, and I'll take you guys out for a posh dinner. I'll be a bridesmaid in your wedding. But can you please hear me out about something?"

"We'll probably elope, just so we don't have to invite you. But go on."

I tell her about Sy, all the details from the beginning, and she listens while I smoke half an ashtray of cigarettes. At the end of it all, she exhales and says, "Well, you messed up, but he's wrong, too, for not wanting to talk it through. You probably don't want to hear this, but I think you have to let it go. You can't change someone who doesn't want to change. Walk away. You'll find someone new eventually, and they'll be more mature and better for you."

"But they won't be as pretty," I whine.

"No," she says. "From the sounds of it, they probably won't."

I move back to my neighborhood. I buy a plant. I take it out of the store and walk it into the sunlight and down the street. Plants like sunlight. I remember that from science class. So far, as a plant owner, I'm doing okay.

Luke and Calvin are outside the Common Room playing hopscotch with beers in their hands. They stop when they see me.

"What is that?" Luke comes over to look.

"It's my new plant."

Calvin thumbs one of the leaves and I tell him to be careful.

"Yeah, I know," says Luke, "but what kind is it?"

"Its name is Umlaut."

"Okay, but, Claire." Luke puts his hands on my shoulders and looks into my eyes. "What varietal of plant is it?"

"Varietal? Is that fancy coffee talk? I have no idea what it is."

"Well, didn't it come with the little pointy tag that tells you the name in English and Latin, and how to care for it?"

"Yeah, it was ugly and poking into the soil, so I threw it out."

"Come on, man," says Calvin, standing on one foot while he polishes off his Pacífico. "Let's get back to the game."

"The guy in the store gave me the pot for free," I tell Luke, holding it up for him to see.

"Yeah, I'll bet," he says. "Umlaut, take good care of Claire, please."

"Don't ruffle my hair," I tell him, shaking free.

I push the library catalog cards and little yellow pencils off the windowsill in my room, and find a good spot for my plant. I pour water into it from a glass, and then I sit in my desk chair and look at it. My roommate Andrew walks past and stops in the doorway.

"What are you doing?"

"I'm looking at my plant."

He comes in and stands behind me and we both look at the plant. It looks happy, if a little lopsided.

"What's it for?" Andrew asks.

"I guess I wanted a roommate who'd shut up once in a while."

"It'll be dead in a week." He ruffles my hair before he leaves the room.

Really, the plant is a present from myself for myself to celebrate my twenty-eighth birthday. Which is next week. It is the way I'm going to prove that I can take care of something. I don't take proper care of myself, or my relationships. I hand my students' papers back to them weeks late, and I forget friends' anniversaries and parties, even though Google calendar reminds me every time. When I was little I had a pet rabbit who didn't get food when it was raining because I didn't want to go out in the cold. It was a London bunny; it went hungry a lot. So this plant is going to be the first thing I take care of. It is my practice dog, and maybe my practice dog will be my practice husband, and maybe my practice husband will be my practice adopted baby from the Near East.

I call up Sy and ask him to come over. He sounds suspicious. It's only been three weeks since we stopped talking. I tell him about the plant and there's slight interest in his voice.

"I just want you to help me identify the varietal. It'll take five minutes."

He comes over and walks inside without hugging me. He enters my room cautiously, like I might have a giant mousetrap in there that will snap onto him and make him stay the night. He opens the blind to get a better look and then tells me that it's a button fern. He touches the soil. "You're giving it too much water."

"Oh no," I say. "I guess I love it too much."

"Just hold off," he says. "You should only water it when it's looking a little dry."

I lean back against my desk. "How've you been?" I ask, trying to sound casual.

"Yeah, really good," he says. "Just tired. I worked both jobs yesterday. I'm dying right now."

"Cool," I say. "I've been good, too."

He looks around my room. The bed is covered in clothes, and bowls with spoons poking out of them, books, pens, scarves, bags, badges, my laptop, my keyboard, a dozen pairs of tights, some necklaces, my tambourine. Somewhere under there are things I've been trying to find for days: my house keys, my mobile phone charger, an Agnès Varda DVD that is way overdue. The floor and the desk and the bookshelves and the closet aren't any neater.

"Look how clean the windowsill is," I say hopefully, but he's staring at the catalog cards spilled across the floor.

This isn't going well. I invited him over to show him the plant, so he'd know that I've changed, and can take responsibility and keep a promise to something. I wanted him to know that I'm not a mess anymore, but he's standing in the middle of it, and I know it's all he can see.

. . .

I catch sight of him a few weeks later, just before he's supposed to leave for the wedding back east. He's riding north
on Valencia Street, and there's a girl behind him on a cute
yellow cruiser, the emo girl from the night at Connor's
house. I'm walking on the same side of the street. He goes
right past without seeing me, and stops at the lights.

"Have you ridden in the city much?" he calls to the girl.
"You have to weave in and out of cars a bit. Don't hesitate.
Just be clear about what you're doing. And make sure you
don't get doored."

"Okay," she says. They turn the corner onto Market
Street and I watch them ride away.

I wish I could say that I feel nothing, but I feel something.
I wish I could say he isn't pretty anymore but of course he is,
though he looks different somehow, smaller and less vivid,
like a postcard reproduction of some painting I once got to
study up close in a museum. By now, I have stopped hoping
that we will get back together, and started hoping that one
day I'll quit wanting him to call. That sometime after that,
I'll run into him again. That maybe then I will be able to
look right at him and see exactly what he is, what he always
was, and what he should already be to me now: just another
kid on a bike.

Head to Toe

Elise and Jenni lost their virginity at twelve and thirteen, respectively. But they were nine months apart in age, so it had happened for both of them at around the same time. In the three years since then, they had both hooked up with a bunch of guys—some from school, some from other schools, a couple of older guys who had already finished school. They had also kissed girls: mostly just for fun, mostly each other, mostly when drunk, mostly to drive some guy at a party insane, sometimes because they were just bored. Both of them had tried MDMA, coke, speed, and mushrooms. Jenni had also taken acid. Elise had once snorted keta, and she liked to smoke weed. But mostly they just drank. Mostly whatever, but beer was fattening and they usually avoided it.

One Saturday night in June, Jenni came over to Elise's

house and they didn't go out. Elise was lying on her bed, on top of the covers, and Jenni came in and lay down next to her, head to toe, and they didn't check their phones to see what their friends were doing, and Elise didn't pull a bottle of anything from under her bed, and Jenni didn't take her cigarettes out of her bag and crack the window. They didn't put any music on, or put on their makeup, or pinch each other's sides, proclaiming that the other one was a fat bitch who wanted to fuck some unattractive member of their class at school. Elise was reading a book about horses, a book she hadn't read since she was a little kid. Jenni lay on her back, cycled her legs in the air a few times like she was at an exercise class, then curled up on her side and fell asleep.

"Lise? Girls?" At around seven, Elise's mum poked her head round the door frame: ready, probably, for the usual fight over curfews or money for taxis or a tube top that was being worn as a dress. "Oh." The two girls were still on the bed, silent, the windows fogged up from the warmth inside and the cold outdoors.

"Shh." Elise lifted her head and pointed at Jenni, who was asleep beside her.

"Oh," her mother whispered. "Okay."

"I don't know." Her voice carried back down the hall from the living room. "They're just kind of—lying there."

The girls were quiet and sluggish when they came out of Elise's room for dinner.

Elise's dad had gotten Japanese takeaway, and the only time either girl spoke was when Jenni accidentally dropped her chopsticks and sent rice flying onto the table and into her glass of Sprite. "Sorry," she said, looking across at Elise, who was cracking up, her mouth half full of food. "What?" Jenni asked, then she cracked up laughing as well.

"That's all right," Elise's dad said, smiling and shaking his head at her mum. The girls went quiet. They leaned over their bowls and lowered their chins so their faces were closer to their food.

"Did you hear about this girl at a uni in America who made a PowerPoint presentation about all the guys she slept with?" Elise's mum asked.

"No," her dad said.

"Yeah. She had everything in there—physical descriptions, photos of the boys. Then, of course, it goes viral, and everyone can read it. I saw it on Sonya's Facebook. She had a link."

"Was this for a class?" Elise's dad asked.

"I don't think so."

"Honestly, I wish one of the young people at my office would make a PowerPoint presentation about anything. They won't do any admin work unless it's fun! Or creative!"

"Maybe they're on to something." Elise's mum stirred her miso soup with the tips of her chopsticks.

Elise and Jenni didn't pay much attention. Both girls' parents were always doing this: latching on to some piece of old news months after the rest of the world had heard about it and already forgotten. It was obvious they pointedly talked about it in front of their kids, but why? To seem cool and casual? To gauge the girls' reaction and find out if they were secretly doing similar stuff? Or maybe just to amuse each other.

"Thanks for the food," Jenni muttered. The two girls stood up, put their bowls in the sink, and went back to Elise's room.

"Check it out." Jenni held up her phone to show Elise the text she'd just gotten: a photo of their friend Bec on a street in the city somewhere, posing with her arm around Adrian Byrne, an ex-football-player for Hawthorn. "That's totally my leather jacket."

"She's gonna stretch it."

"So annoying."

"You wanna sleep over?"

"Okay."

"You want PJs?"

"Yeah."

Elise found two pairs of old flannel pajamas in a drawer. The girls changed, got into bed, and lay like before, head to toe under the covers. Elise turned off the light and they stared up at the glow-in-the-dark stars, which Elise had pasted on the ceiling when she was a kid.

"I've never seen those stars stay so still," Jenni said. They giggled. "Can I have Torco?"

"Why? I have him."

"I want him. Just for a bit. Just till I fall asleep."

"Keep him." Elise flung the stuffed hippo toy at Jenni, who hugged him to her chest. "Don't hump him."

"He loves it."

Elise kicked her shoulder. "He doesn't."

"Oh, Torco."

"Don't!"

"Do hippos have, um, snouts, or—"

"Shut up."

"Ow, that was my head."

"Don't molest him."

"That was Torco's head! Ow. Okay. I'll stop, I'll stop. I'm just gonna hug him. I'm hugging him. Okay."

The girls didn't do much the following week. Jenni made a batch of lemon bars on Sunday night, and Elise went to the gym with her mum on Monday but skipped it on Wednesday. Other than that, they did a bit of homework, watched a bit of TV, messaged each other a bit, but didn't talk on the phone at all. Both girls went to bed around midnight, got up in time for school, and both of them had the glazed, lethargic, agreeable disposition of jet-lagged travelers.

Their parents were worried. "You going out tonight?" Jenni's mum asked her in the kitchen on Friday morning.

"I dunno. Doubt it."

"Did something happen?" she asked. "Are you and Lise fighting?"

"No," Jenni said. "Maybe I'll go over there later."

"I'll drive you," her mum said. And instead of her usual *It's only four stops on the bus,* Jenni shrugged and threw her crusts in the rubbish bin.

"Okay."

That night, Elise's dad went to check on the girls and found them lying side by side, with their heads on Elise's pillow, watching something on her laptop. Each girl had one earbud in one ear; the wire hung across between their faces.

"What are you up to?"

"What?"

"What are you watching?"

"Just a show."

"Which one?"

"It's just this English comedian. He gives celebrities drinks and interviews them."

"Alcoholic drinks?"

"Yeah. They're all over eighteen."

"Is it funny?"

"Yeah."

"Shouldn't you be laughing, then?"

Elise shrugged a shoulder. "I dunno."

At eleven the next morning, Elise's mum opened the bedroom door without knocking. The girls were still in bed.

She picked Torco up off the floor and put him on the bookshelf. "What's happening tonight?" she asked.

"What?" Elise lifted her head. "Nothing."

"No, I know you have nothing planned, but what are the other girls up to? What are Holly and Bec doing?" She reached over the desk and pulled up the blinds. Sunlight beamed through the window. Jenni covered her face with the comforter.

"I dunno," Elise said. "I think Zach's having people over?"

"Good," her mum said. "You're going."

Someone had made a mash-up of Chris Brown's "Deuces" and Rihanna's "Hard" and it was playing loud when they arrived. Zach met them at the door. "Hey." He hugged Elise. "I'm glad you came."

"My parents made us," she said.

He laughed. "Hey, Jen." He hugged Jenni. "How's the puppy?"

"She's good," Jenni said. "She's getting really big."

"You should have brought her!"

"She'd get freaked out by all these people."

Zach looked disappointed when they took off their coats to reveal tank tops, leggings, and Ugg boots. The girls standing around in the living room behind him were way more dressed up.

"You can chuck your stuff upstairs in my room," he said.

"Cool," said Jenni. "Lead the way, Lise."

"Shut up," said Elise.

"That was at my mum's house," Zach said.

The girls waved at some kids in the living room, then climbed the stairs, stopping on the landing to examine a framed photo on the wall of Zach and his brother, on holiday somewhere beachy. Zach was a few years younger in the picture; he had a sunburnt nose, he was holding a snow cone, and there was a ring of blue snow-cone juice around his mouth.

"Don't look at that," Zach called up to them.

"Why not?"

"It's private," he said. "Dump your stuff and come get a drink."

His room was dim and cozy. His curtains were drawn, his floor was clean, his bedside lamp was a globe of the world, lit from the inside. There was a copy of *Persepolis* on his bedside table; they were all reading it for school. Under the pile of jackets and scarves, the bed was made. Someone's phone was ringing inside a pocket or a bag.

"I'm gonna keep my jacket with me," Jenni said, "in case I go outside to smoke."

"Good idea," said Elise.

"Oh. My God!" Holly and Bec screamed when Elise and Jenni came down the stairs. Then Elise hugged Holly, Jenni hugged Bec; Bec hugged Elise, Holly hugged Jenni.

"Where have you Pap smears been?" Bec asked. "We've been messaging you all day."

"Nowhere. Just at home."

"You've missed everything," Holly said. "We have so much to tell you."

"Go get drinks and meet us in the living room."

"We're leaving soon. It's Zoe's sister's twenty-first and she said she can get us in. You should come."

"Yeah, you Pap smears have to come."

There were a few bottles of vodka and bourbon on the kitchen bench, but Jenni and Elise didn't feel like spirits. Jenni opened the fridge and found a half-drunk bottle of Chardonnay.

"Schmance," said Elise. "Get that bowl of jelly snakes and let's go outside."

They went into the laundry and stood aside as some kids from school filed past, smelling like smoke.

"Hi," the girls said. "Hi. Hi. Hi."

"When did you babes get here?" Nico asked.

"Where'd you get that wine?" asked Zach's brother.

"It's cold out there," Sara-Jane said.

"We'll deal."

The backyard was small. There was an empty clothesline in the middle of a patch of lawn, and a cricket bat lying on the ground. The girls sat down in plastic chairs at the edge of the grass. Their breath hung in front of their faces. Jenni uncapped the wine and took a sip. "Party in the USA" came on inside, and a few girls screamed their excitement.

"Should have stayed home," said Elise.

"I know, I'm tired."

"I'm so over it."

They sat, hunched in their jackets, and stared out at the back fence. Jenni smoked a couple of cigarettes, lighting the second one off the first. Elise pushed her teeth down on a jelly snake and yanked it with her hand till its head broke off in her mouth. She could tell without looking that it was a yellow one. They passed the bottle back and forth.

"Did you know," Elise said, "that most foals are born at night?"

"What's a foal?" asked Jenni.

"Seriously? It's a baby horse."

"Am I s'posed to remember that?"

"I dunno. I'll lend you this book I have."

"Okay."

Their phones buzzed. It was Holly and Bec, wanting to know where they were and if they were coming to the next party.

"You go," said Elise. "I'm not feeling it."

"Me neither."

The next time their phones vibrated, neither of them checked. Not long after that, they decided it was time to go home.

On Sunday morning, Elise's mum drove the girls to Highfern, pulled into one of the underground car parks, and stopped in front of the automatic doors. The guy in the car behind her honked, and she waved at him to go around.

"Don't forget, it's winter," she said. "They heat this place like mad but it's still cold outside. So don't buy summer stuff."

"We won't," Elise said.

"Thanks for the lift," said Jenni.

Inside, the shopping center was noisy. The air smelled like roasting nuts, then Lush soap, then Subway bread. The girls passed their usual shops. The mannequins were indeed dressed for warmer weather: onesies over bikinis, leotards under crop tops, stripy T-shirts tucked into shorts held up by suspenders.

"I like that cutout dress," Elise said as they passed Forever New.

"Cute," said Jenni, but they didn't go in.

"Do you wanna maybe see a movie?"

"Yeah, let's go see what's on."

They walked halfway around that floor, past a bunch of shops, and rode the escalator to the next floor up. They walked halfway around that floor, past a bunch of shops, and rode the escalator up again.

"Wait, is this even the right building?"

"Are there toilets on this floor?"

"Can we sit down for a second? I'm thirsty."

Twenty minutes later, they found the cinema. There were lots of new movies out. The girls had hardly seen anything. They decided on *Burlesque*. It was about a girl who moves to the city to fulfill her dream of becoming a performer. After that, they still didn't feel like shopping, so they bought tickets for *Tiny Furniture.* That was about a girl who moves to the city to fulfill her dream of becoming an artist. Then they got popcorn and slushies at the concession stand and went to see *Winter's Bone,* about a girl who goes looking for her dead father. Then, because they weren't hungry for lunch after the snacks, they saw *True Grit,* about a girl who goes looking for the killer of her dead father. Then Elise called her mum and asked her to come get them later than planned because they wanted to see *Somewhere.*

"It's about this girl who visits her dad. She makes him macaroni and cheese, and cheers him up," Elise told her mum in the car later. It was dark outside now. The girls were tired.

"Sounds good," her mum said. "And what else? What did you get?"

"Nothing."

"Oh yeah, I know what that means." Elise's mum reached over and poked her shoulder. "Come on. Show me what you bought."

"We didn't get anything. We just went to the movies."

"That's it? That's all you did?"

"Pretty much."

"Jesus, Lise. How many movies is that?"

"I dunno. Two, three. Four, maybe?"

"What's the point of coming all the way to Highfy to sit on your bum in the dark? You could have watched this stuff on iTunes at home."

"But these movies aren't on iTunes yet."

"You girls," Elise's mum said. But she didn't say anything else. Elise pulled the hood of her jacket over her head and watched the road. Jenni leaned her cheek against the seat and fell asleep. She didn't wake up until they got to her house and her mum came out to say hi.

"How was it?" she asked as Jenni climbed out of the car.

"Hi, girl," Jenni said. She crouched on the ground and patted their dog, Na'vi. "Hi, girl girl girl."

"What did you get?" her mum asked.

"They didn't buy anything." Elise's mum leaned across her daughter and spoke out the passenger window.

"Yeah, heard that one before."

"No, really. They saw movies all day."

"Is that true?" Jenni's mum asked her.

Jenni had her face pushed into Na'vi's neck. "Did you miss me, girl? You didn't miss me, did you?"

"I hate to think how much that cost," Jenni's mum said.

"Don't get me started."

"Thanks for driving them."

"No worries."

"See you soon. School holidays coming up."

"Oh yeah. Can't wait."

Late that night, just after two, Elise was woken by a text from Zach. *You up?*

She squinted at the screen, then shoved her phone under the pillow without answering. Five minutes later it buzzed again.

See ya

Elise sighed and rolled onto her back. The sticker stars above her were all faded; it had been hours since she turned off the light.

Im slee—she was writing back when the phone rang in her hand.

"I got sick of typing," Zach said, "so I just called."

"Okay. What's up?"

"Not much. I can't sleep."

"How come?"

"I dunno. Darren crashed here last night, and we played Wii all day. Now every time I shut my eyes, it's like I'm playing that FIFA game in my head."

"Oh yeah, I hate that."

"Have you actually had that before?"

"Yeah, it used to happen all the time when I played Cactus Ninja."

"Oh, good. I thought I was going crazy. I told my mum and she started looking it up on WebMD." He laughed. "Are you in bed?"

"Yep."

"Me too."

"Cool."

"Where'd you guys go last night?"

"Just home."

"You left so early, you missed everything."

"Yeah, I saw Sara-Jane's pics. Looked like you guys were getting pretty coze." Zach didn't respond to that. Elise heard a rustling sound, like he was turning over in bed.

"We're having another party in the holidays. My dad's going away. You have to come."

"Okay."

"You're not going to, are you?"

"I dunno. I'd have to check."

"With who? Jenni? I'll ask her, too."

"Okay. Don't call her now, though. She's probably sleeping."

"What's the deal with you guys? Holly told me you haven't been answering her messages."

"That's bullshit."

"You should be careful, Lise. You don't want to lose all your friends."

"Whatever. It's not like I'm gonna lose Jenni."

"Yeah, you'll always have Jenni. And Na'vi."

"Exactly."

"And I'll still be your friend, even when you're acting like a total freak."

"Nah, I'm good with Jenni and Na'vi."

"Wow. Such a smart-ass."

"You love it."

"Yeah," he said. "I guess I do. It's so annoying. Good night, Lise."

"G-N."

After school on Tuesday, Elise's mum took her to see Dr. Alonso, the pediatrician she'd been going to since she was born. He was still her doctor but he hadn't looked directly at her since she'd gone through puberty.

"I don't mean to overreact," Elise's mum said, sitting in the chair beside her in his office, "but she's been acting a bit different. We were worried it's chronic fatigue or something."

"Elise?" Dr. Alonso stared at something just to the left of Elise's elbow. "Have you been feeling differently?"

Elise shrugged and leaned her head over to the left, to try to get within the doctor's line of vision. "I dunno," she said. "I just haven't felt like going out as much."

"Any changes in diet or lifestyle? Are you a vegetarian or anything like that?"

"No."

"Everything's okay at school? No problems keeping up with classes? Any issues socially?"

Elise tilted farther to the left. The doctor shifted his gaze accordingly. "No, it's fine."

And just when she thought the guy might be legitimately cross-eyed, he turned and looked directly at her mum. "And everything's okay at home? No major changes?"

"No. I mean, we're busy as usual, but that's nothing new." She looked over at Elise. "Lise is the only thing that's changed recently."

The doctor said he would do some blood tests. He also suggested starting Elise on a low dose of an antidepressant, to even out any chemical or hormonal issues she might be having.

"I dunno," Elise's mum said. "We're not really big believers in that sort of thing."

"Yeah, I haven't heard good things," Elise said. "But do you have any Xanax? Or isn't there something for ADHD that curbs your appetite?"

"Okay," her mum said, standing up. "We'll all discuss it at home and come back."

"I don't wanna go back," Elise said afterward. They were at a café across the street from the clinic. Elise's mum was drinking a mochaccino. Elise had a chai latte with honey. "He's gross."

"He's not gross," her mum said. "He's a hundred years old. He has kids older than you are. Didn't you see the photos? You girls—you think everyone who looks at you wants to sleep with you, and everyone who doesn't look at you wants to sleep with you. Honestly."

Elise didn't respond. She dragged her chair halfway around the table and leaned her head onto her mum's shoulder. "What are you doing?" her mum said. "You're weirding me out."

Her mum smelled exactly the same as she had when Elise was little: a mixture of apricot moisturizer and the mouth rinse they used at the orthodontist's office where she worked as an assistant.

"Can I have the foam off your coffee?" Elise asked.

"No," her mum said. "I want it. Why don't you get your own?"

"I don't want my own."

Her mum tilted her cheek over until it rested on the top of Elise's head. "Elise Ashleigh Jensen," she said. "What are we gonna do with you?"

"What I really want?"

"Yeah?" Her mum sat up. She put her coffee cup on its saucer. "What?"

"Don't laugh."

"I won't."

"You already are!"

"I can't help it. As soon as someone says not to. But go on, tell me."

"I kind of wanna go back to horse camp."

"Seriously?" her mum said. "The one in Daylesford?"

"Just for a few days."

"Wow. I don't even know if that place still exists."

The girls insisted on sitting in the backseat together, even though Jenni's mum complained that she felt like a taxi driver.

"It's not like we'll pay you at the end or anything," Jenni said.

"How are they playing Prince on the golden oldies station?" her mum asked. "You girls know who Prince is, right?"

It was Saturday morning and most of the traffic was going in the other direction: people coming into the city to shop or go to the football match. They took the Monash

Freeway to the West Gate Bridge. The girls looked back at the skyline as they left it behind. Half an hour later they were passing housing developments they'd seen advertised on TV. IF YOU LIVED HERE, YOU'D BE TEEING OFF ALREADY, the signs said. Half an hour after that, they were driving through countryside, past green fields where cows stood around chewing grass and staring out at the road, as though *they* were the scenery.

Elise and Jenni had each packed leggings, boots, flannel shirts, woolen scarves, gloves, and parkas. Elise had half a gram of weed and some rolling papers. Jenni had a six-pack of Vodka Cruisers rolled inside her sleeping bag. Both girls remembered what they used to bring to horse camp: a Ouija board, stuffed animals, a ton of junk food, and a torch with extra batteries, in case they wanted to tell ghost stories, or in case they got scared walking from the dining hall to the cabin at night.

They remembered all that but somehow it didn't occur to them that the other girls at horse camp were going to be the age they had been back then—until they pulled into the campground and saw a group of girls kicking a ball to one another across a soggy field. They looked really young: ten, eleven, twelve.

"Great," Jenni said.

"Can we get a cabin to ourselves?" Elise asked Margot, the older woman who ran the camp, when they went into the office to register and pay.

"Most of the cabins are closed up this time of year," Margot said. "But I'll put you in the emptiest one, just a few other girls in there. They're all friends, from Castlemaine. They'll probably just keep to themselves."

Jenni's mum tore a check along the perforation and slid it across the desk. The girls walked her back to the car. "Have fun," she said as they pulled their bags out of the trunk. She was about to climb into the driver's seat when Jenni came over and gave her a hug.

"Whoa." Jenni's mum lowered her hands onto her daughter's back slowly, as though the girl might detonate at any moment. "I don't think you've hugged me since the day I said you could get a dog."

"That's not true," Jenni said, letting go.

Her mum waved out the window as she circled out of the car park. "Text me if you need anything," she called. Then she pulled her hand back into the car.

The other girls were already in the cabin when Elise and Jenni got there. They were sitting on three different top bunks, listening to music, and passing around a big bag of corn chips. Elise and Jenni had heard them talking when they opened the door, but they'd stopped as soon as the older girls came in. The one closest to them was playing Candy Conspiracy.

"Do you have phone reception out here?" Elise asked her. "I can't get any."

"I can sometimes get 3G. But this isn't a phone, it's an

iPod touch." The girl smiled. She was pretty, in a freckly way, but she was going to need braces.

"I'm Elise, this is Jenni."

"Naomi," said the girl.

"Dylan."

"Indira."

Elise and Jenni took the bunk bed at the back, near the bathroom. "Can I have the bottom?" Jenni asked.

"I wanted it," Elise said.

They scissors, paper, rocked it. Jenni was paper and Elise was paper. They played again. This time Jenni was paper and Elise was scissors. Jenni threw her bag up the top and sat down on Elise's bed to change out of her flats and into her riding boots.

" *'Cause you're a glow stick, girl,*" a Disneyish pop song played through the tiny speakers on Indira's bed. *"Gonna light up this whole world."*

"What grade are you guys in?" Jenni asked.

"We're in fifth grade and Dylan's in sixth," Naomi said.

"How do you know each other?" Elise was in the bathroom, in front of the mirror, reapplying her eyeliner.

"Me and Dylan are family friends, and me and Indira are in the same class at school."

"Cool."

"What year are you in?" asked Indira.

"Tenth grade." Jenni stood up and stomped her feet to get them used to the boots. Elise zipped up her makeup bag.

"Ready?"

"Yep. Let's go."

They left the cabin without saying goodbye to the younger girls.

The horses were standing around in a paddock across from the dining hall. There were about ten of them, all with their heads down, grazing. The girls plucked bunches of long grass out of the ground on their side of the fence and held them over toward the animals. The horses looked up. A few stood staring at them. Some went back to huffing at the ground. "Come here." Both girls shook the grass in their hands. Jenni made kissy sounds with her mouth. Eventually, a few horses wandered over.

The one that came to Elise was acorn brown. "Hey," she said, "are you hungry?" The horse ate the grass straight off her palm. She used her other hand to rub the white patch on its forehead.

Two horses approached Jenni; one was dusty brown with a black mane, the other one was white. At first she liked the brown one better but it tugged the grass out of her hand with its mouth, swooshed its tail, and walked away. The white one stuck around, letting her thump her hand against its side. It had long eyelashes, and its little teeth were all squashed together in its mouth, reminding her of a dolphin's.

"That one's Snowflake," said Margot, squelching over in her gum boots. "You can ride her if you want."

"What's this one called?" Elise asked.

"Glen."

Margot told them their riding group would be the two of them and the other girls in their cabin. Their ride leader would be her daughter Bridget, who lived in Melbourne and had come up for a few days to help out.

The girls found Bridget in the stables, brushing down a black horse that was rolling its eyes with impatience but standing still. Bridget didn't notice the girls until they said hi.

"Oh, hey." She smiled at them. She was petite and wore pigtails. She was probably in her mid-twenties. "Do you girls need to pick your horses?"

"No, we did already. But we're just wondering. We're in your riding group—"

"Great!" said Bridget.

"We're just a bit worried. Because we're pretty experienced. I mean, we've been here before."

"We just want to trot and canter and that, and we're worried that the girls in our group—they're younger and they might be more at the beginning stage."

"Okay. Margot told me you're all intermediate, but I'll check with her again. The ride today is just gonna be, like, a stroll, so everyone can get used to their horses. Tomorrow we'll get into the more intensive stuff." She laid a saddle mat onto the horse's back. The horse stamped a foot. "Shh," she said.

"Okay, sweet," Elise said. "We just wanted to make sure, because—"

"Yep," said Bridget, in a tone that could have been bitchy and could have been businesslike. "Got it."

But once Snowflake and Glen were saddled up and the first ride had started, the girls were just happy to be sitting on their horses. They didn't care how fast they were going, or even where. Bridget had given them all quick instructions in the beginning—reminded them to hold both reins loose in one hand, tug on the left rein to go left, the right one for right, and to pull back on both and say "whoa!" if they wanted their horses to stop. All five girls had paid attention, had sat and listened with straight backs and the balls of their feet pushed out into the stirrups. But none of it was necessary. The horses knew the terrain well, and they walked along in a loose group without any guidance.

Bridget led them through a few open paddocks and up an incline, into some bushland. The path was narrow here, and the horses formed a single line. It was a bit of a climb, and Bridget told the girls to lean forward, to make it easier on the animals.

It was quiet, except for the sound of the horses' feet on the wet leaves underfoot, the breathy sounds they made with their mouths, and the occasional thump of a kangaroo bounding out of the brush, away from them. The gum trees made the air smell like Vicks VapoRub. Every now and then, they passed a pile of horse droppings left behind from a previous ride. The younger girls would point it out to one another and laugh. Jenni leaned forward and rubbed Snowflake's neck. "Hi, girl," she said. Elise stroked Glen's mane. It was sticky and tangled and she couldn't get her fingers through. He tossed his head until she stopped trying.

There were about fifteen other girls in the dining room at dinner, all of them younger than Elise and Jenni. The two girls took a table by themselves. They had just started eating their lasagna when another tray was plopped down beside them.

"Do you mind if I sit here?" asked Bridget. "Margot and the other group leaders eat in the kitchen, but all they talk about is work. And when you grow up at horse camp and you come back to work at horse camp, it's the last thing you want to talk about after hours." Bridget smiled and rolled her eyes.

She wasn't eating lasagna; she had made herself a Greek salad in the kitchen. As she chewed, she asked the girls questions about themselves. Where they lived in Melbourne (Murrumbeena), whether or not they had siblings (Elise didn't; Jenni had a half brother from her dad's first marriage but he lived in Perth and she only ever saw him at Christmas), what they did for fun ("Um, you know, just go to Highfern and hang out with our friends and stuff"), whether or not they had boyfriends ("No"), and what they wanted to do after they finished school (neither of them really knew. Jenni thought maybe marketing. Elise liked taking photos but obviously that wasn't really a job you could count on getting, so she wasn't sure).

Bridget was very encouraging about all of this: the marketing, the photography, the not knowing. She herself was doing a master's in community development at Deakin Uni.

The girls hadn't made up their minds about her. She had changed into a stripy Saint James top and tight jeans, which they liked. But the community thing sounded so boring, neither of them even bothered asking what it was.

"Do you have a boyfriend?" Jenni asked her.

"I have a girlfriend, actually," she said.

Jenni and Elise shot each other a quick look. "Like a girlfriend-girlfriend?" Jenni asked.

"Yeah," she said. "Like a partner."

Her partner's name was Jade. She was two years older than Bridget, and they lived together. Elise asked what they did for fun, and Bridget said lately they'd been staying home a lot because they were saving up for a trip to Cambodia. "We've been watching heaps of TV shows. Jade's obsessed with *The Wire* at the moment. And sometimes we go out with friends."

"Like, to a club or to bars?" Jenni asked.

"Just to our local pub," Bridget said. "Nothing crazy."

"Are your friends guys or girls?" Elise asked.

"Women mostly. Other gay couples. Oh, and one straight guy. Felix." Bridget shook her head. "Poor Felix."

The girls were starting to lose interest in the whole thing when Bridget smiled at them and said, "It's so cool that you guys are such good friends. Female friends are really important, I reckon. How long have you two known each other?"

"Do you mind if we take our brownies to the cabin?" Elise asked.

"We're really tired," Jenni explained.

"Of course," Bridget said. "Just make sure you put the lid on the bin after you throw the wrappers away. The possums like to scrounge around at night."

Before bedtime, when the younger girls were brushing their teeth, Elise and Jenni took their backpacks and left the cabin. They walked out to the car park and sat on a droopy chain fence, facing the road. No cars came past. Elise rolled a joint and lit it. Jenni opened a Cruiser and took a sip.

"Dude," Jenni said, "I can't believe the dress Sara-Jane was wearing at Zach's."

"As soon as I saw it I knew you were thinking that."

"I can't take those clear plastic straps. Everyone can see them. They're plastic, not invisible."

"Zach obviously didn't mind," said Elise.

"Zach was just settling for his second choice."

"Aw, don't be hard on yourself. Maybe you were his second choice."

"Pap smear." Jenni reached over and pinched Elise's arm.

"Ow." Elise pinched her back.

"I was trying to make you feel better."

Elise took a pull on her joint, and exhaled slowly. "Oh yeah, you were." She leaned over and rubbed Jenni's arm. "Sorry, bitch."

Jenni laughed. She leaned her head back and looked at the sky. "Check it out. The Southern Cross."

Elise leaned back, too. "That's the saucepan." She pointed at the sky. "That's the Southern Cross there."

"No it's not. The bottom one's moving. That's not a star, it's a plane."

"Oh yeah." They watched it for a minute. "That seems too slow for a plane. It's probably a satellite." They stared at the moving dot until they lost track of it among the stars.

"Do you believe in aliens?" Elise asked.

"No. I mean, I think there's life on other planets. But I picture them more just like us."

"You mean like maybe there are two girls out there right now, up on some other planet, at horse camp?"

"Yeah! They're probably staring at earth, getting wasted, and talking about whether or not there are girls down here, getting wasted at horse camp."

"Bitching about the alien version of Sara-Jane."

"Which probably looks exactly like the real Sara-Jane." Jenni finished off her drink and burped. They laughed.

"Hey, how many horses do you think there are altogether?"

"I don't know, fifty?"

"No, not here. In the world. How many horses do you think there are on the entire earth?"

"Hmm. Maybe a million?"

"Wow, yeah, you're probably right. It's probably a million horses."

The girls were buzzed and giggly on the walk back. They passed a few other cabins. The lights were out in all of them. The only way to tell which ones were inhabited was by the riding boots strewn about on the porch.

In their cabin, the main lights were off but the bathroom light had been left on. The younger girls were in bed. "Shit." Jenni walked straight into a bag and almost fell over. "I can't see shit."

Elise laughed. "Hey, girls—"

"Shh," Jenni said.

"Mmm." Dylan turned over in her sleep.

"Girls, cover your eyes." Elise flicked the switch and the overhead fluorescents came on. Naomi and Indira lifted their heads and squinted down from their bunks.

"Sorry," Jenni whispered. "It'll just be for a sec."

They changed into their pajamas with their backs to the younger girls. The bathroom counter was splashed wet and littered with hair elastics and Silly Bandz.

"Yuck," said Elise.

Someone had left a tube of toothpaste open and it had oozed onto the bar of soap.

"Gross," Jenni whispered. "It's on my elbow."

They brushed their teeth, turned off the lights, and

climbed into their beds. One of the younger girls was breathing heavily. Jenni leaned over the edge of the bunk and looked down at Elise. Elise could see the outline of her head and her hair waterfalling down. "Hey," Jenni whispered, "can I have Torco?"

"I didn't bring him."

"Boo." Jenni lifted her head up.

A minute later she was leaning over again. "How did you get the bottom bunk, again?"

Elise held up her hand in the shape of a pair of scissors. "Oh yeah," Jenni whispered. "Good night, Leesy."

"G-N."

After breakfast the next morning, the five girls sat in a semicircle on their horses and listened to Bridget talk about trotting. They practiced around home paddock, digging their heels into the horses' sides until they went faster, and sitting up and down in accordance with the animals' movement. Then it was out onto a trail, alternating between walking and trotting. It was a cold morning but the sun was up and bright on their faces. Every time her horse started to trot, Elise laughed.

"What's so funny?" Bridget asked her.

"Nothing. I dunno. I just haven't been horse riding in yonks."

. . .

At lunchtime, the girls sat with their cabin mates and talked about their horses.

"I think Rocket and Snowflake like each other," Jenni said.

"Yeah!" said Indira. "They're always trying to walk together."

"None of the other horses like Glen," Elise said.

"He's just slow," said Naomi.

"He's also the fattest," said Dylan. All the girls laughed.

"He's not that fat!" Elise said.

But when they came out of the dining room, Glen was the only horse leaning over the feed trough. When he lifted his head, he was still chewing and he had bits of hay stuck to his face. The girls cracked up laughing again.

In the afternoon, Bridget led the group out onto the road. They rode on the left shoulder, and the couple of cars that came up behind them gave them a wide berth. Farther along, a logging truck passed by going in the other direction, its tray weighed down by thick tree trunks. The driver honked his horn and waved down at them. The five girls waved back but Bridget didn't.

Eventually, she led them across a field and into bushland. Most of the trees here had blackened trunks or were just pointy stumps sticking out of the ground. "This all got burned on Black Saturday," Bridget said.

Elise and Jenni remembered that weekend well. It had

been unbearably hot in the city. They had both gone over to Bec's house and shut themselves in her bedroom in front of the fan, leaving every now and then to go to the kitchen and take bottles of hard cider out of the fridge, in plain view of Bec's parents and some of their friends, who were crowded around the TV in shock and didn't notice.

"Were the horses okay, on Black Saturday?" Elise asked.

"Yeah," Bridget said, "luckily the fire didn't jump the road. But it was hot and smoky. I'm sure they got spooked. We had to leave them and evacuate into town."

"Oh no," said Jenni.

"Poor horses," said Elise.

When the path widened up, Bridget asked the girls if they wanted to trot. They all did. They knocked their heels into the horses' sides, and the animals took off running. "Okay," she called over her shoulder, "if you girls are ready, this is a good spot for cantering. Just hang on to your reins, keep your backs nice and straight, and stay with the horses' rhythm."

Bridget's horse took off, and the others followed. Indira came up beside Jenni and their horses ran together. "Aww," Jenni said, "they're totally in horse love."

Bridget glanced back. "Those two are brother and sister," she called out.

"Really?" Jenni and Indira grinned at each other. "That is so cute!"

. . .

Bridget cut the ride short because she said she could smell a storm coming. The girls left their horses in front of the stables and walked back to the cabin.

"What does that even mean?" Jenni asked Elise. "She thinks she's, like, Pocahontas." But there *was* something in the air. A damp woody smell that made it seem like the ground and trees were getting ready for rain.

When the five cabin mates were walking to dinner, they saw a flash of lightning on the horizon. "If you count the seconds between the lightning and the thunder, it tells you how far away the lightning is," Dylan said.

"How does that work?" asked Elise. "Like six seconds equals six kilometers?"

"Um, I don't really know." Dylan shrugged.

There was another flash of light and the girls counted aloud together. "One two three four five six seven . . ." They stopped at twenty-five because the thunder never came.

Heavy drops of rain started to fall as they were eating dinner. They were scraping their leftover burgers and thick-cut fries into the bin when hail started hitting the roof.

"Did you hear that?" Elise asked.

"What?"

"I think I heard a neigh. The horses are probably scared."

"Oh no. We should go check on them."

"Definitely."

They told the younger girls they'd see them back at the cabin. Then they stuffed the pockets of their parkas with sugar cubes from the bowl next to the tea bags and water urn, because Elise had read in her book that horses like sugar as a treat. They waited at the door till the hail subsided, then they pulled their hoods over their heads and made a run for it, squinting through the rain.

The big wooden door was unlocked, and the girls yanked it open and closed it behind them. It was dim inside. There was only one light burning, at the other end of the stable. The roof was made of tin and the rain was tapping against it. A few horses were looking out over the doors of their stalls. They had their ears pricked up and were eyeing the girls.

"It's so mean," said Elise, pushing the hood off her head. "They just leave them on their own all night."

"I know," said Jenni. "I wish we could sleep in here with them."

The girls walked down the central aisle, patting the horses, who jerked their heads away from their wet hands. "It's okay," they said. "It's just a little storm. Don't be freaked out." They saw Indira's horse, Rocket, Dylan's horse, Honey, and Bridget's horse, Ovaltine.

Glen was standing at the back of his stall when Elise found him. His eyes were half closed, and one of his back hooves was balanced up on tiptoe. He seemed to be dozing, but he woke when she said his name, and immediately started at the sound of the rain. "It's okay," Elise said, "come here." She took a sugar cube from her pocket and held it

210 HOT little HANDS

out. He approached. "Good boy." He ground the sugar between his teeth and swallowed. She offered him another one. His tongue tickled on the palm of her hand.

Snowflake had her head craned over her door, and she nuzzled into Jenni's face and hair when she approached. There were still some oats in her food bucket, but she gobbled up the sugar as fast as Jenni could feed it to her, until all Jenni had left in her pocket were a couple of sachets of Splenda. She tore one open.

"You can't give her that," Elise said.

"Why not? It's just as sweet."

"It's all chemicals. It'll, like, make her stomach explode."

"No, it won't."

"Seriously, it will."

Jenni dropped the sachet back into her pocket and blew the powder off her fingers. "I'm sorry, girl," she said. "Mean Elise won't let me."

When the rain eased off, the girls kissed their horses on the forehead and whispered their good nights. They were on their way out when Elise glanced into one of the stalls. "Whoa," she whispered, "check out this pony."

Jenni came over. On the floor of the stall, in a pile of sawdust, a light brown pony was lying on its side in the dark. It was moving its back legs and making little nuzzling noises.

"What's wrong with it?" Jenni whispered.

"Nothing. It's sleeping."

"Oh, yeah."

"I think it's dreaming."

"Whoa, you're right."

"I think it's dreaming about running."

They watched the animal rotating its tiny legs. It was panting. They wondered if it was dreaming about running along the trails they rode along all day. Or maybe it hadn't even been on those paths yet; maybe it was dreaming about being in home paddock, running around its mother's legs. Or maybe it was running in some imaginary made-up dream place that it had never been, that didn't even exist; that it wouldn't remember in the morning, but wouldn't quite be able to forget.

"Let's go," Jenni whispered. Elise stayed where she was, watching the pony move through its dream. "Lise, let's go."

"Yep, coming," said Elise. She turned toward the door and they left.

The younger girls were still awake when they got back to the cabin. Naomi and Indira were sitting up on their top bunks. Dylan was perched on the edge of Elise's bed. Elise was about to tell her to get off when she realized the girl was crying. The other two girls looked upset, too; Indira's eyes were red, and Naomi had a wad of balled-up tissues in her hand.

"What's wrong?" Elise asked.

The girls didn't answer.

"What happened?" Jenni asked.

"Nothing." Naomi started to cry.

"Whoa. What's going on?"

"We were playing a game," said Indira. "It was fine and then it turned into a fight."

"What game?" Jenni asked. The younger girls didn't say anything. "What game was it?"

"It's just a game," Indira said. "It was Dylan's idea. You pick someone's name out and write something about her. You have to be totally honest. Then you get your note and read it to yourself, so you know what the others think about you, but you don't know who."

"Secret Swaps," Elise said.

"What do you mean you don't know who?" asked Jenni. "There are three of you."

"You're s'posed to change your handwriting. Like, write with your left hand or something."

"This was a bad idea, girls." Elise sat down next to Dylan. "Secret Swaps is a game for a big group of girls to play."

"It was Dylan's idea," Naomi said.

"And I'm glad we played," Dylan said loudly. She was crying hard now. "Because now I know what you think of me, and you're not a good friend."

"Neither are you, Dylan," Indira said.

"You can't talk," Naomi shouted.

Jenni went into the middle of the room, held a hand up, and yelled, "Girls!" Something about that worked. They all stopped talking and looked at her. "That was a dumb game to play. You should just apologize to each other and go to bed."

"No way," said Naomi. "I'm not apologizing."

"Someone should apologize to me," said Dylan.

"What did your note say?" Jenni asked.

"Don't tell her," Indira said.

"Shut up, Indira," Naomi said. "This is none of your business."

"It's all of our business, Naomi," Dylan said.

"Girls," Jenni said again. "I don't want to get involved. But you're gonna ruin your whole horse camp if you keep fighting, and you're gonna be tired tomorrow. And you're annoying me and Elise." Elise laughed. "Why don't you just tell us what the comments are? They're probably not as bad as you think."

"I wanna go home!" Dylan pulled her feet up onto Elise's bed, put her arms on her knees, and leaned her head on her arms. "I just wanna go!"

Elise looked up at Jenni. "What should we do?"

"Let's go get Bridget."

"She's just gonna give them some touchy-feely girl empowerment talk."

"Maybe that's what they need."

"I think we should find Margot."

"Margot's gonna call her parents."

"So what? They can come and pick her up. Castlemaine's not that far."

"Yeah, but think about when we used to have fights at slumber parties. Was it ever really better when your mum showed up at midnight and took you home?"

Elise shrugged. "Maybe."

"Dylan?" said Naomi. "Don't go home."

Dylan lifted her head. Her face was wet with snot and tears.

"Let's just work it out so you can stay. Here." Naomi held out her slip of paper to Jenni. "I don't care if you read mine."

"Okay." Jenni went over and took it. "Dylan," she said, "do you want us to go get Margot?"

Dylan shook her head. "No."

"Are you sure?"

Dylan nodded.

"All right. I'm gonna read this out loud. But nobody has to say whether or not they wrote it. Let's just keep it 'anonymous.'" Jenni curled her fingers around the word. She unfolded the piece of paper. It said: *You think you're a good dancer and you're not that good of a dancer.*

"I know that was you, Indira," Naomi spat out. "You think you're so much better than me."

"No, I don't," Indira said. "And why do you think it was me?"

"Naomi," Jenni said, "Naomi! Are you taking dance classes?"

"Yes," Naomi said. "I take jazz-funk and hip-hop."

"Okay, good," Jenni said. "She's taking dance classes. So whoever wrote this, just know that she's working on her dancing and she'll probably get better."

"I'm not saying it was me that wrote the note," Indira

said, "but she always acts like she's the best. Whenever we make up dances together, she bosses us around and won't listen to our ideas."

"Okay, first of all," Jenni said, "you girls aren't gonna be making up dances together for much longer. So in, like, a year this won't be an issue. Second, Naomi, if you act like you're the best at something, you're not gonna have any friends. So even if you think you're the best, just keep it to yourself and don't act like it."

"Okay," Naomi said.

Jenni handed the note back to her. "Good," she said.

Naomi seemed pleased, too.

Indira offered up her note next. Jenni read it aloud. *"Your house smells bad, like curry."*

"It's such crap," Indira said. "We have curry, like, once a month. My parents don't even make it. Only my grand-mother does."

"Have you girls ever had curry?" Jenni asked Naomi and Dylan. Neither of them had.

"Oh my God, it's so good," said Elise.

"When you get back to Castlemaine, go over to Indira's place and have curry."

"They're never invited to my house again," Indira said.

"Okay, well, next time you get takeaway," Jenni said, "ask your parents to get Indian."

"Chicken masala," Elise said.

"And a mango lassi," Jenni said.

"You should try saag paneer," said Indira.

"Is that the one with cheese?" Jenni asked. "Isn't it kind of mushy?"

"No, it's really good."

"Okay, get saag paneer," Jenni said, "and a mango lassi. Naomi, Dylan, are you gonna try it?"

Both girls said they would.

"Promise?"

Both girls promised.

Jenni handed Indira's note back to her. Then everyone looked over at Dylan.

"Do you want us to read yours?" Jenni asked her.

"Not really," Dylan said. Then she handed her note to Jenni and put her head back down on her arms.

"You have too much pubes," Jenni read, *"it seriously gross."*

"I wanna go home!" Dylan started crying again.

Elise stood up. "Here, Dylan," she said, "come with me."

"Can you go get Margot?"

"I will," Elise said. "But first, just come with me for a sec."

"No," Dylan said. "Where to?"

"Just to the bathroom. To wash your face." She held out her hand until Dylan took it. The two of them went into the bathroom and shut the door.

"This is a really fucked-up game," Jenni said to the other two. "And I'm not even sorry I said the word *fuck* in front of you."

"We know the word *fuck*," Naomi said.

After a couple of minutes, Elise came out of the bathroom

and closed the door behind her. "So, she showed me," she told Jenni in a quiet voice, "and she doesn't have that much. I told her that in summer, if she wants to swim and that, she could just shave the bikini line. But she really has nothing to worry about." She turned to the other two. "Just so you know, you're all gonna have hair like that, and way more."

The other two were quiet. Behind the door Dylan was running the tap. Then they heard her blowing her nose. When she came out of the bathroom, Indira said, "I'm sorry, Dylan."

Elise and Jenni assumed that meant she'd written the note, but then Naomi said, "I'm sorry too, Dyl."

"That's okay," Dylan said. "I just wanna go to sleep now."

"Me too," said Indira.

"Me too."

After the younger girls had turned the lights off, Jenni and Elise shut themselves in the bathroom and drank the rest of the Cruisers.

"Dude," whispered Jenni. "I'm so glad I'm not eleven anymore."

"I know," Elise whispered back. "It's the worst. Everything's so confusing and, like, no one has their shit together."

"Did you really look at her vag?"

"Yeah. She was freaking out that something's wrong with her. She just flashed it really fast."

"And it was fine?"

"Yeah, completely fine. I *wish* I had that amount of hair."

"Perv."

"How does that make me a perv!"

"I dunno. But it definitely does."

"I hope they're asleep when we go out."

"I know, I can't take much more of their dramz."

It was quiet when they got into bed, and quiet for a few minutes after that. But then from across the room, in the dark, Indira said, "Hey? Jenni?"

"Yeah?"

"Do both of you shave your bikini lines?"

"Um. I shave, Elise waxes."

"Waxing sounds painful," Indira said.

"It is," Jenni said.

"You get used to it," said Elise.

It was quiet for another minute. Then Naomi asked, "Have you ever done a striptease?"

"I mean, yeah, kind of," Jenni said, "but only for a boyfriend or something."

"Did you ever do pole dancing?" Dylan wanted to know.

The older girls laughed. "No," Elise said. "No pole dancing."

"What about, like, having sex on the Internet?" Naomi asked.

"Well," said Elise, "I guess—all you need to know about that is: If you ever do it, make sure the guy isn't taking screenshots. Like, make sure you can see his hands the whole time."

"Okay," Naomi said.

"Also," Jenni said, "if you take naked pics and send them to someone, make sure your face isn't showing. No matter what. Even if he asks for it."

"Yuck," Indira said.

"As if you would ever do that," Naomi said.

But Dylan asked, "Why?"

"Because then it's just out there. And it can come back to haunt you if you ever have, like, a job interview or something."

"Did that happen in your job interview?" asked Dylan.

"I've never had a job interview," Jenni said. "I'm sixteen."

"Oh yeah." The younger girls started laughing.

"Crazy girls."

They were all tired the next morning. They were quiet at breakfast and happy to just walk with the occasional trot in their final ride through the bush.

Jenni's mum was the first parent to arrive. She was standing by home paddock when they all rode up. She pushed her sunglasses up off her face and waved.

"Want me to take a photo?" she called out.

"Yeah."

"Where are your phones?"

"In the cabin."

"Okay, I'll take one with mine."

Jenni walked Snowflake over to Elise and Glen, and the girls smiled for the photo. "Good one," Jenni's mum said, checking to see how it came out.

"Cool," said Jenni. "We'll meet you at the car."

"Are you all packed up? Do you need help carrying your stuff?"

"No. We're fine. Can you just wait in the car?"

The hardest part of leaving was saying goodbye to their horses. "Bye, mister," Elise said, leaning her nose on Glen's face. "Don't forget to miss me."

"I'm sure he won't," said Bridget.

"Bye, girl," Jenni whispered to Snowflake. "Bye, girl girl girl."

"Good luck with everything," Bridget said. "It was great to meet you both. Maybe we'll see you in the summer holidays? Book early for that. There'll be more girls here then."

The younger girls also wanted to know if they'd be coming back. "Maybe," Elise said. She and Jenni were standing on the porch of their cabin with their backpacks on their backs and their sleeping bags in their arms. "We'd have to ask our parents."

"Can you not tell anyone?" Dylan said. "About Secret Swaps."

"Who would we tell?" Elise asked.

"We definitely won't," Jenni said. "Look us up on Facebook. When you're allowed on Facebook." She gave each of the younger girls a high five.

Jenni's mum was sitting in the driver's seat when they got to the car. Jenni got into the passenger seat, and Elise slid into the back.

"You look nice without makeup, Lise," Jenni's mum said.

"Oh my God." Elise touched her face. "No, I don't."

Once they were out on the road, Jenni took a piece of gum from her mum's bag, put it in her mouth, and started flipping through radio stations. "Hey," her mum said, "I was waiting for the news."

"We've been living with eleven-year-olds for three days. I have to hear some music that isn't Taylor Swift or the soundtrack to *Glee*."

"I thought you loved Taylor Swift."

"Yeah, like two years ago, before she got famous."

"Did you hear she was going out with Jennifer Aniston's ex-boyfriend? He must be ten years older than her."

"John Mayer."

"Supposedly he's addicted to porn."

"Everyone's addicted to porn."

"What does that mean, 'everyone'?"

"Hey, Ma, did you hear that Lady Gaga is actually a guy and has a penis?"

"Hilarious," her mum said. "Don't make fun of me." But she was smiling. "So you girls had a good time?"

"Yeah," Jenni said. "I miss my horse already."

"I was just thinking that!" Elise said. "I miss mine, too."

"I'm so glad," Jenni's mum said.

Out on the Western Freeway, the girls' phones started to beep. They were back in range. They had messages from Sara-Jane and Darren and some other kids from school, wondering what they were up to over the holidays. The most recent ones were from Holly and Bec, telling them to come to Zach's party that night. Elise thought Zach might have texted to invite her himself, but he hadn't.

She sent Jenni a text. *Wanna go Zs?*

Her phone said it had sent but it was twenty seconds before Jenni's phone dinged.

"Popular girls," her mum said.

Jenni nodded when she read the text. *Could be fun,* she wrote back. *U?*

Maybe. Elise thought about it for the rest of the drive home.

Five hours after dropping Elise off, Jenni took the bus back over to Elise's house. Elise answered the front door and the two of them headed to her room, passing through the kitchen, where her parents were eating dinner.

"You sure you don't want something?" her mum asked.

"Yeah," said Elise. "We're gonna eat there. But can I have a beer?"

"No way," her dad said, laughing.

"Give us a sip of yours, then?"

He looked at her mum. "Just a sip," he said. Elise picked up the bottle. "That's enough," he said, and she handed it back.

"Better cut down, Dad," she said, thumping her hand on his belly. "Getting a bit tubby there."

"Thanks for pointing that out, Elise," he said.

"Yes," said her mum. "Really helpful."

The girls went to Elise's room and got dressed for the night. Elise decided on a black skater dress with a low-cut back, and a big aqua belt. Jenni wore a gold off-the-shoulder leotard and skinny jeans, with big silver hoops in her ears. Elise wore her Elise necklace and Jenni wore her Jennifer one.

"Let's swap," Elise said.

"Why?"

"Just for fun."

"Okay." Jenni unclasped her necklace and handed it over. "Just as long as Zach doesn't get confused and try to make out with me."

"Yeah, wouldn't put it past him."

They went into the bathroom and took turns cleansing, toweling, toning, and moisturizing their faces. Then they put on foundation, blemish stick, bronzer, blush, eye shadow, eyeliner, mascara, and lipstick and lip liner for Jenni, and tinted lip gloss for Elise. Jenni used a straightening iron to smooth down Elise's hair, and sprayed her own hair with Big Beach to give it some body.

When they were ready, they put their faces next to each other and pouted at the mirror. "We look hot," Elise said.

"You look hot," Jenni said. "I look *fucking* hot."

"You totally wanna fuck Nathan," Elise said.

"Who's Nathan?"

"Zach's brother."

"Oh." Jenni turned and looked at herself side-on in the mirror. She shrugged a shoulder. "Maybe."

The girls were laughing when Elise's mum opened the door. "You girls are gonna freeze in that. I hope you're planning on wearing coats."

"Mum!" Elise said. "Do you mind knocking? We don't live in a tent."

"What does that mean?"

"It means can you please knock before you come in?"

"No need for the attitude, Elise. I was just going to offer to drive you."

"We're gonna take the bus."

"Well, do you want to call me for a lift home?"

"No. Can we just get a taxi?"

On the bus, the girls reapplied their lipstick and lip gloss. Then Jenni played Candy Conspiracy while Elise watched.

"It's the dumbest game ever."

"I know, but it's so addictive."

They missed their stop and had to walk three blocks back to Zach's house. Which sucked because they were both wearing heels.

"Are you nervous?" Jenni asked.

"What, about Zach?"

"Just for the party."

Elise shrugged. "It'll probably be the same as always."

But the party wasn't really a party at all. It was just Zach and Nathan sitting in the living room watching *Tron*.

"We all had a big one at the park last night for Nico's birthday," Zach said. "Most people bailed tonight." He hugged both the girls and said "Whoa" when they took off their coats. "You're looking good. I feel way underdressed."

They looked at his red polo shirt, faded jeans, and white socks. "You are underdressed," Jenni said.

"It's not my fault." He held his hands out. "Our dad gets back tomorrow. I've been cleaning all day."

The girls looked around. The place wasn't too bad, but the carpet was dirty and the coffee table was covered in paper cups and burger wrappers.

"Here," Elise told Jenni, "give me your coat. I'll put them upstairs."

"Wait," said Zach. "I'll come with you."

"Hey, Nathan," Jenni called into the living room, "do you have anything to drink that isn't a Cruiser?"

Elise and Zach climbed the stairs. "Where's the snow-cone photo?" she asked him on the landing.

"I took it down."

"Why? I liked it."

"Shut up," he said. "No, you didn't."

In his room, Zach put the coats on his desk chair. Elise sat on the end of his bed and looked around. It was messier in here than last time. There were clothes on the floor, a pile of graphic novels on his bed, a bowl half full of penne on his bedside table, and the desk was covered with what looked like his dad's mail.

"Sorry about the stuff everywhere," he said.

"It's not that bad."

Zach went over and turned on the bedside lamp. "How was the horse camp?"

"It was awesome," said Elise. "We were drunk and stoned, like, the whole time."

"You girls are crazy." He turned off the overhead light. He had just come and sat down next to her when the door-bell rang.

"That's probably Holly and Bec," he said.

"Should we go down?"

"I don't really want to. Unless, do you?"

"Maybe later?"

"Sounds good," Zach said. He touched her necklace. "Jennifer."

"I forgot about that."

"You're not Jenni. You're way hotter than Jenni."

"That's not true," Elise said. "We're both exactly the same level of hotness."

"Yeah, maybe," Zach said. "More or less." He reached out and put a hand on her cheek. Then he leaned over and kissed her.

. . .

"We're not staying long," Bec said when Nathan answered the door. "We had a really big one last night. We're zonked."

They came into the living room and scrunched up their noses when Nathan offered them a drink. They said hi to Jenni and joined her on the couch.

"Where's Lise?" Holly asked. "Upstairs?"

"Yeah."

"We didn't expect to see you guys here."

"This is boring," said Nathan. It seemed like he was talking about the conversation but then he picked up the remote control and turned off the TV.

"We're not pissed off or anything," said Holly. "We just miss you. We feel like you dumped us or something."

"No no. We just weren't in the mood to go out. And then we were at horse camp."

"What's horse camp?" Nathan asked.

Holly and Bec laughed. "It's exactly what it sounds like," Bec said.

"How was it, anyway?"

"It was fun."

"What did you do there?"

"Just, rode horses and stuff."

Holly and Bec cracked up laughing. "What?" Jenni said. "That's what we did!" Now all three of the girls were laughing.

"What the fuck?" Nathan shook his head. There was a guitar leaned up against the arm of the couch, and he reached over and picked it up.

"Didn't you guys used to go there in primary school?" Holly asked.

"Yeah, but you can go whenever. It's all ages. There was one girl there who's in uni, at Deakin."

"Was she there by herself?"

"Yeah."

"That's just kind of sad," said Bec.

Jenni took a sip of her Southern Comfort and ginger beer. "Yeah, it was a bit. Most of the girls were younger."

"Like how old?"

"Fifth and sixth grade."

"That's my sister's age," said Bec.

Jenni spat a sliver of ice back into her glass. "Yeah, they were so annoying. We had to share a cabin with them. They were all, like, listening to Justin Bieber and braiding each other's hair."

"Any pillow fights?" asked Nathan. The girls laughed.

"No, but guess what they *were* playing?" Jenni turned to Holly and Bec. "Secret Swaps!"

"I used to love that game," said Bec.

"These three girls had a huge fight about it. They were crying and screaming."

"God," Nathan said, picking out the notes to a Bon Iver song on his guitar. "Girls can be so mean to each other."

"I know. They'd written the meanest stuff."

"Like what?" Bec asked.

"Just that one was a bad dancer, and one stank. And— that one had, y'know, more pubes than the others."

"That is so not a game for three people," Holly said.

"But were the comments true?" asked Bec.

"Yeah. I told them they weren't, just to shut them up. But, seriously, they were all kind of true. Like one of them was a crap dancer. And the other one reeked of curry. And this girl, Dylan, she had a super hairy vag."

"What, were you all sitting around staring at each other's vaginas?" Nathan asked.

"No, Elise looked at it really quickly. Just to stop her freaking out."

"Oh my God, what a perv," Holly said.

"She couldn't help it. The girl just flashed her in the bathroom."

"Sounds like the worst," Holly said. "I knew it would suck when I heard you were going."

"I don't know." Jenni shrugged. "I mean, the horses were cute."

"That's just 'cause you like having a big dude between your legs," Bec said.

"My horse was a girl!"

"Nothing wrong with that," Nathan said.

The girls rolled their eyes and laughed.

"So, get this," Bec said. "We have so much to tell you."

"It's crazy," said Holly.

"Hey, is there any more SoCo?" Jenni asked Nathan.

"Yeah, definitely." He put his guitar down and took her glass. The girls watched him leave the room.

"Do you want us to go?" Holly whispered.

"I think he might have a girlfriend," Bec said.

"I'm good," Jenni said. "You should stay. I'm just waiting for Lise."

"That could take a long time," Holly said. "Trust me. Like, a really long time."

Zach rolled on top of Elise. He grabbed her ass. He pulled her dress up and put his hand inside her underwear. "Oh God," he said, "you're so wet already." He stuck his fingers inside her.

She touched his body under his T-shirt. His skin was warm and his back was a little sweaty. He smelled like boy's deodorant, which she liked. She struggled with his belt until he pulled his hand away from her, knelt on the bed, and undid it himself. She unbuttoned his jeans. He took his T-shirt off and pulled his jeans and boxer briefs down. Elise tilted her head and put her mouth on him.

"Oh yeah," he said. "That's so good. Oh my God. You look so sexy. Look at me." She looked up at him. She tried to get all of him down her throat. "Yeah," he said, "holy shit, you're so good at that." She gagged a bit. She pulled back and used her hand. "Yeah," he said. "Now lick my balls. Oh my God, yeah."

When it seemed like he was about to come, he pulled away and told her to get on her hands and knees. She did. He knelt behind her. She thought they were about to have sex, but instead he leaned over and licked her up and down.

"Holy shit," she said. He licked her ass. "Holy fuck." He took his face away and stuck a finger inside her. Then he eased that finger into her asshole. "Holy fuuuck," she moaned.

"You like that?" Zach said.

"Um—"

"I'm pretending you like it," he said.

"So am I," said Elise.

They both laughed.

She gasped when he pulled his finger out. "Do you think they can hear us downstairs?"

"I doubt it, but I can put music on." He stood and went over to his computer. Elise looked at his ass. Then she tried not to look at his ass. She knew what the music was going to be before he pressed PLAY.

"The latest Kanye?"

"Yeah," he said. "How'd you know?"

"It's, like, the hookup album of the year."

"Such a good one," he said.

Nicki Minaj was faking a British accent through the intro when Zach came back to the bed. Elise was sitting up with her legs against her chest, hugging her knees. He leaned over and kissed her. He pulled her by the ankles until she was lying flat. He got on top of her. As soon as he was inside her, she started to moan. He had his head bent over her face. "Fuck, your pussy's so fucking wet," he said.

By the beginning of "Gorgeous," Zach was kneeling in front of her, holding her legs. "I love watching those tits bounce," he said. "Yeah, hold them like that. Oh my God, that's so hot."

By the time they got to "Power," he had rolled onto his back and put her on top of him. "Grind down on me," he said. Elise didn't really know what that meant. "Grind down on it, find your spot." She was moving her hips back and forth and it felt good, but she couldn't find anything that felt like a spot. "Come for me," Zach said. "Come for me. Come for me. Come for me." He probably said it twenty times, but she couldn't do it.

He got on top again. He put his elbows next to her head and leaned down close to her. His chest was rubbing against her nipples. He kissed her, then whispered into her ear, "Come for me, baby. Come all over that big dick."

He was all the way inside her and barely moving at all when she came.

"Good girl," he said. He pushed her hair off her face. "Good girl," he said. "That's my good girl. Turn around."

Her legs were shaky but she managed to get back on her hands and knees. She wrapped her fingers around the metal bed frame. "Yeah," Zach said, "hold on to that bed frame."

Elise laughed.

"What?" he said.

"Nothing. I just feel like if I scratched my ear, you'd be like, *Yeah, scratch that ear.*"

"No, I wouldn't. What's that s'posed to mean?"

"Nothing," Elise said.

"I don't know what that means."

She turned her head and watched him drip saliva from his mouth all over himself. Then he spat on his fingers and wiped it on her.

"I wanna do it hard," he said. "Is that okay?"

"Yeah."

He fucked her hard. "Oh yeah," Elise said. He smacked her ass. "Shit. Shit shit. Shit."

"Yeah," he said. He grabbed a bunch of her hair and yanked her head back. "You like that?"

"Uh-huh."

"Yeah, you take that cock."

Elise moaned.

"Does that feel good?"

"Yeah."

"Tell me how it feels."

"It feels—good."

"Yeah?" he said. "What else?"

"It feels, like, really good and big."

Zach put a hand on her lower back and pushed down. "Arch your back for me," he said. "Yeah, be sexy. Shake your ass. Yeah, shake your ass for me. My God, that's so hot. I wanna fuck your ass."

Elise didn't say anything.

"Can I fuck your ass?"

"No," she said.

"Are you sure?"

"Yeah."

"Have you ever done that with anyone?"

"No."

"Has Jenni?"

"I dunno."

"Are you sure you don't wanna try?"

"Yeah."

"Okay. I want to so bad."

He leaned over her. She could feel his belly and chest against her back. He used one hand to touch her clit. And then he put his other hand around her throat and squeezed.

"Fuck."

"Is this okay?" he asked.

"Yeah, it's just hard to breathe."

"Oh my God, I'm gonna come," he said. "Where do you want my come?"

"I don't know," she said. "On my back?"

"I wanna come on your tits," he said, "or maybe in your mouth." He let go of her, raised himself up, and held on to her waist. "Okay," he said a minute later. "Okay, I'm gonna come. I'm gonna come in your mouth."

He pulled out of her and she turned around fast and leaned down. "Here it comes," he said. She looked up at him. He had his eyes closed. He was gritting his teeth. He came and exhaled and then he opened his eyes and looked down at her. She still had her mouth open.

"Oh God," he said.

She closed her mouth and swallowed.

"Oops." He used the sides of two fingers to scoop some

off her cheek. Then he fed it to her. "Yeah," he said, "you love my come."

By the time they were lying back on Zach's pillow together, "Blame Game" was playing.

"You're so fucking beautiful," Zach said.

"You think so?"

"Absolutely." He lifted the sheets and looked at her body. "You're so hot."

"Thanks."

"How does it feel right now?"

"What do you mean?"

"I don't know. Vaginally, emotionally, whatever."

"Fine."

"You should go to the toilet."

"What?" Elise laughed.

"I don't know. It's good for girls to go straight after. It stops you from getting an infection or something."

"Okay," she said.

"Okay, I'll be here." He kissed her. "You're lucky I'm kissing you. Most guys don't let girls kiss them after they came in their mouth."

"That's not true," Elise said.

"Yes, it is."

"It's definitely not true."

"Huh," said Zach. "I guess guys are fags, then."

Elise stood up, found her coat, wrapped it around herself,

and went to the bathroom. She came back just as Chris Rock was doing his monologue at the end of the song. She dropped her coat on the floor and got back into bed. Zach put his arms around her.

"Hey."

"Hey."

"I'm kind of over this part of the song," she said.

"What? You're crazy. It's hilarious. Chris Rock's the best."

"Yeah, it's funny. But I wish it was its own skit track, so you could skip over it if you want to. I like it. I just don't wanna hear it every time I listen to the song."

"Yeah," Zach said. "Actually, you're right. That probably would have been better."

Jenni was asleep on the couch in front of *How to Train Your Dragon* when they came downstairs. Nathan was on the other end of the couch, watching the movie. The house was cleaner now. The floors looked vacuumed and there were two full rubbish bags sitting next to the front door.

"Whoa," Zach said.

"I did it all," Nathan said. "This one just turned on the TV and fell asleep."

"I offered to help," Jenni said, sitting up and rubbing her eyes.

"Jen, are you ready to go?" Elise asked.

"I thought you were Elise," Nathan said.

"What time is it?" Jenni asked.

"Time to go," Elise said. "If you're ready."

"Nothing really happened," Jenni told her when they were out in the street. "We kissed for a second but he has a girl-friend."

"What, like a serious one?"

"I guess so. He said he felt bad doing anything with any-one else."

"Crazy."

They crossed the street and turned onto the main road. "How was it with Zach this time?" Jenni said. "Your hair's all wavy."

"It was okay," Elise said. "He's a talker."

"Did he give you a bath? Holly told me he gave her a bath."

"No. Seriously?"

"Yeah, he came in her hair, then he put her in the bath and washed it off."

"No, nothing like that. It was pretty vanill." Elise stopped walking. "Which way do we go? I'm disorientated."

"We got off the bus up there, so we should cross and catch it going that way."

"Hey, girls," a group of guys called from a passing car. "Where's the party?"

Jenni and Elise put their arms around each other. "Not telling," Jenni called out.

"Ohhh," the guys yelled and the driver honked as they drove away.

The girls dropped their arms. "I don't think it was that way. Because, look, we came from there and we walked past that corner store."

"Oh yeah. So we take it from here."

They went over to the bus stop; Jenni sat down and Elise looked at the timetable. "Twenty-five minutes," she said. "I hate catching the bus on weekends."

"So annoying," Jenni said. "Should we just taxi it?"

They stood on the curb and looked for cabs. They tried to hail one that came toward them, even though its lights weren't on and it was obviously taken. Eventually, an empty one passed on the other side of the road, but the driver either didn't see them or didn't want to do a U-turn, and he just kept going.

"Maybe we should walk?" Jenni said. "It's not that far."

"Yeah, maybe."

They started walking, but then Elise decided to call home.

"What's wrong?" her mum asked when Elise said hi.

"Nothing. We're ready to go home but the bus isn't coming for ages and we can't get a taxi."

"Do you want me to come pick you up?"

"Do you mind?"

"Not at all," her mum said. "What's the address?"

. . .

Elise and Jenni stood on the sidewalk and waited. Elise crossed her arms over her chest and stomped up and down on the spot to keep warm. She looked down at her shoes and said she wanted new heels. White ones or aqua, or even hot pink, for summer. Jenni said Holly was going shopping in the city the next day and they could join. Then they talked about going to Frankston that weekend because Bec was kind of going out with a surfer who lived there, and there was going to be a bonfire on the beach unless it rained. Jenni had seen pictures of Bec and the guy on Holly's phone, and they looked really into each other and he was hot. In the photos, at least.

They discussed what else they could do in the holidays. They tried to work out if they had one or two weeks left. They were glad someone had made a movie of *Persepolis* so they wouldn't have to read a whole book before they wrote their essays. They wondered why there weren't more Iranian supermodels or movie stars, and thought it was sad but would hopefully happen soon. Then they talked about who the hottest celebrities of all time were, and they debated whether they'd rather look like Beyoncé or Kim Kardashian. They loved Kim because she was beautiful and her body was really curvy but totally in proportion and she had a good sense of humor and didn't take herself too seriously, and they loved Beyoncé because she was completely stunning and her body was perfect and her songs were unique, and you could tell she was the nicest person, and she was always really sweet to her fans. Also, she had a song out with a crazy video in which she did an awesome African tribal army dance. The girls agreed they would watch it later on, when they got home. They were both relieved when Elise's mum pulled up on the other side of the road and waved at them. Jenni had to pee and Elise was hungry.

Plus One

Amelia couldn't finish her book, so she decided to have a baby. She got pregnant with a gay friend, and waited six weeks to make sure it was actually happening. Then she emailed her agent. *It's going to take me longer than expected,* she wrote, even though it had already taken longer than expected and her last email, with the subject line *Any day now . . . ,* had been sent four months ago. *It's early still and I probably shouldn't say anything but—I can't help it. I'm pregnant.*

Her agent, the father of teenage twins, could hardly tell her off for wanting to procreate, but he did express some surprise. Amelia was only twenty-two, after all, and she had never—in conversation or in her writing—mentioned an interest in children. *Of course,* he wrote before signing off, *your mind must be on other matters at this exciting moment.*

Take your time finishing the book. Amelia smiled at that last line. She turned off her computer for the first time in months, and felt a deep sense of relief and calm—a feeling she hadn't imagined she'd experience until the book was done.

She pictured his phone call to the editor and the editor's conversation with the sales team. No longer could they market her as the wunderkind blogger-turned-author fresh out of college. Now she would be this other thing, this uncategorizable shunner of the New York code. While her peers were all busy getting drunk and high, and sleeping their way through three of the five boroughs, Amelia would be at home, sterilizing bottles and feeling sleepy—or whatever it was new mothers did. In any case, she would have good reason not to write. It was a great plan, she thought. Soon morning sickness would kick in and lay her out for hours at a time, her essay collection left unfinished on her computer, and she helpless to do anything about it.

"You won't get morning sickness," her mother said. It was Saturday morning and Amelia was at brunch at her parents' place on the Upper East Side. "I never had it. Auntie Annie never had it. Your grandma never had it. We don't get it. We also don't show till late. Like, five months or so. You've got a while to go."

They were sitting in the living room, eating bagels and drinking coffee. All four of Amelia's sisters were there, too, on the couch, the armchair, and the floor, and their dad was at the table with the newspaper. While everyone else was still gulping back the news, Amelia's mother was dealing with the shock the way she dealt with every uncomfortable emotional experience: with a take-charge attitude. "You'll need to look at your insurance plan," she said. "See what birth options are covered."

"I'm sorry, Mom, but how are you okay with this?" Georgia asked.

"You know she should get it taken care of," Celine said. "Just tell her to take care of it."

"I don't want it taken care of," Amelia told them. "I want this. It's planned parenthood."

"It's fine to want a baby," her father said. "You've always said you would one day. But is now the time?"

"I think so. I don't have much else going on. I'm between things."

"You're between college and the rest of your life," Jane said. "That's not the right time."

"We don't do this," said Georgia. "Seriously. It's just not done."

Everyone fell silent and focused on their bagels. It was clear that by "we" Georgia meant all the Banks girls, and by "this" she meant have children before achieving all your goals and realizing your full potential, fully. It was, Amelia saw now, an unspoken family rule, like "Don't talk during *Gilmore Girls,*" or "Don't ask about Mom's college boyfriend, Claude." It probably went doubly for the two younger girls, and should have applied most stringently to Amelia herself, who was the youngest, the baby, the wunderkind blogger-turned-author-turned-mother-to-be.

Hank usually came back to Brooklyn on Saturdays, and he and Amelia usually fooled around, but today he said he wasn't in the mood.

"What's wrong?" She was standing in their kitchen by the stove and he was at the table. "Don't you think I'm sexy anymore?"

"What? Of course I do. You know I can't resist a girl wearing frilly ankle socks with her glitter jellies."

"So then, what?"

Hank shrugged. "I feel like I'd just be thinking about the baby the whole time. How there's another guy's baby in there. It's kind of a moodkill."

"Oh no, I shouldn't have told you," Amelia said.

"What are you talking about?"

"You get three months before you have to tell people. I should have waited till then."

"Mimi," he said, "I'm your boyfriend, kind of." They'd had an open relationship since June, when he'd moved part-time to Rhinebeck for an artist's assistant job.

"Then fool around with me." She actually had to stop herself from stamping her foot on the floor.

"Maybe later?" he said.

. . .

Later he went out. Amelia stayed in. She had to be careful now, keep away from alcohol and not overdo things. She couldn't remember the last time she had stayed home on a Saturday night. In college, she had gone out all the time just for fun. More recently, since the book deal, she *had* to go out on weekends. How could you write about the habits of a generation without seeing those habits up close? Without getting a plus one, a front-row seat, a backstage pass to those habits. Without sipping, slamming, and snorting those habits, and rubbing the remnants into your gums, just for fun.

Through her window she could see other windows, and in a third of those other windows there was a light on and someone doing something inside. Eating, watching TV, staring at a laptop. Wow, she realized, people do stay home on Saturday nights. Nobody writes essay collections about those people, but they do exist.

She wondered what she should do with the night. What did expectant mothers do? They nested. She looked around. The place was pretty tidy; Hank was better about keeping it that way than she was. She was usually busy, supposed to be writing. There was a teaspoon on the counter. She put it in the sink. She looked out the window again. A woman across the way was applying makeup without using a mirror. Amelia washed and dried the spoon and dropped it in a drawer. That was enough nesting for the night.

She went into the living room, curled up under a blanket, turned on Nick at Nite, and fell asleep. She woke up later when Hank got home. They went to bed and had sex immediately. It was better and more energetic than any they'd had in months. Amelia was on top and she came all over him and all over the sheets. This had never happened before, and she wondered if this was what it would feel like when her water broke. She was careful not to wonder this aloud until afterward, when Hank was lying next to her in the dark, in the wet spot, idly rubbing her back.

"I dunno," he said. He had obviously not spent much time in his life so far wondering about such things. "But that was pretty cool," he said, and fell asleep.

On Sunday morning, Amelia met her friends for brunch at Enid's. When she told them about the baby, they sat and stared at her belly for what felt like a long time.

"There's nothing to see, just my usual pudge." She pulled her T-shirt tight over her stomach. "The baby's the size of a blueberry right now."

"Ew," said Dana.

"Are you hoping for a girl blueberry or a boy blueberry?" asked Gabby.

Amelia practiced a beatific, all-knowing pregnant-woman smile. "I really don't care," she said, "as long as it's a healthy baby. Boy. I want a healthy baby boy."

When their eggs and oatmeal arrived, the other girls talked about their news. Gabby was about to fly to Wyoming to shoot a documentary about Scandinavian cowgirls. Akiko liked her new industrial design job in Dumbo. Dana and her boyfriend were thinking about getting engaged because they wanted to get married on 12/12/12. Akiko was now dating her old boss. Gabby and her boyfriend had been broken up for a month, but they were still living together until their lease was up.

"He has this curtain, in the living room. And he pulls it across when he wants privacy. It's not like he brings girls back there or anything. He just listens to Hot 97 and draws in his sketchbook. It's so weird. Mimi, you should put it in your book."

"I'm not writing the book anymore," Amelia said.

"Are you serious?" asked Akiko. "What are you gonna do instead?"

"Just, like, get ready for the baby."

Everyone went quiet. The waitress, sensing the pause, dropped off the check.

"Let us pay for you." Akiko reached out and touched her wrist.

"Yeah," said Gabby, "as congratulations."

"Thanks," Amelia said, but it felt more like a condolence than congratulations. Or, worse still, like a goodbye. She wondered if her friends might not want her around soon, with her big belly and lack of anecdotes from the night before. Maybe they were worried cute bartenders would stop comping them cocktails and KJs would stop letting them jump the karaoke queue, with a pregnant girl around. Maybe this time next year she would be just another parent trying to push a monstrous stroller past groups of staring Wayfarer-wearers in McCarren Park, on her way to ask suspicious, in-depth questions to vendors at the farmers market. And all anyone nearby would be thinking, her friends included, is that she belonged in *the other park*. So once her friends had piled their twenties onto the tray, Amelia put her elbows on the table and playfully clapped her hands together. "Hey," she said, "who wants to hear about how I got a gay guy to knock me up?"

"Oh, me," said Akiko. "Me me me." They all tilted forward to hear her over the breakfast roar, ignoring the hungry people lining up outside the window with their newspapers and toddlers, waiting to be seated.

Her friends knew some of the story already. Amelia had written thirty pages of prose and a chapter outline, signed with an agent, and, after some near misses and rejections, sold her book to an up-and-coming editor at a good publishing house for enough money to live on for a New York year. She had quit her job with Teach for America and stayed home to write.

After ten years of blogging, she had finally gotten what she wanted. A book deal, and time to write. Only to—falter. Every piece she conceived seemed stupid: maybe worthy of a blog post but not worthy of a book-length collection of essays. Who cared about the purity rings she and her college boyfriend had ironically exchanged? Who cared that they ironically then never actually slept together for the whole three years they dated? Who cared about the drag queen outside Lucky Cheng's who had given her the Heimlich one time when she came out of a nearby bodega and choked on a Sour Patch Kid? Who cared about her internship at a bankrupt roller-skating rink, or her extensive Lisa Frank sticker collection, or her shameful adult Baby-Sitters Club addiction? Or her first memory, her Protestant-girl-at-Jewish-camp story, or even what it was like growing up as the youngest of five sisters? This was New York, she had realized, after months of false starts and thwarted attempts. The city of stories. Everyone had their own tales to tell about internships and drag queens and summer camp. Why would they pay money and take the time to read hers?

This realization had happened about five months into that lost year, and no amount of consoling and encouragement over brunch at Enid's was going to help her. She had made a mistake. The editor had made a mistake. Her agent had made a mistake. And they seemed like undoable ones. *They're waiting for it,* she reminded herself as she sat down at her computer each morning. *They're waiting for it,* she thought as she scrolled through her Twitter feed, posted pictures to her *People Using 10-Color Pens in Offices* Tumblr, resisted the urge to update her blog (she had taken an official break from it while she wrote the book: her editor's idea). *They're waiting for it,* as she brushed her hair, sent handwritten letters, met up with friends, took an afternoon off, had a nap, visited a friend in Barcelona, watched all nine seasons of *Roseanne,* read other people's published essay collections, and took up a few freelance copywriting jobs as supplementary income. *We're waiting for it,* her agent Scott seemed to be saying when he checked in with her periodically—both before and after her missed deadline— just to see how it was going.

Staying in was unbearable, so for a while going out was the only option that worked. It was all—the bars, the openings, the shows, the house parties, warehouse parties, rooftop parties, stoop parties—research for her next essay. *What can I write about my generation?* she wondered. *The Y generation, the entrepreneurial generation, the trophy generation, the Obama generation, the 9/11 generation, the queer, the fun, the public, the digital, the boomerang generation.* From what she saw on her many nightly adventures, it seemed more fun to be someone living in this generation than someone standing apart from it, trying to analyze and write about it.

When she needed the analyzing to stop, there was sometimes alcohol but always Hank. There at the end of the night or beginning of the day to slip into her bed and fuck her until sleep. It was pornier and more banal than she would have liked. The power dynamic was always the same—he was in charge and she was in his thrall—and though sometimes she liked to challenge this way of doing things ("Yeah, suck that dick," he'd say. "Which dick?" Amelia would ask, looking up with faux confusion. She'd point at it. "You mean this one? Right here?"), she was usually just glad for the complete distraction and oblivion that came with that kind of sex.

All of that worked for a while, until a year after she'd

signed her book contract, when Amelia had turned around and noticed that a lot of her friends were actually progressing with their lives. Things were changing, in a way that seemed shocking. Gabby had graduated film school, and she was getting funding to make short films. Dana had met a guy she could viably be with long-term, and had actually fallen in love with him. Everyone they'd gone to school with was busy becoming what they had dreamed of becoming, what they'd trained to become. They were struggling and worried about the economy, and they had too many roommates and loads of debt, but at least they were moving forward.

Her sisters, too, were moving ahead in their careers, chatting excitedly at Saturday brunch about interviews and promotions and press conferences, while Amelia curled up on the beanbag and nibbled at her bagel, hoping nobody would ask her that dreadful question to which she never had a proper answer: *How's the book coming?*

"It's not a book," she always wanted to snap at people when they asked. "It's just thirty pages and a chapter outline. Your drafts folder is more of a book than my book is a book."

She thought about returning to teaching, to save some money and pay back her advance. She thought about telling her agent and editor the truth, that she couldn't do it, that, for reasons that were opaque to her and everyone else, this thing that was difficult but doable for so many was actually impossible for her. She thought about moving to Argentina and changing her name, like a German war criminal. It seemed like there could be a wig involved in that somehow. And then, one afternoon this past August, just hours before the start of Hurricane Irene, when she had finished stockpiling canned goods and was waiting for her best friend, Seth, to come over and spend the weekend, she had flicked through her Netflix queue and watched *Blue Valentine*. And by the time Seth arrived, she knew what she had to do.

"Uh, that's not the message that movie's trying to convey," Seth said, coming in with a paper bag of groceries in his arms.

"I'm ready," Amelia said. "I know it. It's what I'm s'posed to do next."

Seth, having been a bartender for most of his adult life, had a shrug-and-let-live attitude about even the biggest decisions. So his only moment of true consternation seemed to come when Amelia sat him down in front of a paused TV screen, with a bloated and balding Ryan Gosling on it, and told him that he should be the father.

"Think about it," she'd said. "You're always saying you want a family someday. You're also always saying that you never meet anyone you like and you don't want to just screw around. We could have a baby!" She was kneeling on the couch beside him, gesticulating wildly. She felt like a politician. A preacher! A twenty-two-year-old woman whose iPeriod app said she was ovulating that very weekend and she better get to it!

"We love each other," she said. "We're always going to be in each other's lives. You could have weekends. I could take vacations. I trust your diet choices. I know how hygienic you are. You're super hot and I have pretty nice cheekbones under here somewhere. Just please." She fell onto him, her head on his chest, his heart beating against her temple. "Please go halfsies in a baby with me."

Ryan Gosling was still frozen on the TV. A small child by his side. His hand pointing at something offscreen. His character had never regretted having that baby, Amelia thought. There may have been a lot of things he wished were different, but that wasn't one of them.

Outside, rain hit the fire escape and the wind whipped off the water and troubled the tree next to her window. She was glad she had brought her plants in before the storm hit. She was so busy thinking about this that when Seth first said okay, she didn't really hear him.

"What did you say?" she asked.

"Okay," he said.

"What?" She sat up.

"Okay."

"Really?" She grabbed his shoulders. She was wild-eyed with joy. "Really really really?"

"Yes," he said. "Let's go halfsies. All the way."

"Holy shit," Akiko said now. All three of the other girls sat staring at her, with no intention of moving, even though the line outside had grown, and the waitress had already delivered their change. "So you did it the natural way."

"Well, as natural as it can be, with a gay guy. I took off my clothes and stood in the bedroom, in my underwear, trying to dance sexy to the *Grease 2* soundtrack. Then Seth did this freaked-out little yell. It was pouring outside but he ran down the street and bought a bottle of Beefeater, some tonic, and two forties. He drank a quarter of the gin on the stairs on his way back up."

"And that was enough?" Dana asked.

"No. Then he made me shove all my hair up in a beanie. He changed the music to *FutureSex/LoveSounds*. And remember that old Marky Mark Calvin Klein poster I had up in my dorm room, freshman year? We got that out and stuck it on the wall above my bed for us both to concentrate on. Then we dimmed the light and I tried not to make a single sound to distract him from the task at hand. And the guy was a trouper. He was grossed out. But he trouped. Like, three times."

"Did he stay over?"

"Yeah, on the couch. Then the next morning, I made us Froot Loops with chocolate milk and all he said was, 'That was so wrong. But I'm glad we did it.'"

"And what about you?" Gabby asked as they all stood up to go. "Are you glad?"

"Totally," Amelia said. "I'm the happiest I've been in ages."

. . .

If Amelia was worried she might not fit in with her friends anymore, she didn't find a new group or instant community at the prenatal yoga class she started attending at Yogaga on Manhattan Avenue. While the woman behind the desk smiled at her nicely enough, Amelia sensed the other students looking at her with judgment. She was two months' pregnant now, and not showing at all, and she was probably the youngest person in the room by ten years.

The yoga itself didn't feel right, either. They moved from cat-cow into a slow sun salutation into warriors one and two. There was no down dog because it made a lot of pregnant women nauseous, and there was no plank pose or chaturanga because people's bellies would get in the way. The instructor told them the classes would help them breathe through the pain of childbirth, but Amelia couldn't see how that could be true when there was no pain in the class to breathe through. She didn't see how the practice was teaching anyone kindness or compassion, either, when everyone basically ignored her.

In the changing room after class, she listened to the other women chatting about their ob-gyns and midwives, and the pros and cons of getting a doula. It was clear from their conversations that after they got changed, they were heading either back to work or back to other, already-born children. Amelia had neither of those things to return to, and the most she could do was learn the other women's names and say hi and bye to them upon arrival or on her way out. None of them bothered to learn hers.

It was after a midday yoga class one Wednesday that

Amelia came outside and saw her sister Jane waiting on the curb, drinking coconut water from a can through a straw.

"What are you doing here?" Amelia asked. Jane was a deputy press secretary at the mayor's office and usually worked through lunch, and often dinner, too.

"Mom told me you came here. I thought we could talk. Have you had lunch yet?"

"No."

"It's on me."

"Really? Sweet."

"Well, actually, it's on Mom."

"Oh."

"Wherever you want."

Amelia took her to Peter Pan bakery, where she got a jelly donut with vanilla cream. Jane got a cup of coffee.

"So," Jane said when they'd sat down. "Let's be honest. I never really liked your blog. I couldn't see what the big deal was. I can't even say that I planned to read your book." She reached back with both hands and tightened her ponytail. She was all business. It was clear why the family had chosen her as its emissary. Not only was she closest in age to Amelia, she was also a professional communicator. She maintained eye contact and an earnest facial expression as she said, "But now—now I've changed my mind. I think it's a mistake to have this baby. I think you should get a termination and finish your manuscript. Seriously."

Amelia stopped licking the jelly off her fingers. "You never liked my blog?"

"Well—" Jane looked down at her cup until her eyes were obscured by lashes. She was the only one of the girls who'd inherited their mom's long eyelashes. "I guess we were all kind of annoyed by your references to eighties movies and obsession with nineties pop culture. You weren't even alive when most of that stuff was happening, or you were too young to know about it, anyway. The only way you know about *Footloose* or the Bangles or *Punky Brewster* and *Sassy* magazine is from us. It just seemed kind of posey and fake."

Amelia lowered her donut hand to the counter. "'We' were all annoyed? Were the four of you sitting around talking shit about me?"

"No, but—"

"There are other places to find out about the nineties, you know," Amelia said. "The Internet for one. And second"— she looked up at the ceiling—"the Internet."

"I know," Jane said. "I've changed my mind now. I like it. I want to read your book. I was probably just jealous. Who doesn't want to quit their job and write all day and publish a book? I mean, except you."

"I used to want that," Amelia said.

"You still do." Jane sat back in her chair. "You're just scared, paralyzed. That's why you did the baby thing."

"No, I want the baby. It's weird. I actually feel happy for the first time in ages."

"That's just the bonding hormones talking."

"Oh, thank you, *New York Times Magazine*."

"I'm just saying, you don't *really* want it."

"Yes, I do."

"Mom said you don't."

"Mom doesn't know."

"Mom's a therapist."

"Mom's not my therapist."

"But Mom's your mom."

"That's true," Amelia said. "She's your mom, too."

"I know."

The girls sat in silence for a second.

"Have you ever noticed that even when she's talking on the phone, she's liking photos on Instagram?"

"I did notice that!" Amelia said. "She's not just liking them, she's leaving comments. Once she left a comment for me while I was on the phone with her. I confronted her about it, and she tried to deny it."

"She's so clueless."

"I know. How do her clients take her seriously?"

The girls shook their heads, and then Jane checked her phone. "I have to go," she said. "I have two meetings back-to-back, and then a date."

"Ooh. With who?"

"Some guy." She shrugged. "Off OkCupid."

"What's he like?"

"Cute, sporty, ethical investment adviser. Could be good. What are you gonna do now?"

"I have to go home and fill out my yoga journal."

"That's it?"

"It's important to fill it out every day."

. . .

There were baby clothes to buy, and car seat manuals to read, and decisions to be made about the birth, but it really didn't amount to anything like a full-time job. Amelia understood now why maternity leave didn't start until the weeks just before a baby arrived. She got into the habit of taking the subway—the G to the E to the 6—uptown to have lunch with her mother, sitting in the waiting room reading books about how to attachment-parent without ruining everyone else's brunch until her mom had a break between clients. But when Amelia started to show at fifteen weeks, her mom put an end to this, claiming that nobody would want to see a psychotherapist whose smart, talented Manhattan-born-and-bred daughter had decided to put her career on hold at twenty-two and have a baby with a gay man who wasn't her boyfriend.

Seth hated being called a man. He was ten years older than Amelia, but he desperately wanted to be called a boy, and he even more desperately wanted to date boys. He came along for her ultrasound at eighteen weeks, and complained the whole way up First Avenue.

"He was really smart and it seemed so obvious that we would be great together. And I was just about to ask him out, when this little twink, this annoying bear-hunting little twinkie rat wandered in, and they left together immediately. He didn't even say goodbye."

In the past, Amelia would have been paying close attention to the story, taking note of the slang in case she wanted to use it in an essay. But she no longer had to think that way. She reached over and took Seth's hand.

"I'm sorry," she said. "Something will come along."

She held his hand again on the examination table at the medical center, waiting for the ultrasound tech to arrive.

"Thank you for coming with me," she told Seth. "I'll take you out for lunch after."

"Great," he said. "Don't tell me where. There are so few real surprises in life."

The baby was a boy. He was chilling out on his back in a pose that looked nothing like the fetal position, and he had one hand extended out in front of him; the other one was next to his face.

"Looks like it's a Wii kid, not an Xbox one," she said. The tech was concentrating on the screen and said nothing. Amelia looked at Seth for a response. He was sitting beside her, his jaw gone slightly slack, staring at the grainy baby and breathing fast like he might cry. Amelia squeezed his fingers between hers. "Congratulations," she said.

"I can't believe it," he said. "I'm gonna be an uncle."

No one in her mother's family had had a son for as many generations as could be remembered. It had been girls all the way until now, and the other Banks women were taking this hard, considering it a sign that the baby was an aberration and a mistake. Jane's post-yoga visits had become a regular occurrence.

"I was reading this article," she said one afternoon, "about how upper-class Chinese families are actually adopting boys from the States now. Because they have the money to do it and they place such a premium on boys over there. Isn't that a crazy reversal?"

"Crazy," Amelia agreed, biting into a red velvet donut.

"I bet you could get a lot of money for something like that."

"Are you suggesting I sell my baby?"

"No." Jane looked flustered. "I just think—Mom thinks you should consider adoption."

Around the twenty-one-week mark, however, when Amelia had convinced Jane that she planned to have the baby and keep the baby, their conversations devolved into gossip about Jane's work, or her love life, or complaint sessions about members of the very family whose point of view she was there to represent.

Not long after that, the visits stopped altogether, and the family seemed to change tack. Now it was her dad who contacted her, emailing her daily from his office in the History Department at Barnard, with links to random articles about random women in the public eye.

Apparently v. good, he wrote before linking to a book review of *A Visit from the Goon Squad. Didn't know Egan had two sons!*

Remember this? was the subject line of an email containing the famous Demi Moore naked-and-pregnant *Vanity Fair* cover. *This was still so early in her career!*

Interesting idea about leaning in to your ambition, was his analysis of a *New Yorker* article about the COO of Facebook.

And then, Amelia's favorite: a link to the video for Britney Spears's "Piece of Me" with a note about how he *Found these lyrics oddly inspiring.*

"Gee, thanks for the veritable poster board collage of successful working mothers you sent me, Dad," Amelia said one weekend morning in her parents' kitchen. She was the first daughter to arrive for brunch, having been a born-again early riser since her twelfth week. She shrugged and bit into an English muffin. "I guess I really *can* have it all!"

"That's right," said her dad. He was standing by the sink, squeezing fresh orange juice. "You can. No need to give up your writing just because a baby's on the way."

"Well, I—good morning, Mom."

"Mimi." Her mom kissed her on the top of the head and took a seat at the table.

"I have tried to write once or twice recently, but I just got the feeling. This tight, anxious feeling where I find it hard to breathe and nothing that comes out seems good enough. I can hear my heart beating and I feel like I might pass out. That can't be healthy for the baby."

"You just need exposure," her mom said. "You sit there with the anxiety. And you say, *Hello, anxiety,* and then you write anyway, despite the feelings. You know I was William Orton's—"

"Yes," said Amelia. "You were William Orton's therapist when he was writing *The Concierge's Vacation*."

"Don't tell anyone that."

"It's been fifteen years. No one cares."

"He was a finalist for the Pulitzer."

"Well, my book wasn't going to win anything. It was an essay collection about being a young girl in the big city. There was a piece about my method of using candy heart messages to determine what outfit to wear every day. The working title for the whole book was *Don't Mess Up My Mood Board, or My Unicorn Will Cry*."

"Well," her dad said, taking a breath.

"And Other Instructions," Amelia added.

"There's a good market for that sort of thing."

"But I'm not in that market anymore," she said. "I've outgrown it. I can't write it. It's over."

Amelia was preparing to counter whatever argument they came up with next when she looked across the table and saw that her mother was dripping tears onto her placemat.

"Nina, what is it?" Her dad came over and knelt beside her mom.

"It's fine," her mom said. She wiped the inner corners of her eyes with the sleeve of her robe, and then she fanned her face with her hands, trying to stop the tears. She looked over at Amelia, her eyes red, and laughed at herself. "I just love you so much," she said, her voice sounding strained and somehow old all of a sudden. "We both do. All we wanted for all you girls is that you could do anything you want. You wanted to switch schools from Dwight to Hunter, we organized it. You wanted to go to Jewish summer camp? We bought you a Star of David necklace so you'd fit in."

"I love that necklace," Amelia said. "I still wear it on alumni weekend."

"You wanted this book deal so badly," her mom said. "My heart almost broke for you with those first rejections. And when you got it? My heart sang all day. I could barely contain it. I actually told two of my clients the news. I never do that sort of thing."

"I did want that deal," Amelia said, "at the time. But you say we can do anything we want, and now what I want is a baby. And suddenly you don't want whatever I want."

"Because it's just not done," her mother said.

"Some people do it. You had five kids."

"That was a different era," her mom said. "And even then, I was almost thirty when we started. You're going to regret this. Trust me. You're twenty-two."

"Demi Moore was twenty-two," Amelia pointed out.

"Is that right?" her dad asked. He was over by the pantry now, searching the shelves.

"No," Amelia said. "That's not true at all."

"Where are the tissues?" he said. "Oh, never mind, I found them." He brought the box over and set it on the table. Her mom pulled one out and held it to her nose.

"Whoa, what's going on?" Celine asked, coming into the

kitchen, followed by Isobel. They both lived in the West Village, and had probably shared a cab. "Mom?"

"It's nothing. I'm fine," their mom said.

"Did you say something about Claude?" Isobel asked.

"No," Amelia said. "Mom was just telling me how much she's looking forward to being a grandmother."

"Oh God." There was a groan from the doorway, and Georgia came in. "I can't believe I'm gonna be an *auntie*."

"Auntie Annie is an auntie. We're not aunties."

"That baby, that boy, better not call me Auntie."

Amelia thrust her belly in her oldest sister's direction. "You hear that, baby? Auntie Georgie is talking to you!"

"I think I want to be a Papa," their dad said. The girls turned around and stared at him. "That's what I called my grandfather. Papa. I was his favorite grandson."

"Whoa," said Isobel. "This is actually, actually happening."

After brunch, Amelia's mom found a few boxes of the girls' old toys and clothes, stored in the closet in Georgia and Celine's old bedroom. Amelia sat on the floor with her legs splayed out in front of her, picking through smocked pinafores, My Little Ponys with knotted manes, a View-Master with photo reels of baby farm animals and Yellowstone Park, and Guess Who? and Strawberry Shortcake games with pieces either missing or put away in the wrong box.

"I thought this stuff might be worth something on eBay

one day," her mom said. "I hadn't actually pictured any of you girls reusing it."

Amelia had made a small pile of booties and diaper covers when her sisters appeared in the doorway.

"Oh my God," Isobel said, "that's my Snoopy money box."

"And those are my swap cards," Jane said.

"No, they're not." Isobel pulled the album out of Jane's hands. "They're mine. I spent all my pocket money in fifth grade on those."

"Yeah, but you gave them to me," Jane said.

"No, I didn't."

"Yes, you did." Jane grabbed hold of one side of the album. "I gave you my whole eraser collection and my Care Bear. We traded."

"No, we didn't. Mom!"

"Mom!"

Georgia was next to Amelia on the floor now, making a pile of her own. The other girls descended and the five of them rifled through boxes, making piles and inspecting one another's collections for stolen goods.

"Amelia, that's my quilt. Grandma made it when Mom was pregnant with me," Celine said. "I was planning to use it if I ever have kids."

"You still can," Amelia said. "I'm just borrowing it. I'll bring all this stuff back after I'm done with it."

"No, you won't," Isobel said.

"I promise."

Eventually her sisters conceded, but only after drawing up an inventory of everything Amelia was taking, alphabetically, from Bassinet to *The Very Hungry Caterpillar.*

Hank loved all the baby paraphernalia. He made cute noises about the tiny shoes and the fuzzy hats with the animal ears poking out. He loved how much Amelia ate now, and he enjoyed the challenge of fulfilling her cravings exactly, trying to locate lumpy rice pudding or really hard nectarines or chocolate cake with peanut butter frosting, before she either fell asleep or lost the craving. He loved how horny she was all the time. But he wasn't necessarily into the expanding stomach, the vertical line running down the skin below her belly button, her darkening nipples, or the idea of a baby.

"You know you can leave," Amelia told him one afternoon. She was watching him drink a beer and making him breathe in her face after every swig. She missed the smell. "You're not in town that much. And it won't be very fun to stay here once there's a baby on the scene."

"How would you do the whole rent?" he asked.

"If they let me keep the advance, I can manage till the baby's about three months."

"Then you'll finish the book?"

"I'll probably try to freelance from home at first. Then look for something full-time later."

"What about Teach for America? Those kids loved you."

"Yeah, I don't think I'd be considered much of a role model anymore."

Hank took a swig, swallowed, put the beer bottle on the coffee table, and reached for Amelia. He held her face in his hands. "You're gonna be amazing," he said.

"I am already." She wiped the beer off his upper lip with the back of her hand. "Would it be totally weird," she said, "if I named it after you?"

"Whoa, yes," he said. "It really would. But I'd probably be pretty stoked as well."

And that was it. It was Amelia's easiest breakup to date. She thought about writing an essay about it. "The Best Breakup in Brooklyn," she could call it. She considered heaving herself off the couch and scribbling down some notes right away, but then Hank suggested that they paint a mural on the living room wall next to where the crib was set up. A ladybug maybe. Or a robot. Or maybe a huge reproduction of the MTA subway map, because, "Dude, you're never too young to start learning that shit."

That night, as soon as Amelia lay down in bed, the baby started to kick. She slid her legs over to what had been Hank's side of the bed and tried to picture her body the way it looked before she got pregnant. It had had its problem areas, sure, but it was contained and easy to dress and was surely shapeable to perfection, Amelia had always imagined, if she had ever had the motivation or desire. Maybe she should have posed nude for life drawing classes in college like Akiko and Dana had. At least that way there would be a record out there somewhere of how she used to be.

If she was being honest with herself, she also didn't like the vertical line on her stomach, or the changing nipples, or her paunchy face, or the acid reflux she got at least once a day now. She wondered if any of it would go away after the baby was born. She shoved the comforter off her legs. Fuck, you better be worth it, she thought and, probably in direct response, the baby double-thumped a limb against her insides.

She reached across for her phone on the bedside table and texted Seth. *Whatchu doing?*

Mixologizing

Guess what I just realized? I have a penis inside my body.

For 9 straight months? he wrote. *Muy jealous.*

When Amelia was in her twenty-eighth week, Seth called to tell her that he'd told his parents. Within an hour, Amelia and her parents had received a congratulatory email asking if they could meet up one evening soon to "discuss the arrangement."

Amelia took the subway into the city later that week. It must have been around six o'clock because the stations were full of people in work clothes, tapping on their phones. Since quitting her job, she had lost her sense of the hours when other people did their normal other-people things. She felt outside of time. Before the pregnancy, this had been a sad, alienating feeling—she would sit at her desk watching the sky turn dark behind the Pencil Factory, and wonder how her old students were faring under the replacement teacher, and whether Hank might come over that night. Now the timelessness felt like good practice for motherhood, when she would again be outside regular hours, but tethered to the baby's schedule.

As a mostly unbroken rule, Amelia's dad was the most even-tempered person in the family. When the girls had lived at home, he had occasionally gotten flustered by a missed curfew, or a bad grade in history ("It's my field," he would say, his face turning grim over someone's report card. "Why didn't you ask for help?"), or a window left wide open when the heat was running. But mostly he could be counted on to play the bewildered, put-upon dad-with-a-sense-of-humor, sighing dramatically when he was annoyed, and saying things like, "Can you girls turn down the Fiona Apricot music, I'm trying to read," which never failed to make everyone laugh.

So Amelia was surprised to find him being loud and grumpy when she got to their apartment half an hour before the Goodwins' arrival.

"What is all this stuff?" He was bent over the coffee table, tossing magazines around. "Why is it that sometimes I don't feel like I live in my own home?"

Amelia found her mom arranging a cheese plate in the kitchen. "He's in a bad mood," her mom said. "He thinks they want us to sign a contract. They mentioned something in the email. Good heavens." Her hand flew to her chest when Amelia took off her coat to reveal one of Hank's old BROWN UNIVERSITY LACROSSE T-shirts barely covering a seven-months'-pregnant belly. "I almost forgot."

"Me too," Amelia said. "I accidentally rubbed this guy's ass with my stomach on the subway. It was gross."

"Why don't you sit down?" her mother said.

"I will, when they get here."

"Not now," her mom said. "On the subway."

"No one budged," Amelia said.

"They're in denial," her mother said. "We're all in denial."

"Well, now I have to get changed," Amelia's dad said, stomping past the kitchen on his way down the hall. "Why do I have to be here for this? Why is there a 'this' in the first place?"

"Is he talking about the baby?" Amelia asked her mom, taking a seat at the table.

"No." Her mom pulled a bottle of blood-orange juice out of the refrigerator. "It's this meeting. The tone of the email was friendly but your dad's worried about this 'reaching an understanding' business. Joel Goodwin works in litigation. Dad thinks they're worried you'll want money from Seth one day."

"Oh my God, I almost spit out my juice." Amelia cupped her hand under her mouth and went to the sink, laughing. "How could they think that?" She wiped her chin with a dish towel. "Seth is a part-time bartender at (Le) Poisson

Rouge. He has three roommates, and he still has trouble paying his rent."

"Not from Seth. His parents. Dad thinks they're worried you'll go after them."

"So they want me to sign, like, a prenatal agreement? I don't care. I'll do it."

"It's the principle of the thing," her dad said, coming into the kitchen. His face was red above his shirt and tie. "You're not some white-trash girl who got knocked up just so you could scam some of the Goodwins' hard-earned cash."

"That's right," Amelia said. "I had a perfectly good book I couldn't finish."

"Mike," Amelia's mom said. " 'White trash'? That's not okay. I know you're worked up but—"

"There's no shame in that term anymore. My students use it all the time. Mimi? Isn't it okay to describe someone as white trash?"

"Is it? Um, I don't really—" Amelia leaned her elbow on the table and her chin on her fist. "I guess I'm really out of touch these days."

"Congratulations, darling!" Seth's mom was a short happy woman, with a Jersey accent and a year-round tan. She grabbed Amelia's face. "We're so thrilled for you. Really."

"Don't know why Seth didn't tell us sooner," Mr. Goodwin said with a smile on his face, reaching out to shake Amelia's dad's hand, and then hugging both women. "Guess he thought we'd be mad."

"He wanted to come tonight but he's working," Amelia told them.

"A boy," said Mrs. Goodwin. "You're going to have a boy."

"Come in, come in. Would you like juice? Or wine?"

"We brought champagne," Mr. Goodwin said, holding up a bottle. "Of course you can't have any." Everyone looked at Amelia and laughed.

"I'll get the glasses," Amelia's dad said, exchanging a glance with her mom.

"Follow me," her mom said. "Right in here."

The Goodwins had arrived with an agenda but it wasn't a financial one. After a round of cheers and a few questions about Amelia's pregnancy and due date, and a passing around of photos of their existing grandchildren, born to their daughter, Tammy—both of whom were pale-skinned and pinchlipped, and whom Amelia hoped mostly resembled Mr. Tammy—Mrs. Goodwin got to the point. "We're Jewish," she said. "Our kids are both Jewish. Our daughter married a Jewish guy."

"It's very important to us," Mr. Goodwin said to Amelia's dad.

"Amelia went to Camp Tziporah for years," her mom said. "She still has the necklace."

"I'd be fine with him having that as an influence," Amelia said. "You could have him for the Jewish holidays. We could have him for the others."

"And you'd be—" Seth's mother's hand went to her throat. "That would be okay?"

"Of course," Amelia said.

"And what's your plan regarding circumcision?" his dad asked, addressing Amelia directly now.

"Well—" Amelia thought about it, remembering all the nights she'd had to lie around in bed with Hank while he bemoaned the sensitivity he was sure he'd have if he hadn't been circumcised. "You can tell," he always said, "because it's sensitive all around here. So you know that extra skin would have been just as sensitive. I'm missing out. I was robbed. It could feel so much better."

Amelia wished she could explain to Seth's parents that, though she preferred the look of a circumcised one, she was going to forgo the bris to spare some future girl the arduous task of having to placate a guy in an interminable, phallus-gazing, postcoital rant. She said, "I'm not doing a circumcision. But we can talk about a bar mitzvah."

The Goodwins looked at each other and nodded. They seemed happy enough with that. The conversation turned to other issues.

"What are you going to be called, Nina?" Mrs. Goodwin asked her mom. "Grandma? Nanna? Nanny?"

"Oh God," her mother laughed. "I've been so busy, I haven't even begun to think."

"I was like that with the first one," Mrs. Goodwin said. "I felt that I was too young still to be a grandmother. You get used to the idea."

"Oh no, it's not about that," Amelia's mom said. "I just haven't—"

"I'm a Bubba," Mrs. Goodwin said, "and Michael's a Zayde."

"I want to be a Maman," said Amelia. "Like in French."

Amelia's mom raised her eyebrows at the Goodwins. "That's what happens when you have a baby at twenty-two," she said.

"Hey," Amelia said, "at least I'm not getting some bad tattoo or something."

"Yes," her mother said. "What a relief that is to me."

None of Amelia's friends had been to a baby shower before, let alone organized one, and it showed. They arrived at Amelia's apartment on the Saturday night of her thirty-second week, with the makings for whiskey sours, a piñata in the shape of a baby, and a T-shirt saying BIG FUN like the one worn by the fat girl in *Heathers*. ("That's dark," said Amelia. "Super dark." Then she pulled it on over her dress.)

They had a pizza party, immediately followed by an ice cream social. Then the other girls got drunk and watched Amelia stand in front of the piñata with an old tennis racquet in her hands.

"Smash it!" Akiko said.

"I feel bad."

"It's not a real baby."

"You made it look so realistic."

"It's got Melody Pops inside."

"Seriously?"

"And Pixy Stix."

Amelia whacked the fake baby until it was just a mess of plaster, newspaper, and glitter on the floor. The girls ate the candy and did the African Anteater Ritual dance from *Can't Buy Me Love*. Then they changed into pajamas and watched the movie itself. After that, Amelia sat on the couch with her T-shirt pulled up, and they all scrawled with Sharpies on her belly, as though it were a cast covering a broken limb.

GET WELL SOON! wrote Dana. Gabby drew a love heart with an arrow through it and the word MOM inside.

The girls had crimped their hair and were pressing decals onto their fingernails when the doorbell buzzed at around ten o'clock. "Did you guys get me a stripper?" Amelia asked, heading for the door. But it was Georgia and Isobel.

"Are we late?" Georgia asked.

"I didn't think any of you could make it," Amelia said.

"We brought you this." Isobel handed her a paper bag containing a big horseshoe-shaped inflatable cushion: aqua with yellow dots.

"It's to sit on," Georgia said. "When you're breast-feeding."

"For me to sit on or the baby?"

"I dunno," said Isobel. "For the baby, maybe? The woman at Bump said these are the biggest things right now."

"Take it back if you don't want it."

"No, I like it."

"How do you know? You haven't used it yet."

Her sisters came into the living room and looked around

at the other girls. "Cute," said Isobel. "This is just like your slumber parties when you were little."

"Yeah, except now we don't have your diary to read for entertainment," Gabby said.

"Are you serious?" Isobel looked at Amelia. "Is she serious?"

"She's joking," Amelia said. "Totally joking. Do you guys want a drink?" They didn't. Amelia sat on the couch and her sisters squeezed in next to her.

"How come your laptop's out?" Georgia asked. "Were you writing something?"

Amelia felt her face turn warm. "No, we were— Facebook-stalking all my old boyfriends."

"All?" Georgia said. "You've only had, like, two. Unless you count Seth as an ex-boyfriend now?"

"How would you know how many boyfriends I've had?" Amelia said. "You don't know everything."

"Sorry." Georgia tilted her head to the side. "So how many boyfriends have you had?"

"Um, three," Amelia said. "Including Seth." Her friends laughed. Georgia and Isobel visibly elbowed each other.

"Your sisters are bitches," Dana announced after they'd left. Amelia and her friends were lying on air mattresses in the living room—Amelia on her side, the others on their bellies—all sharing three pillows in the middle.

"Massive bitches," Akiko agreed.

"Oh, they're okay," Amelia said. "They try. They brought me a present."

"Your mom probably paid for it."

"True," Amelia said. She looked down at the inflatable cushion, which she'd put between her knees to take the pressure off her back. "Yeah. They are kind of bitches, I guess."

That Wednesday there was a new woman at yoga. She looked like she was about thirty, and she wasn't showing yet. There had been a few new students in recent weeks; a bunch of the women from before had already had their babies, and had either given up their yoga practice or switched to the Happy Baby class on Fridays.

The new woman laid her mat out in front of Amelia's, and she moved through the poses with ease and, Amelia imagined, some impatience. These days, Amelia found it difficult to maneuver herself into even the most basic positions. She was grateful for the slow pace of the class, the breeze-and-bells sounds playing through the speakers, the soothing voice of the instructor. She focused hard when they were told to visualize the beginning of their labor at the beginning of class, and she felt a surge of happiness when the instructor had them picture holding their newborns at the end.

In the changing room after class, the new woman said, "Excuse me?" to no one in particular. "Does anyone wanna go get a juice or something?" Amelia smiled and turned away, letting one of the other, newer students make plans with her. The woman was probably really nice but, with her tiny sports bra and flat, stretch-mark-free belly, she really had no idea what Amelia was going through. The trimesters of pregnancy were kind of like elementary, middle, and high school, Amelia decided. It would just feel weird now to hang out with someone who was so far behind.

When Amelia came out of the studio, Jane was standing in her old spot on the street, waiting.

"I told you already," Amelia said, coming up to her. "I'm keeping it."

"I know," Jane said. "I'm just taking a break from work." She linked her arm through Amelia's. "I'll walk you home."

"Finally," Amelia said, "someone treats me like a pregnant lady."

Jane was having a bad week. "I'm thinking about quitting my job," she said as they turned onto Greenpoint Avenue.

"Why?" Amelia asked. Jane's arm felt tiny against her side. "You love your job."

"I do, but I don't have time for anything else. And how do I know I want to do this forever? I'm twenty-seven. I feel like I'm putting all my eggs in one basket."

"You can change later, though, right?" Amelia said. "It's not like you're tied down."

"I don't know," Jane said. "Maybe I should go to grad school? But I don't know what I'd even want to study. I'd probably be applying for my same job afterward, in an even worse economy."

"So don't go to grad school."

"I guess."

When they got to Amelia's building, Jane turned to face her, reached out, and rubbed her belly. "You look lovely," she said. "Glowing and all that."

Amelia narrowed her eyes. "What's that supposed to mean?"

"Nothing! I really mean it."

Jane followed Amelia up the stairs and they stopped outside her door. "So, I have a yes-or-no question for you."

"Is this from Mom?"

"No. Between me and you."

"Shoot."

"Okay." Jane took a breath. "Should I have a baby?"

"No!"

Amelia was surprised to see Jane looking surprised. "Why not?"

"Because you don't want one."

"But what if I did?"

"You don't. You want to keep working your job. And going on dates. And maybe go back to school, like you said."

"I could have a baby instead of all that."

"Don't be dumb."

"Why are you being so mean about it?"

"I'm not. I just think it's a bad idea."

"Whatever." Jane cocked her head and put her hands on

her hips in an argument stance Amelia recognized from childhood. "You're just scared I'd take the attention away from you."

"Well." Amelia couldn't help herself. "It is kind of my thing right now."

"I knew it."

"Why don't you get your own thing?"

"I can't believe this," Jane said. "Suddenly you own pregnancy? Maybe we should put out a press release to alert the other billions of women on the planet."

"You're just jealous," Amelia said.

"You're just an attention seeker."

"Am not." Amelia reached out and grabbed Jane's ponytail. She yanked. "Take that back."

"Ow!" Jane grabbed a bunch of Amelia's hair. "Get off me!"

"You get off me."

"Take it back."

"You first."

They stayed like that, with their necks craned to the side, grabbing each other's hair with their right hand and using the left hand to try to fend the other girl off.

"Ow."

"Ouch!"

"Get off me."

"I'm going into labor!"

Jane let go. She looked panicked. "What should I do? Are you serious?"

"No," Amelia said. "I just had to get you off me. You psycho."

"You're the psycho." Both girls stood there, catching their breath and rubbing their heads.

"Do you want to come in for a second?" Amelia said. "I have to sit down."

Jane followed her inside and made some ginger tea. They sat at the kitchen table, blowing into their cups without drinking.

"Why don't you wait till I have mine and see if it seems like something you want?" Amelia said.

"Yeah, it was just a momentary idea," said Jane. "Like I said, I'm thinking about grad school." Her tone was still defensive, but when she stood up and put her cup in the sink, she said, "I'm sorry."

"Don't be," Amelia said. "This all just made me really happy that I'm not having a girl."

"Seriously," Jane said. "If I have a child, I'm definitely having an only child."

"Siblings suck," Amelia agreed.

"Sisters especially," Jane said. Then she left to go back to work, and Amelia lay down for a nap.

The editor who had acquired Amelia's book was a woman in her mid-thirties called Camille. She was tall and southern, sarcastic and whip-smart. Amelia had felt intimidated every time they had met or talked on the phone, but never so much as the day they met for a cup of hot cider on a bench in Union Square, a couple of blocks away from Camille's office, during Amelia's thirty-fourth week of pregnancy.

"Congratulations," Camille said, her legs wound around each other like pipe cleaners and her neck decorated with a nautical-themed scarf. "A lot of my friends from high school had babies at your age. You know what the best part is, right? You could be an empty nester by the time you're forty."

"Are any of your friends empty nesters already?" Amelia asked.

Her mind was too buzzy to sit still and listen while the editor answered. Camille had suggested this meeting, and Amelia was certain she was going to be asked about a time line for publication and, if she didn't have one, a time line for paying back her advance. She had spent the morning formulating a financial plan, emailing all the copywriting clients she'd ever had, and scouring baby forums to work out how much it cost to have one, wondering if she could breast-feed till the kid was of paper-route age.

"I'm sorry I let you down," she said. "I know you went out on a limb to buy the book in the first place. I want you to know I'll get the money back to you. I'm happy to commit to a payment schedule, or whatever you think is best."

"Psshhh." Camille shook her head. "You know I'd rather see you finish your book than see that money again. You're so funny, Amelia. You have a great voice. Are you sure you don't want to try to finish it? You could write about the pregnancy and the baby, or pretend neither of those things happened and just continue as you were. Whatever you want."

"I can't," Amelia said. "I just don't think it's gonna happen."

"In that case . . ." Camille leaned over her satchel and pulled out her iPad. "I wanted to ask you something." She went into Firefox and opened up the blog of a pretty young girl, who was pictured in her bedroom, kneeling on the floor in faux worship, in front of a shrine dedicated solely to—

"Stephanie Zinone," Amelia whispered, "from *Grease 2*."

The girl had low bangs and a purple headband in her hair, and she was wearing a Pink Ladies jacket inside out, just like Michelle Pfeiffer in the movie. She was staring wide-eyed at the shrine with a solemn, reverent expression on her face. It was an awesome picture.

"Do you know Sabina?" Camille asked her. "She's been writing a blog called *Rainbow Cake* since she was eight years old. She's a sophomore in high school now."

"No, I don't know it," Amelia said. "Her name's Sabina?"

"Yeah, she's Russian but she was born in Dubai. Her parents are engineers and they were working there. They moved to the States when she was about five. She actually taught herself English by reading Sweet Valley High books."

"Wow, I'll have to look her up."

"I think you'd like her blog. She does fashion shoots, little reviews. That kind of thing. She's got a good following. Anyway." Camille slid the iPad back into her bag. "I'm in talks with her about a book. I just wanted to run something by you. She has a piece about how when she was in grade school, she used to decide what to wear the next day by whatever color Katie Couric was wearing on the evening news. She had a system. I remembered your candy heart piece, which I love, and I wanted to see if you still plan to use it, in your book or your blog, or anywhere else. If you do, it's totally fine. Like I said, I love that piece—"

"It's fine," Amelia said. "She can have it."

"Are you sure?"

"Of course." Amelia rested her hands on her belly and forced a smile.

"So are you excited about the baby?" Camille asked. "Or scared? How does it feel?"

"It feels great," Amelia said, and for the first time, it came out as a lie. "I feel the happiest I've ever felt."

All the way down Broadway, Amelia didn't take in a thing she passed: didn't see a person she brushed by or even glance at the shoes in the window of David Z. Tears prickled on her cheeks and she pulled her hat down over her ears and tried to hide herself. Katie Couric, she kept thinking. Katie Couric on the evening news. She was in grade school. When Katie Couric was on the evening news.

A sob escaped her mouth at the corner of 9th Street. The other people waiting for the light looked over. A guy with a bike. A woman with a Strand tote. A few others. With her puffy coat and her makeup-less face and the big bulge at her midsection, she knew what she looked like to them: a young pregnant girl not even interesting enough to have her own reality show. A bookless writer. A blogless unicorn lover. A big stupid nobody.

The doors of (Le) Poisson Rouge were locked when she got there, and she banged until someone answered: an older man in a turtleneck who took one look at her and didn't try to stop her when she said she was there to see Seth.

She found him downstairs in the quiet nightclub. He was sitting at the bar, on the patron side, talking to a muscly bald guy, and he looked half pleased, half horrified to see Amelia approaching, her belly leading the way across the empty dance floor.

"Mimi," he said, standing up. "This is—what's wrong?"

"Oh, nothing." Amelia looked at the other guy and laughed. "Sorry. I just came to ask you a question."

"What is it?" Seth asked.

"When did—when did Katie Couric take over the evening news?"

Seth looked at his friend and back at her. "Who?"

Amelia started to cry again. Seth put an arm around her. "What's going on?"

Amelia said the first thing that came to her mind: "I just feel. So. Fat."

. . .

Later, after Seth had put her in a cab and given the driver the address, Amelia found herself lying on her parents' couch, her face buried in her mom's lap, sobbing for a good few hours, stopping every now and then to explain to her mom, again, about Sabina and her blog and her book and Stephanie Zinone and the Pink Ladies jacket.

"What does she know about *Grease 2?*" she asked. "What do I?"

"You know a lot about *Grease 2,*" her mom said, rubbing her back, and Amelia started to cry again.

"Why did I do this?" she said finally. "It's like I tried to commit suicide or something. It's like I just couldn't hack it. Who's gonna date me now? Who's gonna marry me?"

"I didn't know you wanted to get married," her mom said.

"I don't," Amelia said. "But why did I do this? It's like I'm nothing now."

"I think—" Her mom went quiet. Amelia stopped crying and tried to slow her breathing. She waited to hear what her mom thought. "I think you just wanted to keep busy and feel involved. And not writing the book made you feel futile. *That* part was the suicide. So you just did this big new thing. That's what I think. And I think you're going to be great at it."

"You do?" Amelia said, looking up at her mom.

"Sure," her mom said. "Better than me, anyway. I had no idea what I was doing. Still don't."

. . .

Amelia wasn't a great mother, or a bad one. She was just a mother. She had a hard first few months, worn down by sleeplessness and feeding difficulties and the urgent and constant recognition that it was her sole responsibility to keep another tiny human alive. When her sisters came over, swanning by on their way home from work or brunch or drinks or a date, Amelia was so excited to have them hold Henry for five minutes so she could shower that she didn't even try to register their feelings about her life or the way she looked or the state of her kitchen or the silent and blank computer sitting in the corner, the keyboard covered in a pile of mismatched socks, each about three inches in length.

"Hey, little perfect," she heard Celine say one day.

"Hi, precious moo," Jane echoed.

"You're not holding him right," Georgia said. "He's uncomfortable, give him to me."

Amelia wondered if her sisters might actually be capable of love and, more specifically, love for the little piece of illegitimate family kicking in their arms.

Her parents came often, her friends now and then, Seth brought his parents over, and Hank would text her on occasion to ask if there was anything she needed.

I'm fine, she'd text back days later, when Henry was in his sling and she finally had the use of her fingers. *You enjoy your feckless youth.*

. . .

The publishing industry was, as ever, teetering on the edge of demise. No one had been ready for e-readers, Amazon was soliciting books for publication all by itself, people were still writing op-eds that said things like "Call me a Luddite, but I just love curling up with a good old bound book, and a screen will never feel the same."

"But it doesn't matter how you feel," Amelia would mutter out loud to whatever well-meaning pundit it was that week.

Her old editor Camille had left her publishing house not long after Henry was born and gone to get an MFA, and either Sabina hadn't yet finished her manuscript or it had been buried at the bottom of some new editor's pile, giving it a long lead time, and a 2013 publication date. Amelia and Henry were on their way home from the park one afternoon, the boy just having learned to walk, when they saw it in the window of WORD bookstore. Amelia bought it and took it home and it sat on her bedside table, topped by book after book, while she was kept busy by her new schedule: freelance copywriting, nap times, mealtimes, playdates with kids from the park and their parents, kids from the YMCA and their parents, kids from Henry's preschool and their parents.

Occasionally, when her own parents offered to babysit, she would go out with her old friends, never failing to be the one who got the drunkest, stealing drags off people's cigarettes in the street. One time she made out with a Pratt student in the back of a crowded bar, declining his invitation to go home together with that glorious and improbable excuse: I have a kid.

"You what?" he shouted over the music.

"She has a kid," Akiko repeated. And the two girls laughed.

"Whoa," the guy said, "that's wild." He grinned approvingly, like she was doing it for a social practice class or a performance project. Then he went and talked to someone else.

And so Sabina's book had been out for a couple of years by the time Amelia found it under her pile, and tried to read it aloud to Henry one night at bedtime.

"Rainbow Cake & Yoo-hoo, and Other Balanced Meals," Amelia read off the cover. Then she opened the book.

"I love sugar cereals," the first chapter began. *"I love sugar cereals so much that the year I experienced my first bout of real freedom—I was eleven and my parents went away, and left us in the care of a crazy babysitter who was a junior at Vassar and had a penchant for giving herself acupuncture—I decided I would eat sugar cereal for every meal every day of that week. This was not an easy feat. Not because of Jasmine. She was in the bathroom carefully sticking needles into her temples. But because of my older brother Sergei. Who had a sweet tooth. And a proclivity for getting cavities. And who could never keep a secret. And who found me one day, outside in our tree house, devouring a bowl of Trix—"*

"What's sugar cereal?" Henry asked. "What's devouring? Where are the pictures? What's—"

Amelia gave up and reached for one of his regular books, the one about the lighthouse and the children of New York.

She left Sabina's book on the blanket beside her. She planned to finish the chapter when she got into her own bed that night but, as usual by that stage, she was too tired to do anything, and she fell asleep before she'd finished calculating how many hours she had of quiet before Henry was up again, singing in the living room. One second she was staring at the alarm clock, counting, and then her eyes were closed and the book fell out of her grasp and slipped down between the headboard and the wall. She found it there months later, wiped the dust off, and put it on the bookshelf. She would get to it later on, she decided, when she had more time.

Your Charm Won't Help You Here

Gallagher is working on his anger issues. Ellis has an infant son who is finally sleeping through the night. Skolski went to Penn State (so did his brother, his father, and his uncles) and he is very upset about the Sandusky scandal. Miller doesn't think men benefit from being married; he himself never resolved a single argument with his, thank God, ex-wife. The Albanian is excited to watch the fight tonight. Morris is on the phone with the relative of an elderly Romanian woman in a wheelchair. Coots is thirty-three and unmarried and, when in conversation, he involuntarily moves his lips as the other person is talking. He's the one fingerprinting me.

"Am I in trouble for something?" I ask as he uses his thumb to press mine down onto the screen.

"I'll explain later," he says.

. . .

Out in the main area, with the line of officers sitting up behind the counter, and the rows of travelers sitting and waiting, Coots lifts my suitcase onto a long table and pulls
surgical gloves onto his hands. He unzips the case and flips
it open. Inside, my clothes are a tangle of T-shirts and cut-
offs, and most of my shoes have escaped the plastic bags I
shoved them into. Everything looks like it's peppered with
sand. "Wow," I say. "It was much neater when I left Istanbul. It must have got shaken up on the plane."

He ignores me. He pulls my hand grinder out of the case,
opens it, and sniffs it. "What's this for?"

"Coffee."

He puts it on the table and holds up a scrap of paper.
"Whose phone number is this?"

"A girl in Istanbul."

"If I called this number right now, who would answer?"

"I guess that girl."

"What's her name?"

"I don't know. She was chatting to me and my friend at a
museum. She gave us her number in case we needed anything while we were in Turkey."

"What did you need?"

"I think she meant if we needed advice about places to
go."

"This isn't a whole lot of clothing. Where's the rest of
your clothes and belongings?"

"Some of it's in London, and some of it's in San Francisco. Oh, and I have a few things in LA, too."

"You can pack this up now," he says. "Bring it into that office when you're done."

"Okay, but what for? What's happening now?"

"For an interview."

"I'm a bit worried I'm going to miss my connecting flight. It boards in an hour."

"Then you better hurry up."

Are you there? I text my sister.

Hey! she responds a minute later. *You back in SF?*

No I've been stuck at immigration for an hour. Maybe they think I have drugs or something from Turkey.

Maybe they heard your music and consider it an act of terror?

Haha maybe I'll show them a pic of your face and request political asylum.

"No phones," Gallagher calls to me. "Put it away."

Coots is sitting behind a desk when I come in. The office is bare except for the desk, two chairs, a desktop computer, and a window on the wall that I assume is a two-way mirror.

"Do you speak English well enough to understand me?" he says as I sit down.

"Sorry?"

"This is the interview," he says. "The interview is beginning now."

"Oh, can we start again?"

"Do you speak English well enough to understand me?"

"Yes."

"Do you understand what I've said to you?"

"You mean, the question about whether or not I speak English?"

"Yes." He lowers his chin toward his chest and glares at me from beneath his eyebrows. "Do you understand me?"

"Yes."

"Where were you born?"

"England."

"Are you a citizen of England?"

"Yes."

Then he asks me if my mum is, if my dad is. He asks where my family resides, and if any of my relatives live abroad. "What is the purpose of your visit to the United States today?" he asks.

"Just a visit, I guess."

"Which country or countries did you visit before your arrival today?"

"I was in Turkey for two weeks. Before that I was in Cyprus, at a conference. And before that I was in London for a month. And before that I was in San Francisco." He's typing all my answers into the PC.

"Am I in trouble for something?"

"I'll explain it later. You used to live here."

"Yes, I lived in California for six years."

"What type of visa did you have at that time?"

"An E. E-40, I think?"

"That's not a visa category."

"Oh. It was a student visa. Whatever the code is for that."

"What line of work are you in?"

"I'm an editor-at-large for a film journal, and I teach now and then, at a few different universities."

He asks me if I'm married, if I have any kids. He asks if I have a boyfriend. "Well—" I shift a little in my chair. "Kind of. I don't really know."

"You don't know if you have a boyfriend?"

"Yeah, because—" I stop talking and his lips stop moving. "I don't know how much information you need. I was playing music with this guy, Lars. We thought we needed a fuller sound, so we could try to play bigger venues. So we got this guy Jacob to play trumpet with us. He's amazing, super talented. Lars made a rule that nothing could happen between me and Jacob because of the band, but then we did kind of start hanging out. Then we accidentally missed a few rehearsals and showed up late for a pretty important show. So then Lars said he'd wasted years of his musical life on me, and he left the band and started a new one. They're really bad, I saw them play. It's all kind of disastrous."

Coots stopped typing thirty seconds ago. "So, you do not have a boyfriend."

"Well—" I look at my reflection in the two-way mirror. If I'd known I was going to be interrogated today I might

YOUR CHARM WON'T HELP YOU HERE   297

have boarded the airplane wearing something other than an oversized NEIGHBOURS T-shirt I usually wear to bed and a pair of tights. I look back at him. "Yeah, I guess not. I guess now I don't have a boyfriend or a band."

The interview goes on, with Coots's lips moving as I talk, his typing ceasing when I'm only halfway into each of my answers. I'm waiting for him to realize that I'm not hiding anything, and let me go catch my flight, but it's hard to convince someone of your innocence when you don't know exactly what their suspicions are. At one point, Miller comes in and puts a stack of papers on the desk. The first page has a photo of me on it, and even upside down I can see it's a printout from the UC Berkeley website. Featuring the Amy Winehouse–style eye makeup everyone was trying and failing to pull off in 2006.

"There's more information online," Miller says, "but I'm sure she'll be happy to tell you *all* about it." He goes and stands in the doorway behind me. Coots leafs through the pages.

"Why didn't you mention any of this?"

"I did. Earlier, at the counter. That's why I initially came to the US. To get a PhD in cinema studies."

Coots types something into the computer. I'm feeling relieved, like the pages will legitimize me in his eyes, so I am completely blindsided when he tells me the interview is over and I will not be going on to San Francisco, that I will be on this evening's flight back to Istanbul, or I will be going to jail.

"But I have a visa."

"We just canceled your visa."

"Why?"

"Because you have an intent to immigrate."

"What?" I turn and look at Miller. His face is a blank, inscrutable wall, like the faces of all the officers here. I turn back. "What does that mean?"

"It means you're trying to make the United States your permanent home."

"But I'm not. My family's in London. I'm about to apply for postdocs in Britain and Germany. I have evidence of that in my inbox. Can I show you?"

"No," he says. "It won't make a difference. You're going back to Istanbul tonight."

My vision grows dark and furry around the edges. I feel like I'm about to throw up, which surprises me. I haven't thrown up from anything but alcohol since I was fourteen. I keep expecting to wake up and find that I'm still on the airplane, up over the Atlantic, my head on a stranger's shoulder, dreaming this whole thing up.

"You can't just send me back to Istanbul." My voice is getting higher now. "I don't know anyone there. I was traveling with a friend, but she's gone back to London."

"Well, you can buy a ticket to somewhere else from there, or you can visit the US embassy in Turkey and see if they'll issue you another visa. But I doubt they'll do that."

"I just got off an eleven-hour flight. You can't put me on another eleven-hour flight back to a city where I don't know anyone."

"That's exactly what we're doing."

"Can I please speak to the branch manager?"

"This isn't a bank, ma'am," says Coots.

"Ha!" Miller says behind me.

"Can I please speak to the manager of the—Secondary Questioning Room?"

"She's leaving," I hear Morris say outside the door. She comes in and stands over me. Morris is dressed like all the officers here: a short-sleeved navy shirt with a HOMELAND SECURITY patch on the sleeve, navy pants, a belt that holds a baton, a torch, and a gun in a holster. A nametag that reads: MORRIS. She has the stoniest facial expression of them all.

"What?" she says.

"I don't understand what's going on."

"Nothing's 'going on.' We're not letting you in." She keeps looking at where my top is slipping down off my shoulder, and I keep pulling it back up.

"But I haven't broken any laws."

"We looked at the dates of your visits, and it's clear that you've been coming in and out of the US for a while now, even after your school program was over."

"But is that illegal if I was issued a visa and adhered to the rules of that visa?"

"I don't have time for these mind games," she says.

"I'm not trying to play games. I have things in San Francisco. I have a storage unit. I have furniture I need to sell."

"You shouldn't have purchased furniture in a country you apparently don't intend to immigrate to."

"My computer's in San Francisco."

"Have someone send it to you."

"I don't understand," I say. "I'm a law-abiding citizen. I mean, not of here, but of the world. I'm a law-abiding world citizen and I've never even been warned about this."

"Well, lucky for us we caught you this time. When's that flight to Istanbul?" she asks Coots.

"Ninety minutes," he says.

"I can't go back to Istanbul," I say. "I feel like you think I'm some kind of wayward vagabond, but I don't just show up in cities unprepared and alone."

"The flight to Istanbul's free, because the airline's obligated to take you back when you're not permitted entry. You can purchase a ticket to England for tonight instead, but it can't stop anywhere in the US on the way. I'm guessing it'll be around three thousand dollars at this point."

"I can't afford that." I start to cry.

She turns to Coots. "Print her up."

Gallagher wants pretzels. Ellis has peanut butter pretzels, but Gallagher doesn't want that kind. The Albanian thinks Skolski should come watch the fight with him tonight, but Skolski thinks it will be too late after he gets home and cleans up. Also, Skolski doesn't really want to watch the fight. Ellis is meeting his wife for a late dinner. They're getting a babysitter. Ellis really likes his babysitter. She's sixteen and really great; the kids love her and she's helping Ellis plan a surprise birthday party for his wife. Miller's seen a photograph of the babysitter and his guess is that Ellis's wife doesn't like the babysitter as much as Ellis does. Ellis stares solemnly at his computer screen while Miller and Skolski laugh.

Do you know any way of getting in touch with m and d? I text my sister. *They still hiking? It's urgent.*

"Give me that phone." Gallagher walks out from behind the counter and comes toward me.

"I'm trying to tell someone what's happening."

"I told you to put it away." He grabs my phone with one hand and I hold on to it with two.

"Can I just send one text?"

"No." He yanks the phone from my hands and walks back to the counter. He puts it on a stack of paperwork, and it buzzes immediately. He ignores it.

Around half an hour later, when my flight to San Francisco is probably taking off, I'm sitting at the back of the room, trying not to cry, when a pair of legs in jeans appears in front of me. It's a tall woman, probably in her late fifties. She leans down and puts her face close to mine. I expect her to ask if I'm okay, but instead she says, "You staying here?"

"I'm not sure. I don't really know what's going on."

"They not letting me go. Why?" She has stringy brown hair and huge blue eyes. "I going Los Angeles, see my friend. I going home Poland April. Now I coming July. Why they not letting me go?"

"I don't know."

"Ma'am," Coots calls to me. "I need you to come over here now. Leave your suitcase where it is."

Along half the length of the long table, Coots has laid out a transcript of our interview, around ten pages in all. "Initial all these at the bottom and sign the final page," he says. "Then you're getting on that flight."

"For San Francisco?" I ask.

"For Istanbul."

"Istanbul, California?" I ask hopefully.

"Don't play games with me," he says. "Your charm won't help you here."

I look at the first page.

Q. Do you speak English well enough to understand me?

A. Yes.

Q. Do you understand what I've said to you?

A. Yes.

I read through the whole page and scrawl my name at the bottom.

"Initial it, don't sign your full name," Coots says. "You need to hurry up."

I try to read through the next page fast, but there are inaccuracies on it. He's misrecorded the number of years I was at Berkeley, and there's no mention of the sponsored teaching job I had at CCA last autumn.

"There are mistakes on here," I say.

"Ma'am," Coots tells me, "just sign."

"She needs to get through those fast," Morris warns from behind me.

"I can't sign something that's wrong. I don't know what this will be used for. Don't I get, like, a court-appointed lawyer?"

"No," Coots says. "You only get that inside the country."

"Where am I right now?"

"You're in the transit zone."

"Do I have the right to remain silent in the transit zone?"

"You can be quiet all you want, but you have to sign the interview."

I look over every page and see more omissions and mistakes. The last two questions he's recorded are:

Q. You may communicate with the consular officer of the country of your nationality. Do you wish to make the telephone call?

A. No.

Q. Being that you have been in CBP custody for more than three hours' time you are afforded a notification call placed to whomever you wish, on your behalf. Is there anyone you would like me to call for you?

A. No.

"Are you done?" Coots asks.

"There are questions on here I wasn't asked. About contacting people." He's still Milli Vanilli'ing everything I'm saying. "It says I answered, but I didn't."

"I was trying to get through the interview as fast as possible, to get you on that plane."

"These forms have factual errors on them. I'm not trying to be difficult, but I can't sign something I didn't say."

"Fine." He steps in front of me and gathers up the pages. "Why don't we do the whole interview again?"

"We don't need to redo the whole thing. But I'd like to correct the mistakes, and speak to my consulate."

"Let's do the whole interview over again," he says. "Why not? You've missed that flight to Istanbul. We have all night."

"This is Officer Morris from the Department of Homeland Security at the Philadelphia International Airport," Morris says. "Morris," she repeats. "We don't give out first names.

"The consulate's closed," she says, handing me the phone. "I got transferred to someone in England."

"Hello?" I say as she leaves the room.

"Hi there," says a weary male voice. It's probably around eleven P.M. in the UK.

"Hi, hello, thank goodness. I'm a British citizen. I'm in transit on my way to California, but I'm being denied entry to the States, even though I haven't done anything wrong."

I swear I hear him take a sip of what is probably a cup of tea before he says, "Yeah, unfortunately we don't interfere with the visa decisions of other countries. It's not in our jurisdiction."

"They're going to put me in jail. Can you at least help me convince them that I've done nothing wrong?"

"Yeah," he says. "Unfortunately, there's nothing I can do."

"Would you be able to call someone I know in London and tell them what's happening?"

"I can't place any calls on your behalf."

"Can you send an email or a text message or anything?"

"I'm sorry, there's really nothing I can do."

"Well, can you maybe pretend to be David Cameron and call the airport and tell them to let me go? They won't know the difference."

"It would be a crime for me to impersonate the prime minister."

"How about Prince Charles, then?"

"I'm sorry. I can't help you. You'll have to do whatever they say."

What's going on?! There's a text message from my sister when Morris hands back my phone. *I called mum and dad but they're in the lake district out of range.*

There's also a dick pic from an Oakland number I don't recognize with a message saying *You back yet?*

"I have no idea who that's from," I tell Morris when she sees the screen, but then I realize that probably makes me look worse than if I did know.

I'm not allowed to reply or send any messages or call anyone from my phone. I have to read a domestic number out to Morris, and she'll dial it from the phone on the desk, and let me speak.

I try to think of someone to call, someone decisive and levelheaded; someone with some knowledge of the legal system or the immigration system, or someone who might know someone who knows about those things. But I don't know anybody like that. So I just call the person I always call when I'm having a freak-out.

"Luke."

"Hey, brat."

"I'm having a freak-out."

"Why you calling from a blocked number?"

"I need to talk to you," I say. "Are you sitting down?"

"No, I'm at the sample roaster. Lydia's competing in the barista competition, and I want her to use this El Salvador I just got in. So I'm standing up. Well, I'm kind of leaning, against the roaster."

"Okay, that's good enough. Listen." I tell him the details of what's been going on, but he can't understand what I'm saying, so I stop crying long enough to tell him again.

"Oh my God," he says. "I've never heard of this. What's an 'intention to immigrate'? Is that a thing?"

"I don't know. It's like a pre-crime. I seriously feel like I'm in *Minority Report* right now."

"What can I do? Would it help to call nine-one-one? Just to see if this is even legal?"

"I don't think so. I think these people are more powerful than the police."

"Should I call Gabe and ask him to drive down and bail you out? He lives on the East Coast now, in Ithaca."

"I don't think this is a bail situation. Can you do me a favor, though, and look up flights to London from Philadelphia, leaving tonight?"

"Of course," he says. "It's Claire," he tells someone else. "Calvin says hi. He says to remind you he has your projector and a bunch of your Criterions."

"Okay, tell him to just keep that stuff for now."

"She's crying but she says hold on to it."

"Luke! Don't tell him that! I don't want him to know that. I don't want anyone to know."

He looks up flights on his phone and finds a British Airways one, leaving in an hour. It costs three thousand, three hundred dollars.

"Do you have that?" Luke asks.

"I have it. But it's all I have."

"Well, I hate to say it, but if the flight back to Istanbul's free, maybe you should just take it. That way you can go to the embassy there and work this out."

"The thing is," I say, "I don't think I can handle a night in jail. I'm freaking out from being detained at the airport. I think I'll completely lose my shit if I get put in jail."

"Come on," he says, "you're tougher than that."

"I'm really not."

"You've gotten through stuff before."

"Not on my own."

"You moved to a new country by yourself."

"I got so stressed out, I gave myself mono."

"Oh, yeah. You bounced back from the mono, though."

"I gave it to you and you got over it before I did."

"Oh, right. Huh. Well, you survived your relationship with me."

"That's true. That's definitely the most trapped I've ever felt."

"See?" he says. "You got this. One day it'll just be a crazy story you'll tell of something funny that happened."

"But it's not funny."

"Time's up," Morris says from the doorway.

"Who's that?" Luke asks.

"It's Officer Morris from the TSA."

"I hate the TSA," Luke says.

"I work for the Department of Homeland Security," Morris says.

"I hate them, too," he says. "I'm so ashamed of my country right now."

"Don't say that. They're probably recording this."

"Let's go," says Morris.

"What should I do?" Luke asks. "Should I call Jacob?"

"No. We're not together anymore."

"What about James and Amanda? Brook? Rafael?"

"No. Please don't say a word to anyone."

"Can I at least tell Lydia?"

"Of course, but no one else. I don't want anyone to know this is happening. I just don't want people to think of me like this."

. . .

The walk through the airport is slow because I have cuffs around my ankles as well as my wrists. And because they took the shoelaces out of my plimsolls so I sort of have to slide my feet along the floor. They took my hair elastic, my necklaces, and my earrings, and they made me pull the drawstring out of my hoodie before I put it on. They took the Klonopin I had in case I couldn't sleep on the plane, and said they'd give it back to me later. They took my suitcase and carry-on bag, and locked them inside an office.

The airport is completely deserted. The line dividers are still up in the customs area, but there are no people waiting, or officers waiting to stamp them through. The baggage carousels are stationary, the arrivals screens are blank, and the PA system is silent. The liquor and perfumes are all locked up inside the duty-free shops. It would all be eerily serene, except that the Polish woman is also here, also being escorted in cuffs, and she is screaming. "Why? Why you take me? I am not Al Qaeda! I am not terrorist!"

"Looks like it's ladies' night tonight," Skolski says.

"Uh-huh," says Gallagher. "Looks like it."

"I am not terrorist! I am not bandit!"

"Jesus Christ," Gallagher mutters, "shut up."

"Can I ask why she's being detained?" I ask the officers flanking me.

"We're not gonna tell you that," Gallagher says.

"I just want to know if it's something violent or danger-ous, because I assume we're going to be transported and locked up together."

"Even if it's something violent," says Ellis, "she's not gonna do much harm to you with her hands and legs in cuffs, is she?"

"Fuck!" she screams. "Why you taking me?"

"How long is the drive to the jail?" I ask.

"About an hour," Ellis says.

"Why are you answering her questions?" Gallagher asks him. "If you answer her questions, she's going to ask more questions."

Ellis shrugs. "I'm just trying to get outta here."

We go through a pair of double doors, down a long corridor, and into a freight elevator. The Polish woman stands next to me. She's a lot taller than I am. She's wearing jeans that cinch over her waist, white socks, black sandals, and a red nylon zip-up sweatshirt. I'm pretty sure her hands are the most enormous hands I have ever seen on any person in person.

All the officers are here, too: Coots, Morris, Ellis, Gallagher, The Albanian, Skolski, and Miller. Out in the customs hall, when I first arrived, there were officers of all ages and ethnicities—black, white, Asian, Hispanic, in their twenties, forties, sixties—but the staff of the Secondary Questioning Room are all of one type: white and military-aged, with the close haircuts of soldiers and the aggressively washed faces of people who believe they're dealing with scum all day.

The Polish woman looks down at me. "Why? Why they taking me?"

"I don't know," I say. "I don't get it, either."

The officers ignore us. If I were Nicolas Cage I'd be elbowing someone in the jaw right now, but I'm me, so I cry tears onto my feet and watch them sink into my shoes.

The van is dark gray and windowless. It's hard to climb up without the use of my hands. Morris steps in after me and tells me to sit on a narrow steel bench that runs along one wall.

"Can I just please sleep in the airport?" I ask her.

"No."

"I can sleep on a chair."

"You can't stay here. We're not a twenty-four-hour facility."

"Is there an airport motel I can stay in?"

"We wouldn't allow that. You might run away."

"I won't. You can put an ankle monitor on me."

"We don't do that." She reaches across me for a strap.

"I really, really don't want to go to jail."

"You should have thought of that when the flight to Istanbul was leaving and you were playing word games and arguing semantics with me."

"I wasn't playing games."

I hold my hands up while she straps me in. When she's done, I'm pinned to the wall like I'm on an amusement park ride that's about to start spinning. She turns to leave. "Can I just ask you one more question?" I say.

"What is it?"

"How likely is it that I'll be granted another visa anytime soon?"

She shrugs. "It's very unlikely."

"How long till I'll be allowed back in, do you think?"

"Years, probably. Ten years, twenty years. Maybe never. It just depends."

"Oh my God." For some reason, I think of my bike, locked to a street cleaning sign outside Jacob's place, and I wonder what will become of it.

"Listen," says Morris. "You're acting—" She glances over her shoulder and lowers her voice to an almost-whisper. "You're acting like this is the end of the world. It's not the end of the world. I won't lie to you. You're going to have an unpleasant—what? Forty-eight hours. But then you'll be back in Turkey."

Suddenly Morris's face is different. It's not stern and unreadable. It's—a face. A nice, kind face. Suddenly she looks like someone I could imagine sitting with at a kitchen table, drinking tea and talking about my disastrous love life and how horrendous her job is. I look at her hands and notice she's wearing a wedding ring. I picture her lying on her side at night, with someone's arms around her, hugging away her day.

"It's just forty-eight hours," she says again.

I want to say that it's not always the amount of time you experience something that determines its impact on you. I also want to mention the bike. But I don't want to be accused of playing games, and I don't want her face to go back to how it looked before, so I don't say anything.

"Do you want to take that Klonopin now?" she asks. "Then you can get to jail and fall asleep."

"I can't. It'll totally zonk me out. I need to be awake to deal with whatever happens when I get there."

It's hot in the van—it's a hot night in Philadelphia—but once we start moving, the air conditioner comes on. There are no lights back here, it's very dark, and for the first time since I landed at the airport, five or six hours ago, I'm not under fluorescent lights. I don't have to answer anyone's questions, or defend myself, or ask what's going on, or what's going to happen next.

To my right, there's a caged plastic window that looks into the front of the van. Miller is driving and Coots is riding shotgun. To my left is the Polish woman. She is sitting behind a thick cage wire divider, and she's still shouting. "Why? Why you taking me? America. Ha!"

I stare at the wall opposite me. My head is aching and my eyes sting from all the crying. I also, I realize, haven't eaten or drunk anything in a long time. The last thing I had was a bottle of raki with Ellie at the airport in Istanbul, before she left for London, and I ran to catch my flight to the States.

"Why you taking me?" the Polish woman yells. "You no taking me. No!"

"Hey," I say.

She stops shouting but doesn't say anything.

"Hello?" I say.

"Yes?" she says in the dark. "They taking us jail? I don't believe."

"What's your name?" I ask. "I'm Claire."

"What my name is?"

"Yes. Mine is Claire."

"Boleslawa," she says.

"Okay. Boleslawa. They told me the drive is one hour."

"One hour?" she repeats. "Why?"

"I don't know. That's where the jail is."

I turn my head and try to see through the window and out the windscreen. I can tell we're on a highway, but the plastic is too fuzzy for me to read the signs above the road. Miller and Coots are talking to each other, but the drone of the air conditioner drowns out their voices. I wonder what this van looks like to the Philadelphian people passing us on the road.

I'm amazed by how sterile it is back here. Everything is stainless steel and bolted down. You could bang against the cage or try to break the plastic window with your feet and nothing would budge or crack. You could puke or bleed, and they would just hose it off and erase all signs.

"Boleslawa?" I say, practicing my pronunciation.

"Bobbi," she says. "Is easy, just Bobbi."

"Bobbi," I repeat. "Cool." She wouldn't exactly be my first choice of companion in a Pussy Riot–type situation, but she's who's here.

. . .

When we walk into the jail, it's like we're interrupting a joke. There are two officers in uniform behind a window, and a guy in scrubs leaning against a wall. They're all grinning like someone said something hilarious just before we came in.

Coots unlocks my handcuffs and tells me to turn around so he can unfasten the big leather belt they're attached to. "Watch out for this one," Miller says. "She has a problem with authority." I'm taking in this information about Bobbi when I realize that everyone's actually looking at me, including Bobbi.

"I don't have a problem with authority," I say. "I just didn't want to be deported."

Coots and Miller hand over some paperwork and leave. We're no longer in their custody. We're now in the custody of an older white guy with a sweaty forehead, and a pasty-faced younger white guy with glasses.

"Which one of you's from England?" the older guy asks.

"Me."

"Why you here? If I was you, I'd be in London, getting ready for the Olympics. Wanna switch places?"

"That depends. Can you get Netflix on that computer or is it just Solitaire all night?"

The younger officer comes out to where we are. "Whose is the Klonopin?"

"Mine."

"Do you want to take it now?"

"Are we going to sleep now?"

"You've gotta be processed first."

"Okay, I'll take it later then."

Bobbi has some medication, too, for her blood pressure. The officer says he'll keep our pills and pass them on to the nurse.

"All right," the older guy says from behind the glass. "Go to seventeen."

"Sorry?" I ask.

"Go to cell seventeen. Up there, on the left."

We walk up a short corridor and look in. It's a tiny, windowless cell, probably two meters by three, with a bench along one wall, a small metal sink, and a steel toilet bowl with no seat. The younger officer comes up behind us and tells us to step in. Bobbi goes in. I step in and, as I do, I see the officer go to press a button out on the wall.

I step out. "I changed my mind," I say. "I want the Klonopin. I'd like to take that pill now."

"It's too late, ma'am," he says.

"Please. Can I just take it now?"

"You'll have to see the nurse. Step in."

I step into the cell again and, again, I see him go to press the button. I step out.

"Yes?" he says.

"Can I please see the nurse now?"

"No."

"When can I see the nurse?"

"After we've processed you."

"When is that?"

"I'm not sure. We'll let you know when it's time."

"I'm very scared of being locked inside a cell."

"You should have thought of that before you went and broke the law."

"Can I talk to you about that? Because I don't think I did break the law."

"Ma'am." He shakes his head. "I was born *at* night, but not *last* night."

"I'm being accused of a pre-crime."

"You need to stop talking now and step into the cell."

I step in and he presses the button, and the door closes behind me.

Bobbi is sitting on the bench. I go over and sit on the other end of it. I look around. There's a meshed window in the door and below it a slot where I guess people get their meals. On the wall next to that, what looks like an intercom, with a speaker and some buttons. The overhead lights are fluorescent, the walls are white cinder block, the bench and the floor are concrete. Above the sink, stenciled in big black letters it says:

WASH HANDS

I pull my hood onto my head, put my feet up on the bench, and hug my arms around my legs.

"What we doing?" Bobbi asks.

"I guess we're waiting to be processed."

I try not to think about the locked door. I try to ignore it completely. When that doesn't work, I try to remember other situations when I was locked inside somewhere and didn't even care or think about it. The eleven-hour flight I just took from Istanbul, for example.

"We are here"—Bobbi points down—"every night?"

"Just tonight," I say. "Tomorrow I go back to the airport. I'm assuming you do, too?"

"They take us airport this?" She holds her wrists together.

"You mean with handcuffs?" I look from her enormous hands to her worried face. "I'm not sure."

I stare at the WASH HANDS. I decide to make as many words out of the letters as I can, but then I don't make any.

"We are here every night?"

"Just tonight," I say. "One night."

"Tomorrow they take us this?" She puts her hands together.

"I don't know," I say, "but I assume so, yeah."

"No!" Her eyes widen. "But tomorrow will be people in airport. See us, this?"

I'm on a fault line, I'm on a fault line.

"What we doing?" Bobbi asks.

"We're waiting for someone to come and get us, so we can be processed. Whatever that means."

I'm on a fault line and I'm losing ground.

"We are here every night?"
"You mean all night? Yes, we're in jail all night."

I'm on a fault line, I'm on a fault line, I'm on a fault line, and I'm battening down.

It's a song Lars wrote after he left our band and started a new one. I saw him play it onstage at the Hemlock, the last time I saw him. I haven't thought about it since then, but it's running through my head now, over and over.

"Why? Why they taking me? I going Los Angeles, see my friend. He say no."
"What did they tell you? Did they give you a reason?"
"They not saying me nothing!"
"Do they think you're trying to live in the States?"
"We are here every night?"
"Just tonight. Tomorrow we go back to the airport."

I'm so damn tired of waiting for the crash. Turning under tables and praying it'll pass. I'm on a fault line—

"Tomorrow we go airport?" Bobbi asks me. I know when I look over, she's going to have her wrists together. "With this?"
"I don't know," I say. "If we do, maybe you can put your sweatshirt over your hands so no one can see."

"No," she says. "With this? Would be bad."

"Why is it so bad that people at the airport see that? Why do you care? Are you worried someone's gonna film it and put it up on YouTube? That would get like twelve views. I wouldn't even worry. Unless you're on the run or something?"

"We are here every night?" she asks.

I'm on a fault line, I'm on a fault line, I'm on a fault line and I'm losing ground.

"What we doing?"

"We're waiting."

"Tomorrow we go airport this?"

"I'm not sure. Maybe we can ask the wardens when they come and get us."

"What we doing?"

"We're just sitting here."

"What we doing?"

"We're just sitting in a cell."

"What we doing?"

"I don't know. I guess we're kind of—languishing."

It goes on like this for hours, with Bobbi asking and me answering, and Bobbi asking again. I can't tell whether she's hiding something or having some kind of psychotic episode, or maybe it's a reaction to her blood pressure. I feel like my own blood pressure's starting to rise, and I want to ask her to stop talking, but I'm scared she'll start screaming like before or have some kind of meltdown, so I answer every question in a calm voice and then try to ignore her and do steady yoga breaths until the next question comes.

I have to pee, but I don't really want to pee ten centimeters away from her. I stand up and go to the door. I can't see anything through the window but a section of empty hallway. I press a button on the intercom thing. Nothing happens. I press it a few more times. No one comes.

"I don't believe it," Bobbi says. "I don't believe it. Tomorrow we go with this?"

I sit down and lean my head back on the wall. I try to work out what time it is. If I was at the airport for, say, six hours, then in the van for one hour, and in here going on maybe four hours, it's probably around two in the morning.

Not feeling steady on my feet. Don't feel at home on my own street. I'm on a fault line.

I close my eyes and I start picturing my friends, my American friends—in San Francisco, Oakland, LA, and New York. In New Orleans, Austin, Atlanta, and DC. And Ithaca, wherever that is. I think of my friends who took teaching jobs in small college towns I've never been to: Auburn, Alabama; Moscow, Idaho; Gambier, Ohio.

I think about my American friends and wonder if I'll ever get to see them again. I think about them and I wonder if it's possible to be a patriot of a country that isn't yours. Not an intent-to-immigrate-type patriot. Just, like, a spectator on the sidelines, eating cotton candy and waving at the big parade.

I think of my American friends and I hope they'll never picture me here, powerless and nullified, locked inside a jail cell, somewhere in Philadelphia. Because I'm scared that if they knew about it, they'd believe that if I wasn't allowed in—if I got locked up and sent away—I must have done something wrong, and deserved this somehow.

"We are here every night?"

"Hey, Bobbi, do you have a family?"

"If I have family?"

"Yeah."

"I having one daughter. And ex-husband."

"I have a brother and a sister," I tell her. "My brother and his wife are gonna have a baby. So I'm gonna be an auntie soon!"

"We staying here every night before airport?"

It's just a fault line posing as a punch line, says it won't hurt me but just give it time.

It's just a fault line posing as a friend of mine. Say you'd never hurt me but that's just your line.

I close my eyes again and see myself back at the airport. I see all the officers, sitting around talking. But in my mind, I'm not sitting across the room from them like I was earlier today; I'm sitting among them, and we're chatting. Miller says something rude about his ex-wife and I say, "You know what? You shouldn't judge all relationships by one bad one.

It sounds like you ended up with the wrong person. But you could meet the right person one day. It's just a matter of chemistry." Miller smiles and admits that I may be right.

"And you," I tell Coots in my mind. "You could probably do pretty well for yourself. You kind of look like a skewed Ryan Phillippe. Maybe you could grow your hair out a bit. And honestly, you should probably think about switching jobs. This one isn't doing you any favors." The other officers laugh and tell him maybe he should listen to me. I'm basking in the feelings of camaraderie when I hear voices outside the door. I open my eyes. Two officers are escorting a girl down the corridor in the direction of the front desk.

"You'll have to take the laces out of those sneakers," the male officer tells her.

"Okay," the girl says.

"Is that your real hair?" the female officer asks her.

"Yeah." Half the girl's head is shaved, the other half is in braids. She tugs on the braids. "They're real."

Bobbi gets up and bangs on the door. "Hello? Hello!"

The female officer looks in at us. "I'll come back," she says. A few minutes later, she opens the door and we flutter to it.

"What we doing?" Bobbi asks her. "We sleep this?"

"I don't know," the officer says. She's short and black, and she's smiling at us like she actually wants to help. "I'll go find out."

"Thank you," I say. "Also, I have to pee. Is it possible to do that somewhere a bit more private?"

"Okay."

"Seriously?"

"Nineteen's empty now. You can use that one."

"Oh my God, I love you."

"No need for that. Come on out."

Cell nineteen is identical to cell seventeen, except for a few pieces of toilet paper that someone stuck in the air-conditioning vent. It's not really that much more private in here; the officer stands outside the open door the whole time, keeping an eye on both cells. Three or four nights ago I was at a party in Istanbul, peeing in a doorless bathroom while a gay guy called Zeki kept watch for me, looking back every few seconds to see if I was done. I try to pretend this is exactly like that. I try to pretend this isn't that weird.

The girl with the braids is sitting in the nurse's office. She has her arm on the desk and her head down on her arm. She's black and she's wearing a pink tank top, and she has the word CAT tattooed above her right shoulder blade. On the desk in front of her, there's a pile of orange prescription pill containers.

"Catherine?" the processing officer says.

"I have Catherine here," the nurse calls out.

"Okay." He looks over to where Bobbi and I are sitting against the wall. "Claire?"

I go and sit in the chair opposite him. He's a middle-aged Latino man with hunched shoulders and a worry line across his forehead. On the wall behind him is a handwritten sign that reads: ALL NIKE X SHOES HAVE A HIDDEN COMPART-

MENT IN THE SOLE. THEREFORE NIKE X SHOES ARE NOT PER-
MITTED TO BE WORN BY INMATES OR STAFF IN THIS FACILITY.
On the wall to my left is a printed sign about sexual assault.
There is a zero-tolerance policy toward sexual assault in this
jail, it says, and inmates should report any incidents to the
officer in charge.

The processing officer asks for my birthdate, my eye color
and hair color. He asks me where I'm from. "What did you
do?" He leans back in his chair. "Overstay a visa? Work il-
legally?"

"I don't really know. They think I'm trying to immigrate
here. I still don't quite understand it."

"Ah, yes," he says. "America isn't the same place since
September eleventh. There's a dark side now. Okay, look in
the camera." Before I have a chance to locate the camera—
a spherical ball on a stem sitting next to his computer—he's
taken my photo. He prints out a card with my details on it,
and laminates it. CLAIRE OGLIND, it says, FEMALE, AGE 30.
EYES BROWN HAIR BROWN. STATUS: NONRESIDENT ALIEN. In
the photo, my head is bowed and I'm looking down into my
lap. I have an expression on my face sadder than I knew I
was capable of. Like, Mother Mary sad. "Can I get a copy of
that?" I ask him.

"No," he says, "it's for your cell door."

When it's Bobbi's turn to be processed, I go back and sit
against the wall. Catherine is still leaning on the desk, and
the nurse, a wan white woman with cropped red hair, keeps
waking her up to ask her questions.

"You'll have your medical intake in the morning," the

processing officer tells Bobbi and me. He hands us each a Styrofoam cup of water and a small envelope with our pills in it. Bobbi puts her medication in her mouth and swallows. I slip my Klonopin into my pocket and drink the water.

On our way through the jail, we pass a bunch of other cells. Some of them still have the lights on, and I catch sight of the people locked inside. One woman is standing with her hands on her hips. She's wincing and rotating one of her ankles like it's injured. In another cell, two women are sitting on opposite ends of the bench, heads leaned back against the wall, staring at nothing. One of them looks about fifteen. Everyone seems bored, miserable, and calm—either they're done freaking out about being in here, or they didn't freak out to begin with. We must be in a women-only section, because all the inmates are female. And though I've heard the statistics, and I thought I understood the crisis, I'm still stunned to realize that every woman in here is black.

Cell twenty-three is the same size as the other cells, but it has two concrete benches in it, running along adjacent walls, with a flat rubber mattress on each one. Next to each mattress is a pile of sheets, a thin gray blanket, and a mini toothbrush and tube of toothpaste.

"Make your beds," the processing officer tells us from the doorway. My mattress has a huge rip down the middle with stuffing coming out, but I don't care. I'm so relieved to finally be going to bed.

"Okay," he says when we're done. "Go to sleep."

I slip my feet out of my shoes and lie down. "Do you know what time they're coming to get us in the morning?" I ask him.

"Early. Maybe six o'clock."

"What time is it now?"

He checks his watch. "Ten of four. Go to sleep now." He leaves the cell. The lights go out and the door slides shut.

"We have two hours to sleep," I tell Bobbi.

"Two hour? Only two?"

"Apparently."

The room is dim now, with a slant of light coming in from the hallway. "I have to pipi," Bobbi says.

"Okay." I turn over and face the wall while she goes. When she's done, I get up and brush my teeth. Then I get back into bed. I look around at the benches, the toilet, the sink.

"I don't believe it," Bobbi says. "Why? Why they taking me?"

"Hey, what's your daughter's name?"

"My daughter? Jadviga."

"That's a nice name," I say.

"Thank you."

"What town do you come from in Poland? Warsaw? Krakow? Where's your home?"

"My town? Is Lubin."

"I've never heard of it. Is it nice there?"

"Why I no going Los Angeles?"

"I don't know."

"Why? Why they not let me go?"

"Bobbi, I'm gonna go to sleep now," I say. She doesn't answer. "Good night."

After a long pause she says, "Good night."

I pull my hood onto my head, pull my sleeves down over my hands, and yank the blanket tighter around me. I reach into my pocket, pull out the pill, bite into it, and swallow half. I lay my head down and, with a camera behind plastic in the high corner of the room filming me, I fall asleep.

There are voices in the corridor and they wake me. I go to the door. I can see three other cell doors from here, but I can't see inside. I see shadows moving in all three windows, though; inmates hovering around their doors. I sit on my bed and wrap the blanket around me. About ten minutes later, the lights blink on and the young officer with glasses opens the door.

"Time to wake up," he says. Bobbi lifts her head.

"Are we going back to the airport now?" I ask.

"No," he says. "You're seeing the nurse for an intake."

"But we're leaving today."

"Everyone has to see the nurse."

This morning's nurse is a black woman in her thirties, with blue scrubs and a tattoo of a kite on her left forearm. She asks me a bunch of questions about my medical history. I tell her I'm allergic to bee stings, I've been a vegetarian for fourteen years, and I used to smoke cigarettes but I quit a couple of years ago.

There's a note stuck to the side of the PC that says the rules have changed and female inmates now have to discard their own pregnancy samples. I'm wondering what that means when the nurse hands me a small plastic cup, and tells me to go into the bathroom and pee in it.

"Why?"

"For a pregnancy test."

"I don't need that. I know I'm not pregnant."

"Everyone has to do it."

The bathroom door locks from the outside so after I pee I stand inside, holding the cup and knocking, until Bobbi finally lets me out. The nurse takes the cup and puts a pregnancy test stick in it. Then we move onto the psychological part of the exam.

"Have you ever hurt yourself or had thoughts about hurting yourself?"

"No."

"Have you ever threatened to hurt yourself or others?"

"No."

"Do you ever feel like life is a roller coaster of ups and downs?"

"Yes, sometimes I do."

"Do you ever get angry or irritated that people you know are talking to you about their problems?"

I sneak a look back at Bobbi. "I try to be patient but occasionally it can get overwhelming, yes."

"You're not pregnant," the nurse says, and even though I wasn't worrying about it, I exhale with relief. "Take the test and throw it out in the bathroom." She rolls her chair over to a dispenser of hand sanitizer on the wall and pumps some onto her palm.

When I get back from the bathroom, I keep staring at the dispenser. Eventually I ask, "Would I be able to use some hand sanitizer?"

She glances at it. "Okay."

"Really?"

She nods.

"Oh my God, thank you." I go over and pump some gel onto my hands and rub them together. I feel so sticky, I wish I could rub it all over my arms and face. I wish I could dive into a pool of hand sanitizer right now.

When I sit back down, the nurse is holding a syringe. "Have you ever had a tuberculosis test?" she asks me.

I have no idea, but I stare at the needle and say I have.

"When?" she asks.

"Like, two months ago."

"Well, I have to give you another one. It's an airborne disease, so you might have contracted it since then. I'll inject this into your forearm and you keep an eye on it. If it gets swollen or hard in the next few days, go see a doctor."

"I really don't want to have that test."

"I have to give it to you."

"But I'm leaving this morning."

"Everyone has to be tested."

"Why does it even matter if I have TB? I'm leaving the country. I'm not gonna spread it to any of your citizens."

"It's mandatory procedure," she says.

"I know you're just doing your job and I don't want to make it harder, but I really don't want to have an injection."

"If you don't let me give you the shot, I'll have to get someone else to do it by force."

She puts on surgical gloves and comes around the desk and sits beside me. She holds my forearm with one of her hands. "It'll just be a quick prick," she says, "and then it'll be over."

I squint my eyes closed and wait for it to happen. But nothing happens. She runs a gloved finger along my forearm, probably looking for a vein. "When did you get these marks?" she asks.

I open my eyes and look. There are tiny red bumps on my skin, three on my hand, and around seven on my arm. "I don't know," I say. "They weren't there yesterday."

"Do they itch?"

As soon as she asks me that, they start to itch. "Yes." I scratch at them. "They really do."

"I think you may have contracted bedbugs."

"Oh my God. Please don't tell me that."

"Which cell were you in?"

"Oh my God. Twenty-three. And seventeen and nineteen."

"Okay. There's nothing we can really do about this here. When you go home, put all your clothes and everything you have with you in the dryer or in the freezer straight away. Take a shower, and don't scratch the bites."

"Maybe they're just from mosquitoes?" I say, examining them.

"No, they're lined up like that," she says. "I'm pretty sure it's bedbugs."

"I can't believe this," I say. "Can I please at least not have the TB test now?"

"You still have to have it. It'll just take a second." She holds the needle just above my forearm. "And then you can go back to your cell." Then she presses it in.

"Why you crying?" Bobbi asks me when she gets to our cell. She shows me the plaster on her arm. "Why I having this?"

"I don't know." She sits down next to me.

"You should stay away from me, Bobbi, and my bed, and probably yours, too."

"Why I having pregnancy test? I too old."

"I don't know."

"I fifty-nine. I sixty!" She gets up, goes to the door, and looks out. "Why they taking me? I go Los Angeles, I come back. I not doing nothing."

"I didn't do anything, either," I say. But I'm starting to doubt if that's true. Would all these people go to the trouble of putting me through all these steps and systems if I hadn't done anything wrong? Would those airport officers have questioned and fingerprinted me and interviewed me and interviewed me again and cuffed and escorted me to jail if they hadn't looked at the details of my life and seen that something wasn't right?

Would Lars write scathing songs about me if I hadn't been careless and selfish, and hurt him without even considering that I might?

Would Luke suggest that one day I tell this as a crazy story, if I didn't always view my life as something detached from me, reducing everything to a series of funny anecdotes to tell a group of tipsy couples at a Friday-night dinner or a Sunday lunch?

I know I didn't have an intention to immigrate. I always assumed that I'd take all my stuff and say goodbye and leave San Francisco permanently one day, just like all my academic friends had already done. But I never made plans to actually do that. I didn't have an intention to immigrate, I just didn't *not* have one. And maybe, in the end, it equals the same thing.

Breakfast is a brown tray separated into sections like a TV dinner. There's a slop of porridge, a piece of dried-up French toast, a sachet of table syrup, a small carton of milk, and a carton of orange drink with, the box says, up to 2 percent real juice in it. Bobbi drinks her milk and then her juice. "You can have mine, too," I tell her.

"You don't have?" she asks me.

"I know it's a waste of taxpayer money, but I really don't want any." I sit on the bench next to my bed and try not to scratch my bites.

"Bobbi," I say, "at the airport, did they ask you how much money you have?"

"Yes. I showing them."

"What did you show them?"

"I having three hundred dollar. I showing them."

"Maybe that's why they wouldn't let you in? Because they didn't think you had enough money to cover your time here."

"Why I need money?" she says. "I not eating much. I just taking sometimes fruit."

"If you don't have enough money, they're probably worried you'll work or do something illegal."

"My friend Los Angeles, she pays me food. Why it's their business? We go vacation Las Vegas. She pay everything. What I need? Nothing."

She gets up to pee. I look the other way.

"America," she says when she's done. "This is America. Ha!"

"Would this kind of thing happen in Poland?" I ask.

"Yes," she concedes, "happening most place."

Apparently the officers from the airport usually transport deportees to and from jail but, starting today, the Department of Homeland Security is outsourcing its transportation services—to the jail. The young officer with the glasses comes and gets us and takes us out to the entrance area, where the Olympics enthusiast from last night is waiting with a table covered in chains and handcuffs.

"Well blimey, mate," he says in a fake British accent. "If it isn't the Spice Girls." He looks from Bobbi to me, waiting for a response.

"Yep," I say. "Here we are."

It turns out the guy with the glasses is a new employee, and the Olympics guy is training him. He instructs him on how to fasten the big leather belt around my waist, while another guy leans in the doorway of an empty cell and watches.

"We going this airport?" Bobbi asks.

"Will we be taken through the airport in handcuffs?" I ask them.

"That's up to Homeland Security," Olympics says. "They won't be taking our cuffs, though. This equipment's expensive."

The rookie tightens the cuffs around my wrists, and then Olympics instructs him to put the leg shackles on me.

"We going this airport?" Bobbi asks again.

"They don't know," I tell her.

"No. With this?"

"She just told you she didn't know," says the guy in the doorway.

The officers glance at him and look away, but I can't help

grinning. He's young—eighteen, nineteen years old. A black kid in red shorts and a green Eagles T-shirt, with a layer of teenage baby fat he hasn't lost yet. "Do you work here?" I ask him.

He shakes his head. "I'm just waiting to go upstairs."

"Is that, like, the guys section?"

"Yeah."

"What are you in for?" Rookie asks him.

"I didn't show up in court," the guy says.

"Failure to appear?" Rookie stands up. "So, what, you're here for the weekend?"

"Yeah. Three days."

"It'll be okay," Rookie says. "You'll just be here for a few days and then you can go home."

The guy doesn't say anything.

"Next time, show up to court, okay?"

"Yeah."

It's probably before nine in the morning, but the air outside is already muggy as we shuffle across the car park. The whole place is surrounded by barbed-wire fences. It looks like we're in a pretty desolate area, at the end of a dead-end street in a half-rural, half-industrial part of town.

The van is exactly like the one from last night, except this time Bobbi and I get put into the front section together, she strapped against one wall, me against the other. Rookie steps out and slides the door shut. A minute later there's the whiny clicking sound of the engine turning over, but the van doesn't start up. It goes quiet for a second, and then there's the same clicking sound, followed by silence. I look through the little window and see Olympics in the driver's seat, turning the key. He tries a few more times and gives up. He and Rookie get out of the van.

We sit and wait. It gets stuffy really fast.

"Is hot," Bobbi says.

"I know."

"Hey, Galvarez, you got cables in your car?" Olympics calls to someone I can't see. "No way am I calling Triple A. Get your ass over here."

An officer pulls up in an SUV. He and Olympics attach jump leads between his car and the van. The SUV guy doesn't want anyone else touching his engine, but he also doesn't seem to know how to jump-start a car. "It's red to your positive and my negative," he says.

"I don't know about that," says Olympics.

"It goes on both positives," Rookie says. "It's definitely red to both positives."

"Is too hot," Bobbi says.

She's starting to ask about the airport again when I wriggle my hands and realize something amazing. "Guess what?" I say. "I can get out of my handcuffs." She watches as I wriggle my right hand and squeeze it through. I do the same with the left one. It's really tight but it comes out. "Oh my God," I say. "This is crazy."

I look around the van, wondering what I can do with my

hands. I could untie the leather belt but then my ankles would still be shackled, and, anyway, there's no door handle on the inside of the van and, anyway, I wouldn't try to escape. I'm not about to tap on the window or draw attention to the fact that my hands are free. So I just sit around and play with my hair for a bit. I chew on a fingernail, but it tastes like hand sanitizer. I'm trying to show Bobbi a shadow puppet of a reindeer on the door when the door slides open and Olympics sticks his head in.

"This won't take—"

I put my hands in my lap.

"What are you doing?" He pushes the door all the way open. "Are your hands free?"

"Yes."

"How did that happen?"

"I can get them out of my cuffs."

"Are you kidding me?"

"Sorry, I'll put them back in now."

"No, don't," he says. "Wait here." He goes and gets Rookie, and brings him over. "With the smaller ladies, you have to cuff them like this," he tells him, grabbing both my hands in one of his. "One wrist on top of the other, one cuff around both."

Once they get the engine going, the air-conditioning comes on. As we leave the car park and get out on the road, I peer through the front window and try to make out the street names through the windscreen. I see one called Prison Farm Road, another called Visitation Street. I decide that even if I am allowed back into the States one day, I will never come back to Philadelphia. I probably won't even eat the cream cheese. I won't watch the Tom Hanks movie, or the Katharine Hepburn one, and I won't listen to the Fresh Prince theme song, even though I love it. And I will never, ever call this place Philly. That's too cute a name for a place like this.

Because it's the first day of the new system, the officers don't know where to go. When we get to the airport, they drive around, stopping at different side entrances. Olympics makes some calls on his phone. Eventually they get to the right place, and Rookie comes in to unstrap us and let us out. I step down onto the pavement and see Miller, Skolski, and Gallagher standing there.

"Looks like someone made it through the night," Skolski says.

"Sorry about the delay," Olympics tells them. "We got a map but it's not too clear."

Bobbi climbs out of the van and stands beside me.

"So you're transporting both ways now?" Miller asks.

"Yes, sir. Here's my card," says Olympics, passing one over.

"I didn't hear about this."

"Yes, sir," says Olympics. "We'll be doing your transportation services from now on, so you can just go ahead and call that number when you require us."

Miller looks at the card, then hands it back to Olympics. "Okay," he says, "let's get them inside."

"Why is she cuffed like that?" Gallagher asks as Rookie unlocks my hands.

"She slipped out of her cuffs earlier," Olympics tells him.

"Are you serious?" asks Skolski.

"I put the two of them in back of the van. Next thing I know, she's waving her hands around like a little Houdini."

"Unbelievable." Miller and Skolski start to laugh. When I look up at Gallagher, though, he's not smiling at all; his jaw is clenched and he's glaring at me like I just ruined his day before it started.

"I assume you'll be recording this as a UO?" he asks.

"I hadn't thought about it," Olympics says. "Really, no harm was done so——"

"I'll make a note of it on our end," Gallagher tells him.

Finally, Bobbi has her answer: The Homeland Security officers lead us through the airport unshackled—down a series of corridors and into the elevator, where she and I stand together, listening to the officers talk.

"I never heard about this," Miller says.

"Morris briefed us last week," says Skolski. "It costs less if they do it."

"You think he's getting kickback?" Gallagher asks. "Seemed pretty damn eager for the work."

"You been over there?" Skolski asks. "I'd want a reason to get out, too."

"Skolski," Bobbi says. "I knowing this name." The officers look over at her. She points at Skolski's name tag. "Is Polish name. Are many Skolskis Poland."

"Oh, yeah?" Skolski says. The other officers don't say anything. They purse their lips and stare at the door till we reach the right floor and it opens.

It's quiet in the Secondary Questioning Room this morning. Flights haven't started arriving, and most of the officers aren't here yet. Gallagher tells us to go sit against the far wall, on the other side of the long table. He hands us each a Styrofoam cup. "You can get water from the bathroom," he says, "but hang on to those cups. You're not getting another one."

There are three chairs against the wall and for some reason, Bobbi sits in the middle one, directly beside mine.

"The flight to Istanbul leaves at eight ten tonight," Gallagher says. "The Warsaw flight's at nine thirty."

"So do we just sit here all day until our flights board?" I ask.

"Yep. Unless you don't like those seats, and then you can sit in a cell out back."

". . . Okay."

"Would you prefer to sit in a locked cell?"

"No, I'd prefer to sit here."

"All right, then." He goes and sits behind the counter and shakes his head at his computer.

Ellis comes in for a minute and then leaves to get coffee.

"You ever thought how much cash you'd save if you made your own coffee?" Gallagher asks.

Ellis shrugs. "Just a matter of time before they start giving me freebies."

"Oh my God, coffee," I whisper to Bobbi.

"We can take?" she asks.

"I don't know."

"Did you eat?" Gallagher asks us. "Are you hungry?"

"We didn't eat," I say.

He opens a cupboard behind the counter. "Do you want Tuscan Vegetable or Chicken Parmesan?"

I look at Bobbi. "Um. The vegetable one, please?"

He comes over with a white electric kettle and two foil packets of food. He tears the bags open and pours hot water into the chicken one. It's some kind of astronaut food, where you add water and it makes a meal. He hands the bag to Bobbi with a plastic spoon. She starts eating it straight away. He's pouring water into the other packet when I see that the label reads *Tuscan vegetables with beef pieces.*

"Oh, I'm really sorry, I don't mean to be difficult, but I can't eat that. I didn't realize it has meat in it."

He stops pouring. "Are you kidding me? You're telling me this now?"

"I'm sorry. I didn't see the label before. I'm vegetarian."

"Seriously? Grow up." He looks down into the bag. "What am I supposed to do with this now? Give it to a homeless person outside?"

"I mean, I can try and pick out the non-meat parts?"

"Don't play games with me."

"Do you have anything in the cupboard that doesn't have meat in it?"

"No." He takes the bag and kettle and walks away.

"Would it be possible to go to a vending machine," I call after him, "and get something from there?"

"No," he says. "This isn't the Four Seasons."

"Why you no eating?" Bobbi asks me. "Is okay. Not bad."

When I look over at Gallagher again, he's sitting at his computer, eating the Tuscan vegetables with beef pieces. "I'm making it," he says when Miller comes in, "I'm halfway through making it, and she tells me she's not gonna eat it. She tells me she's a vegetarian."

"Uh-huh," Miller says. "What did you expect?"

Gallagher has been researching his family on Ancestry.com. Coots has the day off today. Skolski wants to get tickets to a festival that Jay-Z is putting together in a couple of months. Skolski doesn't really care for Jay-Z's music, but Pearl Jam is playing and he wants to see them. Skolski loves Pearl Jam. The Albanian is happy with the result of the fight last night. Ellis watched the highlights on TV and he's glad he didn't put money on it. Gallagher thinks Ellis would have more money to bet with if he stopped paying through the nose for coffee at the place downstairs, waiting for a free drink they'll never give him. Miller's pretty sure you can never expect a single thing for free in this life. He learned this lesson from his, thank God, ex-wife.

The first flights of the day start landing. A couple of travelers come in, looking groggy and confused. An old man traveling alone from Ghana doesn't know if anyone's meeting him, and he doesn't speak English, except for the word "priest," which he says quietly with a smile, his index finger prodding his own chest.

"They bring priests over to give sermons for big church events. It's probably something like that," Skolski says.

"Do they pay them for that?" Ellis asks. "They give you money?"

"Priest," the priest says.

"It might just be food and board."

The priest has a list of local phone numbers. Ellis calls a few of them before someone picks up and explains the situation to his satisfaction. He stamps the guy's passport and hands it back to him.

"Thank you, Father. Enjoy your visit."

"Priest," the priest says, smiling. He stands where he is until Morris comes to escort him out to baggage claim.

"Later, Father." Ellis waves at him and turns to his computer.

"Anyone got any pretzels?" Gallagher asks. "Hey, Kristy. Got any pretzels?"

"Go to the vending machine," Morris tells him.

"Kristy," I whisper to Bobbi. "Her name's Kristy." I feel like I just received a valuable piece of information, but there's nothing I can actually do with it.

Bobbi asks me what time it is, and I guess that it's elevenish. She asks how long till our flights and I say I think about nine hours. She asks if we're going to sit here all day, and I say yes.

"Did you see the lookout?" Ellis asks. He turns his computer monitor toward the other officers.

"This guy," Skolski says. "Look at this guy."

"Morris," Ellis says. "You seen this?"

"The one-day?" Morris walks over to them. "Yeah, it just came in."

"You think he really looks like this?" Ellis asks. "He won't get in anywhere in the Northeast looking like this."

"This fucking guy," Skolski says.

The Albanian is at the long table in front of us, searching through the suitcase of a middle-aged Bangladeshi woman in an orange sari. On the other side of the table, Morris is showing a Chilean couple where to sign a form, while their baby sleeps in a pram beside them. At the counter, Gallagher is questioning a South African girl with a fiancée visa.

"Who paid for your ticket?" The Albanian asks the Bangladeshi woman.

"Okay, that's it for now," Morris tells the couple.

"I don't believe that you paid for that ticket," The Albanian says.

"Don't take an attitude with me," Gallagher says.

"Your actual green card will arrive at this address in three to six months," Morris says.

"What's this?" The Albanian asks.

"A calendar," the woman says.

"I know it's a calendar. But what are these numbers? What does this writing mean?"

"If I showed up to the airport in South Africa and had that attitude, do you know what would happen? They wouldn't let me in."

"Thank you, thank you." The Chilean couple take their papers and wheel their baby and luggage out, smiling.

"I would get in a lot of trouble," Gallagher says, "so I advise you to treat me and our country with the same kind of respect I would have to have if I showed up in yours."

"How do I know it's your niece's wedding?" The Albanian says. "How do I know you're not on the way to your own wedding?"

The workday revolves around the arrival of flights, and the few passengers who get sent back here from each one. In their downtime, the officers leave in pairs to get something to eat, or they sit around and talk about the people they've been dealing with.

"I say, 'San Jose, California, or San José, Costa Rica?' He doesn't know which one he's trying to get to," says Miller.

"She had one of those old green cards," Ellis says. "The really, really old ones. Like, the ones that were actually green."

Customs officers come in to use the bathroom or file some papers. "Did you see the lookout?" they ask each other. "That guy's not getting in anywhere today."

The travelers become an indistinguishable loop of worried faces, overtired children, and couples who seem sick to death of each other. Occasionally the pattern is broken by the appearance of someone stylish and put-together. Two Austrian tennis players. A catalog model from Thailand. An Iranian woman who left her passport on the plane. The attractive women don't get special treatment from the officers, but their appearance back here is so rare—a fresh vision among all these other bodies, slumped in chairs, in their sneakers and travel fleece and zip-off cargo pants—that I feel it, too: the charge of sex in an otherwise indifferent environment.

"Do not come back here," Miller snaps at the Austrian girls when they step forward to look at his computer. He's angry because one of them said they're not being paid to be here and the other one said they're getting two thousand dollars. He gets on the phone with the person sponsoring them. "They can't come in on B-2s if it's pay for play," he says. He pauses to listen. "Yes, there certainly are more important issues in the world I could be dealing with, but I'm not dealing with those issues right now, am I? I'm dealing with you and your amateur tennis players."

"What time do you think it is?" I ask Bobbi. She has no idea. "I'm guessing around two," I say. I'm starting to feel lightheaded.

"What I wanting," Bobbi says, "is cake! Coffee and piece of cake."

"When I get on that airplane," I tell her, "I'm going to be so decadent. I'm gonna get a glass of champagne. And I'm gonna pay for Wi-Fi."

Ellis walks past us, whistling. He opens a filing cabinet and drops a file folder in. "Did you get something to eat or drink?" he asks us.

"They're fine," Gallagher tells him.

Morris is searching through the suitcase of a PhD student from Belgium. All his clothes are clean and neatly folded; he has a Tupperware container filled with blocks of Belgian chocolate to give as gifts to his American friends, and a thousand dollars in an envelope that his parents gave him as a going-away present.

Morris asks him if he has any tattoos and he pulls up the sleeve of his T-shirt to show her some text on his left shoulder.

"What does it say?"

"It's a quote from Rilke."

"What does it say? Translate it for me."

"Uh, it translates to something like, 'Let life happen to you. Believe me. Life is always in the right.'"

"Very wise," Morris says.

"Thanks."

"I wasn't complimenting you. You didn't write it, did you?"

"Is this you?" Skolski calls over from his computer. "*Dis-*

ruption and Attenuation of the American Dream in Mexican American Literature, 1964 to 1971?"

"Yes," the guy says.

"Sounds like a real page-turner," Skolski says. "I'll have to read this later."

"Maybe I'll go to Belgium and write about the Belgian dream," Miller says. "How would that feel?"

"I don't know," the guy says. "We don't really have a Belgian dream."

When he's allowed to leave, the guy smiles at me and Bobbi on his way out. I make a plan to look him up online when I get out of here, but ten minutes later I've lapsed into some sort of exhausted, hunger-induced daze and I've forgotten his name, the university he's studying at, the topic of his thesis, or any other Googlable details.

Gallagher is staring at his computer when I walk partway to where he is. "What?" he says.

"Is it possible to get a drink that isn't water?" I ask. "A juice or soda? Something with sugar or caffeine? I'm not feeling—"

"No," he says. "Sit down."

He's going over some papers with Miller when he notices me watching them. "Keep looking over here and you're going in that cell," he says. I look away.

. . .

Five hours from now I'll be on an airplane, drinking a beer and watching *Wanderlust,* feeling like Justin Theroux might be the most attractive man in the world, but probably just because he's not wearing a uniform or carrying a gun.

Half a day after that, I'll be at the American consulate in Istanbul, talking to officers with walls for faces. Two days later I'll be in a middle seat on a flight to Heathrow, having nightmares that I'm still locked inside a jail cell until I remember the half pill in my pocket, and take it to knock myself out.

Six weeks from now, I'll be camped out on the sofa bed at my parents' place, surrounded by my suitcase and all my stuff, staying up late at night to talk to my American friends online. Telling them to come visit me and not believing them when they say they will. Asking Lars to forgive me so we can get the band back together. And when I finally tell them all the story of how I got deported, they'll laugh at how scared I was for them to know. "What did you think we'd say?" my friend Amanda will ask. "Everyone knows the system's broken."

Four months from now, I'll get my period for the first time since being deported, because my body will have recovered from the stress. I'll rent a room in a friend's flat in Dalston. Luke will send me my computer and I'll update my CV and apply for postdocs and teaching jobs. Nine months later, he and Lydia will get married at San Francisco City Hall, and they'll text me the photos from the steps out front.

Three years from now, I will still not be allowed back into the States. I'll just be watching it from afar, like everybody else. And strangely, it will only be when I'm in yoga class, holding certain poses, that I'll remember myself back there, in the Bay Area, as though the memories are somehow locked inside my muscles. Riding my bike up Guerrero Street. Walking into the café and seeing his face. Daydrinking margaritas in the park, not too far away from places where people get locked up and sent away all the time. Before I myself got turned around and kicked out. Before I came of age long after I had come of age. Before I took the journey back to where I started, and started again.

But right now, still waiting in this room, in the transit zone, I lean my head onto Bobbi's shoulder, and doze on and off for the hours until my flight. "I really don't want to give you bedbugs," I tell her, but she doesn't shake me off, even when I start to drool.

ACKNOWLEDGMENTS

Thank you to the Stanford University Creative Writing program for bringing me to the States and teaching me so much once I arrived. Thank you to my extraordinary teachers and mentors: Tobias Wolff, Elizabeth Tallent, John L'Heureux, and Colm Tóibín.

For their wisdom, faith, and perpetual good humor, thank you to everyone at Spiegel & Grau, especially Cindy Spiegel, Julie Grau, and Laura van der Veer. Enormous thanks, too, to my agents Peter Straus and Melanie Jackson, Mary Mount at Viking UK, and Ben Ball and Arwen Summers at Penguin Australia.

I am grateful for the support of the MacDowell Colony, Tin House Writer's Workshop, Virginia Center for the Creative Arts, the Ucross Foundation, and MacDowell again. I'm grateful, also, to the editors who have published my work in journals and anthologies.

Thank you to my friends, readers, and hand-holders, and especially to these amazing people, who are all three of those things: Hassan Javed, Alexandra Teague, Suzanne Rivecca, Stacey Swann, Josh Tyree, Skip Horack, Jim Gavin, Stephanie Soileau, Nellie Bridge, Ryan Brown, Andrew Braddock, Craig Cox, and Fleur, Jase, and the Market Lane team xo.

Finally, and most of all, thank you to my incredible family: Vivienne, Ross, Kate, Meg, Emily, Bren, PJ, Indigo, Jarrah, Pepper, Zeph, Woody, and D'Ange.

And a special thank-you to my grandfather, who put us to bed on Friday nights when we were kids with the story of "How Saul Met the Beautiful Lucy." It's one of the first stories I ever knew, and it's still one of my favorites.

ABOUT THE AUTHOR

Abigail Ulman was born and raised in Melbourne, Australia. She has a Bachelor of Creative Arts from the University of Melbourne and was a recent Wallace Stegner Fellow in Fiction at Stanford University. *Hot Little Hands* is her first book.

ABOUT THE TYPE

This book was set in Granjon, a modern recutting of a typeface produced under the direction of George W. Jones (1860–1942), who based Granjon's design upon the letterforms of Claude Garamond (1480–1561). The name was given to the typeface as a tribute to the typographic designer Robert Granjon (1513–89).